Christmas in Good Hope

Also by Cynthia Rutledge / Cindy Kirk

Christmas *in* Good Hope

CINDY KIRK

Montlake
Romance

Text copyright © 2015 Cynthia Rutledge
All rights reserved.

Published by Montlake Romance, Seattle

www.apub.com

Amazon, the Amazon logo, and Montlake Romance are trademarks of Amazon.com, Inc., or its affiliates.

ISBN-13: 9781503949652
ISBN-10: 1503949656

Cover design by Mumtaz Mustafa

Printed in the United States of America

To Renee Ryan and Nancy Robards Thompson, fellow authors and fabulous friends. As a writer I should be adept at coming up with something brilliant that conveys how much your friendship, love, and support mean to me. But I've never been good at such things. Just know that while a love of the written word may have brought us together, mutual respect, friendship, and love are the glue that binds us. You are truly the sisters of my heart. Thank you, thank you, thank you for your unfailing support!

Chapter One

It may have been only the first of December, but historic Hill House in the small village of Good Hope, Wisconsin, was already gussied up for Christmas. In spite of the festive evergreen wreaths with red ribbons at each window and pinecone garlands around the white porch rail, the home reminded Amaryllis Bloom of an aging film star trying to conceal wrinkles beneath a thick coat of greasepaint.

If anyone understood a desperate need to hide flaws beneath a polished veneer, it was Ami. God knew she'd tried. But she finally had to accept that guilt wouldn't go away just because she prayed and that past errors, no matter how much she regretted them, couldn't be undone.

Old memories dipped her sunny mood briefly into overcast. But the clouds cleared when Ami entered the 1870s home. She perked up, eager to see what decorations the historical society had in store for visitors this year.

It certainly wasn't off to a rockin' start, not if the gold bows and garland draped on the massive staircase to her right were any indication. The greenery was a nice touch, although also a tad boring.

Things improved significantly when Ami reached the parlor. Her gaze was immediately drawn to the corner where a seven-foot Fraser fir stood. Though Ami was normally a fan of bright holiday colors, the dark green foliage decorated in an understated color scheme of silver, gold, and bronze took her breath away. Instead of a traditional star, fresh holly and large gold temple bells adorned the top.

The elegant scheme extended to a mantel arrangement. There, peacock feathers and mirrored ornaments coupled with curly willow branches added accent color, complementing the tree.

After admiring several less prominent touches the volunteers had added to the room, including shimmering oversize Mercury glass ornaments in a basket by the fireplace, Ami heeded the five-minute warning and took a seat.

The monthly meeting of the Women's Events League began precisely at one. As red, tart cherries were the main crop on the Door County peninsula, the group had been dubbed the Cherries. These prominent women planned all holiday events in the village of Good Hope.

As the treasurer launched into the financial report, Ami glanced around the semicircle. She caught sight of Anita Fishback at the far end of the horseshoe. It had recently become obvious—at least to Ami—that the midfifties divorcée had Ami's widowed father in her crosshairs. Ami couldn't imagine a worse match than one between the piranha and her sweet dad.

Ami averted her gaze and focused her attention on the other members.

While some of the women were near her age, many were old enough to be her grandmother. Or, in the case of the current treasurer, her great-grandmother.

Ninety-six-year-old former community theater star Gladys Bertholf went for flair as she reported on the organization's current financials. Cadaver thin with a shock of dark black hair boasting a swath of silver, Gladys gestured broadly as she reported, the sleeves of her purple caftan dress fluttering around birdlike arms.

The older woman's voice carried easily throughout the richly decorated room. Unfortunately, there was only so much even a former actress could do with pitch, tone, and movement to make a P&L statement interesting.

While a trifle eccentric, the woman was amazing. Not only was she a whiz with figures and a master of public speaking, as of last month Gladys was now the oldest member of the Cherries.

Her elevation to treasurer had occurred when MarJean Thorpe had passed away at 103. And it had been MarJean's passing that had opened a spot for a new member.

Ami had been the chosen one. She'd been thrilled to be asked. But sitting here now and feeling completely underwhelmed made her wonder if this was freshman year in college all over again. She'd gone through rush only to realize several months later that sorority life wasn't for her.

Give this a chance, she told herself sternly and refocused on Gladys.

Ever since her mother died three years ago, Ami had been even more determined to receive a coveted invitation to join the group. Some of this desire sprang from the fact that membership had been something her mother had pursued but never achieved. But mostly it was because Ami, like her mother, believed strongly in their mission.

From a merchant's perspective, she recognized the financial value of celebrations. The events planned by the Cherries brought much-needed tourist dollars to their small township. But for Ami, the increased revenue was an added benefit. It was the warm sense of community and camaraderie, the way holidays brought people together, that made the planning worthwhile.

As far back as Ami could remember, she'd been a holiday planner. The oldest of four girls, Ami recalled with much fondness the cookie-baking marathons, the ice skating races on Rakes Pond, and all the neighborhood Fourth of July parades she'd helped her mother organize.

Sarah Bloom had loved everything about holidays and had gone out of her way to make them special for her family and neighbors. Her mother would have been an asset to the Cherries, but a stay-at-home mom and wife of a high school teacher hadn't been on their radar.

Ami found it reassuring that once she got past the sixty-day probationary period, she would be a member for life.

So she had to sit through a few boring meetings to get to the fun stuff. What else was there for an almost-thirty-year-old single woman to do on a snowy Monday afternoon? An image of a roaring fire, a book, and a glass of wine flashed before her. She shoved it aside and caught the tail end of the report.

As Gladys returned to her seat beside Ami, the executive director, Eliza Shaw, took the podium. With her tall, slender figure and natural elegance, she looked more like a New York model than the owner of a general store in upper Wisconsin.

As usual, Eliza was dressed more for style than the weather. While Ami wore tweed pants and a bulky cable-knit sweater with her beloved UGGs, Eliza had chosen black pants that hugged her slender legs like a second skin, a tunic of cherry red, and shiny heeled boots.

When Eliza's gaze scanned the group of women, it passed over Ami as if she weren't there. It pained Ami to remember that at one time she and Eliza had run in the same circle of friends. But that had been a lifetime ago.

"We'll start with our biggest problem first. Beckett Cross." Eliza's voice snapped like a freshly washed sheet hung to dry in a brisk wind. "Mr. Cross absolutely refuses to allow his home to be part of the tour."

A murmur of disbelief rose like an orchestra's crescendo through the group. Eliza quieted them with a hand.

"He actually said no?" Gladys's rich voice filled the momentary silence as she slapped a hand sparkling with jewels to her breast.

"Oh, he did more than that." Katie Ruth Crewes, who'd gone to school with Ami, spoke without waiting to be called upon. "Mr. Grumpy Pants threw Eliza out of his café. I was headed to lunch and witnessed it firsthand."

Katie Ruth grinned. The pretty blond retained the perky bounce she'd had in high school. Now, instead of leading cheers, Katie Ruth was the front desk manager at the BayShore Hotel.

In her spare time she served as editor in chief of the *Open Door*, a daily electronic newsletter. Targeted primarily to peninsula residents, it included local news and events as well as a popular gossip feature.

"That man is impossible," someone muttered in an overly loud voice.

"I believe that is something all of us agree upon . . . with perhaps one exception." Eliza shifted her gaze to Ami. "Do you realize that your friend will likely—out of sheer pigheadedness—disrupt one of our most cherished traditions?"

Though *cherished tradition* might be stretching credulity, there was no denying that the annual Victorian Tour of Homes was much loved by residents and tourists alike.

Traipsing through prominent and primarily historic homes festively decorated for Christmas definitely drew the crowds. Since the event had begun, the historic Spencer-Shaw house—the one Beck purchased last summer—had always been the first on the tour. Not to mention the most popular.

Ami frowned. While Beck could be a bit gruff at times, he wasn't an unreasonable man. "Did you mention to him that touring the Spencer-Shaw home is a tradition in Good Hope?"

"He doesn't give a fig about traditions." Eliza flung a frustrated hand in the air. "He pops up here from God knows where, and not only buys the café but snatches my cousin's home out from under our noses. None of the family had a clue Katherine was even considering selling it."

Perhaps if any of you bothered to visit her, she'd have told you.

Ami kept the uncharitable thought to herself. She and the spry octogenarian met weekly for tea, and the sale had been as much of a surprise to her as it had been to Katherine's family. Never once had her elderly friend mentioned selling her home and moving to Arizona. Not until it was a done deal. But then Kate had always been an intensely private person and a little eccentric.

"We must stay focused." Gladys raised a clenched fist, much like a general rallying the troops. "We can't give up."

"Since Eliza wasn't able to persuade Mr. Cross to open his home, perhaps Ami should try," Katie Ruth suggested. "She might have better luck."

The cushioned seat beneath Ami turned rock hard and she shifted uncomfortably. All eyes were now on her. "I'm sure Eliza laid out the facts quite clearly. I don't know what I could do. Mr. Cross has made his decision."

Though she wanted to help, Ami's contact with Beck was minimal. Sure, she saw him every morning, but theirs was a superficial relationship, kept alive by a mutual predilection for pastries and strong coffee. She had no more insight into what made him tick—and regardless of what Eliza believed, no more influence on him—than any other woman in the room.

"I don't believe what I'm hearing." Eliza's gaze narrowed. "Are you refusing to help?"

The direct question, and the venomous undertone, caught Ami off guard. "No. No. Of course not. I was merely saying—"

Eliza leaned forward, resting her arms on the podium, her gaze riveted on Ami. "Though some in the group expressed concerns about bringing you in as a member, the majority was convinced you strongly supported our mission in this community."

Ami had no doubt one of those who'd expressed concerns had been Eliza. She knew why the woman hated her, understood and accepted the animosity. But Ami wouldn't allow her—or anyone—to impugn her loyalty to Good Hope.

For years, Ami had worked tirelessly to increase participation by the merchants in the holiday celebrations planned by the Cherries. As owner of Blooms Bake Shop, located in the heart of the Good Hope business district, Ami knew the extra revenue these celebrations generated.

This was especially true in December, when the entire village was transformed into a winter wonderland for the Twelve Nights celebrations.

"I have always supported the group's efforts. I believe strongly in the mission." Ami spoke slowly and distinctly so there could be no misunderstanding. "But Mr. Cross isn't from here. He—"

"—refuses to be a team player," Eliza interrupted, pulling all eyes back to her. Her dark hair, cut in a stylish bob, swung like a shiny black curtain as she whirled to directly face Ami. "You will make him see the error of his ways and secure his cooperation."

When Ami opened her mouth to reiterate—again—that she had no control over the man, Eliza lifted a hand, palm out. "Don't bother to deny your connection. We're all aware of your tête-à-têtes when the café is closed."

Heat rose up Ami's neck at the openly speculative looks directed her way. "His café is next to my shop. We—"

"It's settled." Eliza's tone brooked no argument. "Your first official assignment as a Cherrie is to convince Beckett Cross to open his home to the tour."

Irritated by the autocratic tone, Ami took a few seconds to rein in her temper. She drew in a breath, let it out slowly. Somehow, she managed a smile. "I'll give it a try."

"Trying isn't good enough. Take whatever measures necessary to achieve the goal." Eliza lifted a shoulder in a careless shrug. "Otherwise . . ."

"Otherwise what?" Ami asked bluntly, her patience gone.

"Just make sure he agrees." Though Eliza smiled, her eyes remained cool. "That will be in everyone's best interest, including yours."

Ami thought about Eliza's threat on the short stroll to her apartment over the bakery. Considered it again as she polished off a late lunch of corn chowder. It was obvious that if she didn't get Beck to agree, the vote to grant her full membership in the Cherries might not go her way.

Who needs them anyway? But then Ami remembered her mother's unfulfilled dreams. She'd give the next sixty days her all. If they booted her out, well, she'd have done her best.

At peace with the plan, Ami slipped downstairs to the shop she considered her second home. A scent of yeasty earthiness with a dash of cinnamon teased her nostrils. She paused in the doorway to survey her kingdom and experienced a rush of pride.

The interior was still very much a work in progress. Yet every day, with each acquisition, it became more her own. Ami adored the antique chandelier and the exposed brick walls she'd painted a soft turquoise.

She let her gaze linger on the bright yellow shelving holding vintage tea tins, each brimming with an assortment of growing herbs.

As most of the business was carryout, seating in the shop was limited to two tables and a counter with stools by the window. Wanting to build on the boho-chic vibe, Ami had sanded down the tables to bare wood, then painted one a bright watermelon pink and the other an eye-popping cobalt blue. Brightly colored mismatched chairs added to the vibrancy of the room.

When the bakery was closed, Ami liked to sit at one of the tables and enjoy a scone with a cup of tea. She always took her time picking from the eclectic mix of china cups dangling from the mug tree on the counter. With the shop now on winter hours and only open Friday through Monday from ten to four, Ami had plenty of time to sit and savor.

When she'd first purchased the bakery several years earlier, she'd felt like a slacker working such short hours during the winter. After a couple of summers working ten-hour days, seven days a week, she'd come to see this as a much-needed opportunity to relax and recharge.

Until Ami expanded the bakery hours in February, her only employee was Hadley Newhouse. With curly blond hair and expressive blue eyes, the young woman from North Dakota—or so she said—reminded Ami of her sister Marigold.

Perhaps because of that resemblance, Ami had liked Hadley the instant she'd strolled into the shop last spring with the Help Wanted sign from the front window in her hand. Once she tasted Hadley's Scandinavian breads and pastries, she'd hired her despite a dearth of references.

Ami was a big believer in second chances. Over the past six months, Hadley had proven herself to be hardworking and honest. A friendship between the two women had blossomed, fueled by a mutual passion for baking.

Although her sisters were all proficient in the kitchen, from the time Ami had been a small child, she'd shown an aptitude for what her father called the "womanly arts." Pies and cookies were now her specialty.

"How was the meeting?" Hadley asked when Ami entered the shop.

Ami rolled her eyes.

"That good, huh?"

"I'm not sure *good* is the right word," Ami said with a wry smile.

"Now I definitely want details." Hadley glanced at the It's Cupcake Time clock on the wall and grimaced. The small hand pointing to the carrot cupcake with cream cheese frosting showed her shift had ended.

Hadley removed her apron and sighed heavily. "Darn second job. I need to scoot. Promise you'll tell me tomorrow?"

"I'll give you all the gory details." Ami shivered for effect, then paused. "Is it cold in here?"

"I can't believe you just noticed." Hadley laughed. "I can practically see my breath. Old Ralph hasn't kicked on since you left."

Old Ralph was the ancient furnace she'd hoped would last at least another year. By then she planned to have enough money saved to get a new one. With parts impossible to find, replacement was the only option. "I asked for a bid, just in case Ralph croaked. I wanted to know how much a new furnace would set me back."

Hadley inclined her head. "What did you find out?"

When Ami told her the quote, the other woman whistled.

"That's a chunk of change. Do you have it?"

Her directness was only one of the many things Ami liked about Hadley.

"I have some of the money. I suppose I could charge the rest." A knot formed in the pit of Ami's stomach. "The problem is I use that credit card for business expenses. Right now I'm able to pay off what I charge each month. Carrying a balance would mean paying high interest."

Hadley tapped a finger against her lips. "I may have a solution."

"You're a rich heiress and I can be your philanthropy?" Ami joked.

A startled look crossed Hadley's face, then she laughed. "Yeah, right. I'm wealthy. That's why I work two jobs."

Ami snapped her fingers. "Bummer. Okay, what's your idea?"

"Muddy Boots is looking for a cook." Hadley cast a speculative glance in Ami's direction, then pulled a tube of lipstick from her bag and expertly applied it to her wide mouth. "Janey got a call and left right after lunch today for Milwaukee. Something to do with her mother. Supposedly she won't be back until the first of January."

"I'm sorry to hear that." Ami knew Janey Eversoll's mother had been struggling since her stroke last month.

"It'd be a perfect way for you to earn some extra cash over the holiday," Hadley said, returning to her earlier point.

Ami hadn't considered taking a second job, but it might be the answer. If Beck would allow her to work in the café on the days the bakery was closed, it could be a win-win for both of them. Assuming he'd hire her, of course.

"I am a good cook," Ami murmured.

"You're an excellent cook." Hadley added another coat of mascara to her already thickly coated lashes. "Not to mention you have an in with the boss. You and Mr. Cross have quite the thing going in the mornings."

"It's called being neighborly." Ami ruined the righteous tone by flushing like a guilty teenager.

That made her angry. At herself. At the gossipmongers. She had no reason to feel guilty. It wasn't as if her banter with Beck had ever had any *sexual* connotations.

Simply thinking of *sexual* and *Beckett Cross* in the same sentence caused her cheeks to burn. Out of simple embarrassment, she told herself, nothing more.

Thankfully, Hadley's gaze was on her purse as she rummaged through the contents. Emitting a sound of triumph, she pulled out her cell phone.

"Now that I've found my baby"—Hadley gave the phone a loving stroke before her gaze pinned Ami—"let's talk about what being neighborly means to Amaryllis Bloom. I mean, some neighbors have sex. And Beckett Cross *is* überhot."

"I'm not sleeping with Beck," Ami protested.

"Even if you are, it's not my business." Though Hadley's hands rose in a gesture of surrender, a smile played at the corners of her lips. "Though if you'd want to share what he's like in bed, I'm willing to listen."

"I don't even like the man," Ami retorted, then immediately felt a flash of guilt. Okay, so that wasn't entirely accurate. Still, all the talk linking her and Beck—a man she barely knew—flustered her.

"Methinks the lady doth protest too much," Hadley teased.

"I thought you needed to get to your other job."

Hadley glanced at the clock. The small hand was now on the chocolate cupcake. She yelped. "One more thing, real quick. When you interview with Mr. Sexy, don't sell yourself cheap. He'll be desperate. That means he's likely to agree to any demands."

"But I don't have any experience. I've never cooked for anyone but family and friends."

"That won't be a problem. You'll simply pretend you're cooking for your sexy next-door neighbor." Hadley slung the bag the size of Texas over her shoulder and winked. "The one you're not sleeping with."

Ami laughed and shook her head.

Hadley had barely disappeared down the block—headed to her other job as a server at the Flying Crane—when large white flakes appeared outside the picture window.

Ami shivered. The heat still hadn't kicked on. If she didn't take care of this furnace fiasco soon, her pipes would freeze, and then she'd have an even bigger expense.

With a resigned sigh, she pulled out her phone. By the time she hung up, she had an installation date for Wednesday and her credit card had sustained a massive hit.

She wished she could speak with Beck about the job right this minute. But he was likely occupied with the supper rush, and her dad would be here any minute to pick her up.

Tonight they were attending an all-you-can-eat fish fry at the high school. One of her father's fellow teachers had been recently diagnosed with cancer—the same type that had taken her mother's life—and the staff had organized a fundraiser to help with medical expenses.

It was these types of events that brought a swell of pride to Ami's heart and made her love Good Hope all the more. Friends helping friends was a way of life in this corner of the world.

Later, after she'd eaten her fill of whitefish and fries, she would stop by Beck's home.

Once there, she'd tackle the tour issue with him first. Hopefully it would be a simple matter of putting things in perspective for him.

Of pointing out that when he moved here, he hadn't just gained a beautiful house and a business; he now had an extended family that would always be here for him.

Ami would lay it out in such a way that Beck couldn't help but see that with such blessings came certain responsibilities. It certainly didn't hurt that they were headed into a wonderful time of the year, when peace and joy filled every heart.

She could see it now. Beck would catch the spirit and agree to open his house for the tour. Once that deal was struck, he'd generously offer Ami a job with the hours and pay she requested.

Hey, if a girl was going to dream, she might as well dream big.

With a light heart, Ami hummed a tune as she went upstairs to grab her coat. She had a feeling this was going to be the best Christmas ever.

Chapter Two

Beckett glanced around the now-empty café and breathed a sigh of relief. His business had survived the evening rush, thanks to Janey's helper. The former navy mess hall cook, Tom Larson, had stepped up and done his best.

Though there had been a few rough moments tonight, thankfully, business had been slow. The real problems lay ahead. Beck had no doubt that once the Twelve Nights celebrations began, the Muddy Boots café would be swamped.

While Tom was willing to handle the primary cooking duties short-term, he'd made it clear he hadn't signed on to be in charge of the kitchen. Beck knew if he didn't hire someone quickly, Tom would be out the door and he'd be left manning the grill. *That* would be a disaster of epic proportions.

Beck had no doubt there were qualified cooks in Good Hope. And he was willing to pay top dollar. The problem was, who would want to take a job for only one month, and over the Christmas holiday to boot?

Blasted holiday season.

The bells over the front door jingled, a grating sound that scraped against his last nerve. Busy tallying the figures for the day and counting cash, Beck didn't look up. He resisted—barely—the urge to snarl. "We're closed."

"Bah humbug to you, too."

Beck jerked his head up at the familiar voice. Despite his foul mood, he couldn't help but smile.

Max Brody, a local CPA and one of Beck's few friends in Good Hope, pulled the door shut behind him. After making a big production of flipping the sign on the door from Open to Closed, he sauntered across the room to where Beck stood beside the ancient cash register.

Dressed in jeans, a red ski sweater, and Columbia snow boots, Max looked like he should be crossing the countryside on skis rather than quoting tax codes.

Although Beck was several years older than Max, both were athletic men, standing just over six feet two inches. That's where the similarities ended. Instead of a dark brown, Max's hair was the color of dirty sand. His body was also more muscular than Beck's leaner frame. The biggest difference, though, was the accountant's face held a perpetual smile. Max loved life and it showed.

It had been that way for Beck once. He'd had everything.

"If you keep that scowl on your face, Santa is going to bring you a lump of coal." Max's tone might have been light, but his eyes held concern.

Beck lifted a shoulder, let it drop. "I'm not much for holidays."

"I'd never have guessed." Max laid an envelope before him with a flourish. "Merry Christmas, anyway."

Beck raised a brow.

"What I anticipate will be your fourth-quarter estimates for the IRS." Max rocked back on his heels, grinned. "Now you can't say I never gave you anything."

Beck laughed as he picked up the envelope and dropped it into the open leather briefcase at his feet. "You didn't need to bring it over."

"The café is on my way home." Max glanced around the dining area and gave a low whistle. "You've made some changes since I was last here."

Beck assumed the CPA was referring to the spatter of cobalt-blue paint on the white walls and the new mural.

"The blue reminds me of rain. And that mural is amazing." Max strolled to the far wall and studied the scene, which had been completed only days earlier. It was of a young girl in a bright red jacket with shiny red boots. She stood in the rain, kicking up water. "Who's the artist?"

"Her name is Izzie Deshler. She also painted the walls. She's relatively new in Good Hope. Do you know her?"

Max thought for a moment, then shook his head. "How did you find her?"

"She approached me." Beck saw no reason to mention Ami had given Izzie his name. He'd discovered—just as Ami had said—that the woman was desperate for work.

He'd hired her, figuring whatever she came up with was bound to be better than boring white walls. If it hadn't turned out to his liking, he would have had her paint over it.

"She's good," Max said with what appeared to be genuine admiration. "These changes give Muddy Boots a modern feel."

Beck hadn't been keen on the café's name and had seriously considered changing it. But the place had been Muddy Boots for over forty years. Everyone but him seemed to love the name. "The reaction of patrons to the mural and the paint has been overwhelmingly positive. But really, anything would be an improvement over what was here."

Last summer, when Beck had walked into the café, he'd been stunned. The pictures the realtor had e-mailed him prior to the purchase had been heavy on the quaint exterior: the large windows facing the main street and a new, crisp blue awning with the café's name and the trademark bright red boots.

The interior shots had primarily focused on the recently updated commercial kitchen. Nothing had prepared him for the 1970s decor in the dining area. The Formica-topped tables and yellow vinyl chairs were acceptable in the short-term. Likewise, the gray-tiled floor might be scarred from years of wear but would do until he found time to get hardwood down.

But it was the wallpaper, a hideous coffeepot pattern in harvest gold and mud brown, that had to go. He'd wished there had been time to remodel. But Independence Day had loomed, and holidays in Good Hope meant lots and lots of tourists spending boatloads of money.

Beck had settled for having a crew come in and remove the wallpaper. Since he hadn't yet decided what he wanted to do with the interior, he'd had the walls painted white. The neutral color ended up being the perfect backdrop for Izzie's blue "rain" splatter.

The accountant returned to the counter where Beck stood. His friend reminded him of a bloodhound that had just caught a scent when he sidled up to the jar holding round, chocolate-covered mints. A popular item, they sold for ten cents each or three for twenty-five cents.

Max unwrapped one of the shiny silver wrappers and popped a mint into his mouth. "You're making progress, but you've still got work ahead of you."

"I like to keep busy." Beck had discovered that being exhausted helped him to sleep and not think. "Is there something else I can do for you, Max?"

Beck didn't mean to be abrupt, but talk of the holidays had given him a headache. All he wanted was to take a couple of ibuprofen and head home.

Apparently finding the first one to his liking, Max grabbed a couple more mints. "I hear you refused to allow your house in the tour."

"Is that what the *Good Hope Gazette* is reporting?" Beck said with obvious disdain, referring to the town's weekly paper. Hearing that news was already making the rounds didn't surprise him. It hadn't taken him long to discover there was no privacy in a small community.

"Actually, I read it in the *Open Door*."

Beck gave a derisive snort. He'd only opened the daily online newsletter once. The gossip feature had turned him off and he hadn't looked at it since. "Tabloid rag."

Max inclined his head. "Is the news accurate?"

"It is." Beck finished closing out the cash register and added the money bag to his briefcase.

The day had started off okay with a red velvet doughnut and coffee for breakfast. It had been all downhill from there.

When Eliza Shaw had approached him, he'd been polite but firm. Finally, when she became a yappy dog that wouldn't shut up, he'd shown her to the door. "I can't see having a bunch of people I don't know traipsing through my house."

Though some might say his house was too big for one man, the place was slowly beginning to feel like home. It had become Beck's sanctuary, the one place in Good Hope where he could fully relax.

Max shoved his hands into his pockets, for the first time looking uncomfortable. "The thing is, it's—"

"Stop right there." Beck cut him off before he could finish. "Be warned, if you say the word 'tradition,' I may have to punch you."

"Then I guess I'll have to appeal to your mercenary side." Max grinned, not at all intimidated by the scowl or the growl. "The home tour is a big moneymaker for the community. It'll bring in business to the café and all the merchants."

"I venture that people will still come to Good Hope for the tour, even if my house isn't open."

"Probably," Max reluctantly acknowledged. "But it's tra—" Catching himself, the accountant stopped, changed direction. "Where's your community spirit? All I'm asking is that you consider participating. Come on, I know there's a heart under that scrooge exterior."

"Oh, so now I'm a scrooge?" Beck lifted a brow. "You seem to be forgetting who gave who a tax bill for Christmas?"

Max's expression turned sheepish.

Just like he used to when he'd been a defense attorney, Beck drove the point home. "You gave me a tax bill while I gave you chocolate mints. I ask you, who's the scrooge?"

———

Ami gazed through the frosted front window of her shop and watched her father's car drive away in the falling snow. She could have told him to drop her off at Beck's home, but the request would have provoked questions she had no desire to answer. As she was the only one of his four daughters still living in Door County, his overprotectiveness sometimes bordered on stifling.

Some women might have chafed under his constant questions and concerns, but Ami understood. Her dad worried about her. Worried she'd never find a husband and have children like her sister Primrose. Worried about her decision to remain in Good Hope rather than moving to Chicago like her sister Marigold. Even though he wanted her here, he knew she'd stand a better chance of finding a husband in the big city.

Steve Bloom was a traditional man. He'd been happy in his marriage and wanted the same happiness for his daughters. As much as she understood, Ami was grateful there was Delphinium to take some of the pressure off.

Her father worried almost as much about Fin as he did about her, but for different reasons. The young woman who'd been their father's fishing buddy and was the next stair step down from Ami hadn't been back to Good Hope in several years.

Ami jerked the hood of her parka up, zipping it until only her eyes peered out. The gloves on her hands were rated for subzero temps, so when she opened the door and stepped into the night air, she was warmer than she'd been in the bakery.

She didn't mind the walk. As Ami didn't drive, she normally got to where she was going on foot or by riding her trusty Schwinn.

Snow crunched under the heels of Ami's boots, and flakes of white clung to her coat and gloves. Street lamps bathed the sidewalks in a golden glow. Distant music from the Flying Crane wafted on the night air.

Ami hummed along to the popular tune and felt the weight of the day lift as she found comfort in the familiar. Many of the shops had been in existence since she was a child.

There was the Good Hope Market. Next to it was Hill's General Store, a business that had been in Eliza's family for six generations. The Muddy Boots café, the business Beck had bought last summer, was dark now, the sign on the door flipped to Closed.

Ami had been as surprised as anyone when she'd learned someone from out of state had purchased the café. What had shocked her more was learning that same person had bought the Spencer-Shaw house.

Her secret wish had been to one day buy the house and turn it into a B and B. She'd done cleaning for Katherine Spencer when she'd been in high school and had fallen in love with the home. Kate, as she'd instructed Ami to address her, had no husband or children and wasn't particularly close to any of her family.

Ami had hoped by the time Katherine decided to sell the home, she'd have the income that would allow her to buy it.

Obviously not meant to be, she thought with a sigh.

When she reached the intersection, Ami crossed Highway 42, the roadway that ran the length of the peninsula. The Spencer-Shaw place, *er, Beck's home*, sat at the corner of the highway and Market Street, directly across the street from Hill House.

The house was impressive: a two-story white clapboard with green shutters and stained glass topping each window. A black iron fence enclosed a yard that spanned two lots. In the spring and summer, leafy trees shaded a spread of sprawling green accented with clusters of colorful flowers.

Those in the community who cared about such things had worried the new owner might not keep up the property. That hadn't been the case. Though Katherine had used a lawn service, Beck tended the grounds himself.

Ami recalled the time she'd been biking to the library and seen him mowing. His white T-shirt was stretched tight across broad shoulders, and worn jeans hugged long, muscular legs.

She smiled at the pleasant memory and opened the gate. Like the sidewalk on both sides of the property, the walk leading to the house had been recently shoveled.

There were lights on upstairs, but the main floor was dark. Ami knocked on the door, then took a moment to brush the snow from her coat and stomp her boots on the mat.

After several seconds with no response, she knocked again, using more force.

This time, lights on the main level flicked on. Seconds later she heard the dead bolt snap. The door swung open and Beck stood blocking the doorway, wearing jeans and a navy, long-sleeved Henley.

He was tall, with a lean, rangy build and a striking face that was all hard angles and planes. He wore his rich chocolate hair longer than when he'd first arrived. The slightly wavy strands brushed the top of his shirt. His eyes, the same color as his hair, held intelligence and perpetual wariness.

"This is a surprise." Puzzled, his gaze searched hers. "What brings you by, Ami?"

The way he spoke her name—Am-mee—in that soft southern drawl always made her shiver. She supposed all southern drawls were supersexy.

"Hi, Beck." She gestured to the warmth flooding from the inside out. "Invite me in?"

After a barely perceptible hesitation, he moved back, giving her space to enter.

As she stepped inside, Ami was struck by the clean, fresh scent of him. He smelled of soap and shampoo and an indefinable male scent that had desire curling low in her belly. The thought that she might indeed be lusting after Beckett appalled her.

She'd only recently gotten to know the man, yet here she was, wondering what he looked like naked. The heat that rushed through her was surprising in its intensity. Though Ami was no shy virgin, her two love affairs had been eons ago, and physical intimacy had been a carefully considered decision.

There had been no punch of lust.

No spicy thoughts heating her cheeks.

Coming here, in this frame of mind, had been a mistake.

The odd thing was that Ami hadn't known she was in this frame of mind . . . until she'd seen Beck.

She edged back into the open doorway. "We can talk about this tomorrow. Just so you know, I'm planning on bringing Cronuts. I don't know if you've ever had one, but they're really good. Are you familiar with them?" Without giving him a chance to answer or her to take a breath, she continued, "They're a croissant-doughnut hybrid. My customers love them. I'll bring a Danish for you, just in case you don't share my enthusiasm."

She was babbling, knew she was babbling, but couldn't seem to stop herself.

When he stepped closer, her speech came even faster. "Cronuts were invented by a sous chef in New York City. Right away they were this huge success and—"

"Ami."

Something in the way he said her name silenced her, even as her heart continued its erratic rhythm. "Yes, Beck?"

"It's cold out there." He took her arm and tugged her farther into the foyer and shut the door firmly behind her. "Now, tell me why you came."

Buying some time, Ami shifted her gaze from those smoldering eyes to the parlor. She blinked. Looked again.

The home that had once boasted luxurious Persian rugs and an amazing decor, looked sad and empty and old. The wallpaper—a delicate rose pattern—had begun to peel. It was obvious now that those beautiful floor coverings had been cloaking hardwood in desperate need of refinishing.

She turned to Beck. "It's empty."

His quicksilver smile was gone so quickly she wondered if she'd only imagined it.

"Stellar observation skills, Miss Bloom."

Ami inclined her head in a regal arch. "Noticing when a room is empty is a particular talent of mine."

This time she was certain his lips twitched.

"What can I do for you?" he asked.

She had to give the guy credit. Beck obviously subscribed to the notion if you don't get an answer when you first ask, try, try again.

"I'd say you could invite me to sit." She gestured with a sweeping hand toward the parlor. "But as I don't see any chairs, that might prove difficult."

"How about you simply tell me what brought you by?"

Yes, indeed, try, try again.

"How about you find a chair and offer me something hot to drink?" Bantering with Beck was familiar territory, and Ami felt herself relaxing. Contrary to what Hadley intimated, the banter had nothing, absolutely nothing, to do with sex.

Beck studied her for a moment through narrowed eyes. "You won't leave until I do."

"I knew you were a smart guy." She took off her gloves, stuffed them into her pockets, then began to unzip her coat. "Too bad you don't have a fire in there."

She gestured with her head toward the dark and cold hearth.

"I've got the one upstairs. That's where I spend most of my time." Before he finished speaking, he raised a hand. "That part of the house is off-limits to you."

"Don't flatter yourself, Cross." Ami gave a dismissive snort. "You act as if I have some burning desire to visit your bedroom."

Yet she could see it all so clearly: snow falling outside the window, a cheery fire in a hearth, and Beck next to her in a four-poster bed, na—

"Actually, the upstairs fireplace is in the sitting area, not in my bedroom." Beck sounded amused.

"Oh. Yes, of course. I knew that." In an attempt to regain control of her wayward thoughts, Ami brushed past him. "Do you use the kitchen much?"

"Hey, where are you—"

Ami didn't stop until she reached the large room at the back of the house. She'd spent many a pleasant hour in this kitchen.

Now, Kate was far away in Arizona, and she'd probably never see her old friend again. Ami experienced a little pang in the vicinity of her heart at the thought. "I remember when Katherine—Kate—had this room updated."

Beck watched her warily. It was apparent he was still trying to figure out why she was there.

"Built-in cabinets didn't exist at the time this house was constructed. Everything was freestanding and moveable." Warming to the topic, Ami hung her coat on a vintage wall hook by the back door. "Back then the work surfaces were tables, not countertops. Kate was determined to stay true to the era. The only exception she made was the built-in cabinet that houses the dishwasher. This is definitely a twenty-first-century kitchen with a Victorian feel."

"She did it up right," Beck acknowledged.

"It cost her a whole bucketload of money." Ami paused. "After the kitchen was done, she replaced the old boiler. She didn't tell me what the new modulating-condensing one cost, but I got the impression it was pricey. I wonder if the cost of keeping the place up was part of the reason she decided to sell? Or maybe she had all the improvements made because she planned on selling?"

"Didn't she tell you why?"

"By the time I heard, it was a done deal. She was already on her way to Arizona." Ami tried to keep the hurt from her voice. "Kate was a very private person."

His gaze searched hers. "Sometimes, a person needs to make a change, and they don't tell others because they don't want anyone making them second-guess their decision."

Something told Ami he wasn't speaking about Kate. She thought about asking him again what had brought him to Good Hope, but refrained. When he'd first arrived, Beck had made it clear his past was off-limits.

Ami plopped down into a chair and realized, for the first time since she'd left her house, she was warm. "A cup of tea would be nice."

"Would you like a cookie, too?"

Sarcasm laced through the words like a pretty ribbon. Ami hid a smile. "No, thank you. I had a piece of kringle earlier. But I appreciate the kind offer."

———

Beck wondered why he didn't simply toss her out. Actually, he wondered why he'd let her in. He didn't want visitors, especially not a brown-haired pixie with green eyes and a spray of freckles across the bridge of her nose.

Ami, not A-mee, but Am-ee, as she'd told him the first time they'd met, wasn't like anyone else in Good Hope. For one thing, she never took him seriously when he growled.

Back when he'd been a trial attorney, one look had been enough to send junior associates in his firm scrambling. This woman seemed immune to such tactics.

Beck couldn't figure her out. He'd noticed that while *Am-ee* appeared to know everyone, she seemed to hold part of herself back. But she didn't ask him questions about his past and he didn't ask her.

He wondered what she'd say if he told her he'd picked Good Hope by closing his eyes and settling down where his finger landed on the map.

"Since you seem to be moving slow tonight, I'll brew the tea." She rose and went to the cabinet. "You do have tea?"

He shook his head.

She rolled her eyes. "Good thing I came prepared."

Her hand dived into the pocket of her pants and she pulled out two individually packaged tea bags. "I hope you like Earl Grey."

He was beaten. He knew it. She knew it.

"I'll get the cups."

Chapter Three

Beck took a drink of Earl Grey and listened to Ami's spirited account of the fundraiser she'd attended with her father earlier in the evening. He wondered if she was aware that her face glowed whenever she spoke about helping someone in need.

Ami had a giving spirit. It was one of the first things he'd noticed about her. Shortly after he'd moved to Good Hope, she'd strolled through the door of his café at the absolute worst time. The crew he'd hired to tear off the hideous wallpaper had just arrived.

After introducing herself, she'd handed the foreman a box of doughnuts. Then she'd turned those sea-green eyes on him. With a cheeky smile and a sassiness he found refreshing, she'd swung the bag in her other hand back and forth and announced she'd saved several of her favorites for them to share as they got acquainted.

Beck had been powerless to turn her away. She'd plated the pastries. He'd poured the coffee. A morning tradition, which continued to this day, had taken root.

He'd told himself many times he should put a stop to it. The fact that it was becoming harder to take his eyes off her mouth when she wrapped those luscious lips around a cruller only emphasized the danger she posed.

"I put Cory's name into the Giving Tree."

"Cory?"

"Cory White." She stared down into her tea. "The teacher fighting leukemia."

"You went to a fish fry for him tonight." That should show her he'd been listening.

"I did." Ami lifted her gaze. "The event coordinator announced over a thousand dollars was raised for the family. It's money they desperately need. Cory and his wife have three small children. His wife—Jackie—was diagnosed with multiple sclerosis last year. Stress makes her illness worse. Between the kids and taking him to the doctor for treatments . . ."

Ami's green eyes turned dark as jade. "We're lucky, Beck. You and I are so very lucky."

The words sliced his heart like a meat cleaver. *Lucky* was not a word he'd use to describe his life. He opened his mouth, prepared to tell her just that, but came to his senses in time. Mentioning his past would only lead to questions. Questions about a time in his life he was doing his best to forget.

"I really hope Cory and his family will get assistance from the Giving Tree."

"How does that work?" Beck latched on to the offhand comment as a way of getting the conversation off his "lucky" life. Too late he realized he should have steered it in the direction of why she'd come over. He still hadn't received an answer to that question.

"It's actually pretty simple." Ami rose and refilled her mug. She held up the kettle and gestured toward his cup.

What the heck? He nodded.

Her smile was like the sun breaking through the clouds. Before Beck could steel himself, a wave of warmth washed over him. He realized the feeling of contentment he experienced when around her was another reason he hadn't told her to stay away.

After filling his mug to the brim with steaming water, Ami resumed her seat across from him. Wrapping small, sturdy hands topped with short-cut light pink nails around the red ceramic mug, she leaned forward.

"The Giving Tree started out as a Christmas gift project sponsored by the rotary." Her eyes took on a faraway look. "As kids, my sisters and I would do bake sales and car washes in the summer specifically to raise money to buy the gifts. Our dad was very active in the rotary. Still is, for that matter."

"I don't understand how the charity works."

Ami stiffened ever so slightly. If he hadn't been observing just how nicely she filled out her sweater, he might have missed the subtle response.

"It's not a *charity*." She paused, took a deep breath. "Not that *charity* is a bad word. In the most basic terms it means voluntarily giving, typically money, to those in need. But in some circles, it carries a negative connotation, a one-upmanship that I find offensive."

Beck had never given the matter much thought. His parents were both very philanthropic. He'd carried on the tradition. In his former life he'd generously donated to numerous charities in the town where he lived.

"I never considered the one-upmanship angle." He rubbed his chin. "I have to admit I'd probably be one of those too proud to take money or help."

"If you had a family who depended on you, like Cory does, I imagine you'd find a way to overcome your reservations." Ami sipped her tea, her green eyes thoughtful. "That's why it's so important to always stress this isn't charity. The Giving Tree is basically neighbors helping neighbors who've fallen on hard times. We help in many ways, not just by giving money."

"Do the *Cherries* have their fingers in this pie?" Beck barely suppressed a sneer. Eliza and her troop had been a thorn in his side from day one.

The slight twitch of those red lips told him Ami knew exactly how he felt about Eliza Shaw. No doubt she'd heard about his altercation with the group's executive director.

"There is some crossover, but the rotary remains in control of the Giving Tree. It takes many community volunteers working year-round to meet the needs of Good Hope citizens. This year, I'm the chair of club projects, which means I'm in charge of Christmas gift distribution."

Her gaze suddenly narrowed on him. When she tapped a finger against her lips, the hairs on the back of Beck's neck prickled.

After a long moment she spoke. "Being a rotarian is an excellent way for a business owner to become involved in the community."

"I don't have time." Beck raised a hand, palm out, deciding it was best to put a stop to her pitch before it went any further. "With Janey gone and—"

"I don't need you to do me—" Ami inhaled sharply, then emitted a nervous giggle. "I mean, I don't want you to—"

Beck inclined his head and watched a hint of red creep stealthily up her neck.

Interesting.

"I'm sorry. When I get tired, I get a little punchy. Let me start over." This time she spoke slowly and deliberately, as if carefully plucking each word from a specially selected basket. "I'm not asking you to join or to participate in any fundraising for the club. Though if you would like to, we'd be happy to have you."

She looked so intense, so serious, Beck couldn't help but smile. He'd only known one other woman with such passion . . . and he'd married her. The loss of her still haunted him. He felt his smile slip.

The realization that Ami reminded him of Lisette had Beck's next words coming out more abruptly than he intended. "What is it you want from me, Ami? Spit it out."

Her smile vanished for a second, then reappeared, though not as bright. With precise movements, she placed her cup on the table, then met his gaze. "I'd like to use one of the rooms in your house to store the gifts we purchase. It'll only be for a few weeks. Whoever we find to play Santa will deliver the presents on Christmas Eve."

Had she really asked him to turn his home into a warehouse? "Absolutely not."

The smile remained on her lips. She leaned forward and rested her forearms on the table. "Tell me your reservations."

The request was offered in an easy, conversational tone, but Beck noticed the slight lifting of her chin. The determined look in her eyes, well, he didn't like that one bit, either.

He didn't blurt out all the reasons he was opposed to the request. That would be pointless. She'd only attempt to allay his concerns, and he wasn't interested in platitudes.

Instead of pushing for an answer, Ami took a sip of tea and studied him in the curious way one might study a particularly interesting bug.

"I don't want strangers in and out of my house." Beck sat back, pleased to have come up with the perfect response. A personal preference was difficult to argue against. Besides, with almost the entire main floor empty, he could hardly assert he didn't have room.

Ami dipped her head as if graciously accepting defeat.

Beck relaxed, feeling as proud as the day he'd won his first case. There was nothing like—

"I wouldn't want that, either." She offered him a smile filled with warmth and understanding.

An appropriate response, to be sure. Yet something in those sea-green eyes put him on high alert.

"I'll make you a deal."

Deal? He wasn't interested in any deal. His decision was final. "What kind of deal?"

"I promise I'll be the only one who'll bring gifts to your home." Her gaze locked on his and the pleading look in her eyes tugged at his heart. "Please, Beck. The guy who used to store the packages got married this year. His house is small and his wife doesn't want the clutter."

Say no, Beck told himself. *Stop the dialogue. Just say no.*

"Where are you keeping the gifts now?"

"In my living room." Ami sighed. "I barely have room to walk, let alone a spare foot or two for a tree."

Beck had never been inside Ami's apartment. But he was familiar with the bakery and knew she lived directly above the small shop. No, there probably wasn't extra space for storage.

He considered all the empty rooms in his home.

When she'd shown up at his door tonight, he assumed she'd stopped by to badger, *er, persuade*, him to open his house to the home tour. Compared to a request of that magnitude, this was a small thing to ask. The promise that she'd be the only one bringing over the gifts had him reconsidering. "Okay. You may store them here."

Her face lit up and Beck basked in the glow.

He congratulated himself on picking his battles. Always better to agree to something small than to get roped into doing something huge like opening his house to the public.

"I suppose I should be heading home." Ami pushed back her chair and stood. "I've imposed on your generosity long enough."

Beck rose to his feet. This would be the time to mention that in the future he'd prefer she called before stopping over. But when Ami rounded the table and placed a hand on his sleeve, the words died in his throat.

"Thanks for agreeing to help, Beck. And for sharing an Earl Grey moment with me." She flashed him a quick smile. "Up to this point, my night had been a bit rocky."

Without further elaboration, she strode to where she'd hung her coat.

"Why?"

With one hand resting on her jacket, she turned. "Pardon me?"

Though whatever had gone on earlier wasn't any of his concern, Beck was curious. In all the months he'd known Ami, this was the first time Miss Holiday Cheer had mentioned any cloudy skies. He couldn't help wondering what had brought her down and if there was something he could do to help.

"Tell me what happened at the fundraiser," he suggested, surprised by his willingness to extend her visit.

"Memories." She lifted one shoulder, let it drop. "They slam a fist into your heart at the most unexpected times."

Beck concurred with the sentiment. In the past two years he'd discovered that something quite innocuous could flatten him.

Apparently mistaking his silence for confusion, she added, "Cory's cancer is the same kind that took my mom's life."

Several months ago, during one of their morning coffee breaks, Ami had confided that her mother had been diagnosed with leukemia during her senior year in high school and passed away three years ago.

He saw no need to mention something Ami already knew: each person's prognosis was different, and just because Cory had the same cancer didn't mean he faced the same outcome. "What else?"

Ami averted her gaze. "What do you mean?"

"What else made the evening difficult for you?"

"It's stupid." She made a dismissive sound. "Silly."

He gestured to the chair she'd just vacated. "I have time, a warm house, and Earl Grey."

That brought the smile back to her lips. Instead of taking a seat, Ami began to pace.

Lifting his mug of lukewarm tea, Beck rested his back against the counter and followed her strides with his gaze.

He knew she didn't have any idea how beautiful she was with her golden-brown hair brushing her shoulders and her green eyes reminding him of stormy seas.

"Anita Fishback was at the fundraiser."

An image of an attractive woman in her midfifties popped into his head. Beck had met the vivacious brunette at a business function when he first moved to Good Hope. Their paths had crossed several times since.

The woman struck him as pleasant, if a bit intense. She reminded him of his mother's Maltese, Brandie Sue. The fluffy puffball might appear innocuous, but those engaging brown eyes belied a will of steel.

The last time he'd spoken with Anita, she'd steered the conversation around to what she needed to do to get the contract for desserts at his café. A contract currently held by Blooms Bake Shop. "She's your competitor."

Ami made a face. "Crumb and Cake may be another bakery, but Anita is not my competitor."

By the dismissive tone, Beck surmised whatever trouble existed between the two women was personal.

A frown furrowed her brow as she continued to pace. "I think she's got the hots for my dad."

Beck tilted his head ever so slightly as he studied her. "Is that bad?"

"Yes. No. Oh, I don't know." Ami blew out a breath and came to an abrupt halt. "Anita was once married to my dad's best friend. Richard died of a heart attack back when I was in middle school. She dated around and finally married Bernie Fishback, the Bagel King. They divorced several years ago."

Ami pressed her lips together as if realizing she'd been rambling.

"Your father and Anita are both single," Beck pointed out, wondering what he was missing.

"You don't understand." Exasperated, she flung her hands into the air. "She's manipulative and sneaky. When I run into her and my father is with her, she acts like we're buddies. But if I see her on the street and she's alone, she barely acknowledges me. I know I'm protective when it comes to my dad, and I suppose that could be influencing my impression of her, but the truth is, she doesn't think highly of me, either."

Beck couldn't hide his surprise. "Why not?"

Ami's voice dropped to a whisper, though they were the only ones in the room. "It's complicated."

She looked so miserable he found himself moving close.

"Your father is lucky to have you looking out for him." He placed a hand on her shoulder, hoping to comfort, wanting to soothe. He felt the tension ease out of her.

"I love him so much." Her voice trembled with emotion.

Beck thought of his own parents and how long it had been since they'd spoken. They worried about him but were determined to give him the space he needed. He needed to remember that building a new life in Good Hope didn't mean cutting off contact with those he loved.

She chewed on her lip. "I'm probably being silly."

"I don't think so."

His quietly spoken words appeared to surprise her.

"You—you don't?"

"You have good instincts." Beck kept his tone matter-of-fact. "From what I've observed, you look for the best in everyone. If this woman sets off alarms, I'd trust my gut."

Beck met her gaze, willing her to see he meant every word. In the court system he'd seen many instances in which the outcome might have been different if the individuals had paid attention to red flags instead of dismissing them.

"Thank you, Beck."

He wasn't certain what she was thanking him for, but he was glad her smile was back and the frown that had worried her brow had vanished.

Beck helped her on with her jacket, and with the subject of Anita Fishback apparently now off the table, they strolled to the parlor, leaning into one another like old friends. As they passed the front window, Beck saw snow had continued to fall. Though the street lamps were valiantly attempting to light the darkness, it appeared to be a losing battle.

When they reached the foyer, Beck rested his hand on the newel post, suddenly conscious of how close she stood and how good she smelled. Like cinnamon and sugar and everything sweet. "Appears the snow is picking up steam."

"Welcome to Wisconsin."

The teasing words drew his attention back to her mouth. To the lips that reminded him of plump, red strawberries. When he'd moved in last summer, Beck had located a berry patch in the far end of the yard. He wondered if Ami's lips would taste as sweet.

A curious energy infused the silence. Her cheeks went a little pink, but she didn't say a word. And neither did he . . .

Though Beck and Ami had shared coffee and pastries almost every morning for months, only recently had Beck begun to see Ami as more than the shop owner next door.

That didn't mean he planned to act on the attraction. He wasn't looking for a *relationship*. Nothing could replace what he'd had with Lisette. And Ami didn't seem like the type of woman who'd be interested in a fling.

Slowly, Beck drew air into his lungs.

"Well, thanks again." Ami paused, as if not sure what more to say. She lifted her hood, then began wrapping yards of a multicolored scarf around her neck as if preparing for the next ice age. "See you in the morning."

Finally able to focus, he stepped between her and the door. "Not so fast. I'm driving you home."

Surprise skittered across her face. "It's only a few blocks."

"It's a blizzard out there."

Ami laughed, a short, nervous burst of air. "Hardly a blizzard."

"I'm driving you home," he repeated in a gruff rasp, his tone brooking no argument.

"Okay, but on one condition." Her eyes seemed to glitter. "Tomorrow morning we meet at my apartment instead of the café." Her request made no sense. Then again, nothing about this evening had followed a scripted path. Beck dropped his gaze from her warm green eyes with their flecks of gold to those full, plump lips that tantalized, and grinned. "Shall I bring the coffee?"

Chapter Four

The snow continued through the night and into the early morning hours. Beck was covered in the white stuff by the time he reached the bakery.

He dusted the snow from his coat while he waited for Ami to unlock the door. After years of wearing a suit and tie every day, it felt strange to be dressed so casually on a workday. But casual was de rigueur in Good Hope.

Like him, Ami wore jeans. While he'd chosen a navy ski sweater he'd purchased on a trip to Aspen several years earlier for this snowy December morning, she'd gone ultracasual and donned a red-and-white-striped hoodie with a scowling badger on the front. He recognized the strutting animal with the arrogant attitude as the University of Wisconsin's mascot, Bucky.

Though the oversize sweatshirt gave no clue to the womanly figure beneath, the jeans clung to her toned legs like a glove. She opened the door with a broad, welcoming smile. He noticed the tips of her hair were still wet. Instead of smelling like cakes and cookies today, the faint floral scent from her shampoo teased his nostrils.

He must have been staring, because she laughed and grabbed his hand. "You'll freeze if you stand out there much longer."

She ushered him inside and quickly shut the door behind him.

After hanging his jacket on the downstairs coat tree, he followed her to the stairwell at the back of the shop. The journey up the steep steps to her second-floor apartment was made more pleasant by the enticing view of her backside.

"This morning I have an extra-special treat for you," she promised, her voice a husky caress.

His gaze returned to the sway of her hips as she took another step. His mouth went dry. Was there something more than pastries on the menu this morning?

For a second he let himself fantasize what it would be like to hold her, taste her, touch her. When the urge to do just that threatened to overwhelm Beck, he shifted his gaze to the lavender walls of the stairwell.

"Aren't you curious?" she asked, sounding perturbed.

Beck struggled to remember the conversation. "As to what pastry you're serving?"

"What else?"

His gaze returned briefly to her derriere. *What else indeed?*

"It's called kouign amann," she continued. "It's a traditional French pastry."

"I've never met a French pastry I didn't like." A lifetime ago, Paris had been a favorite destination when he and Lisette had needed to relax and recharge.

"Just wait until you taste this one." Ami chuckled as they reached the landing. "It's *sinfully* delicious. It resembles a puff pastry with its layers of buttery, sugary dough. But, in my opinion, it's the caramelized crust that makes it *très magnifique.*"

Beck's mouth began to water in anticipation. He had no doubt the pastry would be every bit as good as she promised. He'd never been around a woman with such an aptitude for baking.

Ami flung open the door to her apartment and stepped inside, glancing back at him over her shoulder. "Watch where you put your feet."

The warning came in the nick of time. Beck's boot missed an iPad box encased in bubble wrap by a centimeter. Deciding to play it safe, he paused to survey the apartment from where he stood.

An unusual wall clock with framed photos instead of numbers drew his gaze. If the floor hadn't been so cluttered, he might have moved closer to see if Ami was in any of the pictures.

He shifted his focus straight ahead to the galley kitchen with a small dinette table. Off to the right was a hallway that he assumed would lead to a bathroom and bedroom.

Though the living room was small, because of the relatively open floor plan, it looked more spacious. Or, Beck qualified, it would have appeared larger if almost every available surface, including the floor, weren't covered with gifts. Some of the items were already wrapped and tagged, while others were still in original packaging.

Beck had expected the toys and electronics, but not the household items, blankets, and clothing. He even spotted a power saw in one corner.

"As you can see, there's still a lot of wrapping to be done." Ami smiled at him from across the room. "If you don't have a spare table, I'll bring one. That way I can finish wrapping these and the new gifts as they arrive."

Beck cocked his head. Had she mentioned she'd also be stopping over to wrap? No, she'd definitely left that part off of her "I need your spare room" spiel.

Before he could mention the oversight, Beck caught a whiff of fresh coffee. Unless his nose was mistaken, she'd brewed the dark chicory blend they both preferred.

Beck carefully picked his way through the chaos of the living room to the kitchen. The wall behind Ami was a bright, cheery yellow. The white lacquered dinette table had multicolored flowers painted across the top.

It was the curtains that had him looking twice. His first impulse was to label the holdbacks as ridiculous. He went with his second. "I like the forks."

Ami grinned. "I think of them as both clever and unique."

The white curtains with their border of sewn-on flowers were held back on each side of the window by an oversize bent fork.

"Very unique hardware." Beck couldn't recall ever seeing anything remotely like it. His parents' home in Fairview, Tennessee, as well as his prior home in Bogart, Georgia, had been professionally decorated. Not a single bent fork in sight. Still, he liked the novelty. The bright colors suited the small space. The vibrancy of it fit Ami's personality.

"Have a seat." She gestured to the table, where two bright purple plates each boasted a pastry so perfectly formed it could qualify as a work of art.

Turning from him, Ami moved to the counter and poured coffee into two red mugs from a vintage silver percolator.

"Where did you get the coffeepot?" The last time Beck had seen one like it had been years ago at his grandmother's house.

"My dad is hooked on his Keurig and didn't want it anymore. I was the lucky recipient of his castoff." After placing the steaming mugs on the table, she sat across from him. "Try the pastry. Let me know what you think."

Beck bit into the round, crusty cake. The sweet, buttery layers and caramelized crust came together in his mouth in an almost orgasmic explosion. He groaned.

Ami had been right.

Anita Fishback was no competition when it came to baking skills.

"I'll take that as a yes."

Her lighthearted laugh brought a smile to his lips even as his mouth closed over the pastry for another bite.

"I heard about Janey leaving."

The abrupt change of topic barely registered. Beck had grown used to her jumping from one subject to another. He took a sip of coffee before responding. "Only for a month. She'll be back after the holidays."

Ami's gaze was now firmly focused on him. "She left you in the lurch."

"Her mother had a stroke." Beck had seen the fear on Janey's face. He knew all too well how it felt to have an unexpected phone call rock your world. "I hope, faced with the same situation, I'd do what was necessary to help my mother."

"Are you and your mom close?"

"We used to be." Beck leaned back in his seat and studied her. He noticed the tight grip her hands had on the mug. She hadn't yet touched her pastry.

Unable to resist, Beck took another bite of his own.

"I want you to hire me as your cook." The request burst from Ami's lips, and the abrupt delivery appeared to startle her almost as much as it did him.

With the entire building imbued with the aroma of fresh-baked bread and cinnamon, one fact was indisputable. "You're a baker."

"I cook every bit as good as I bake." Ami placed her cup on the table and leaned forward. "I'd be a terrific asset to the café."

"I don't doubt that in the least." Beck warmed his hands around his mug and considered her request. "You already have a job. Why work two?"

"Ralph." The word came out on a sigh.

Something that felt an awful lot like jealousy flashed. "Who's Ralph?"

The edge to his voice had Ami blinking.

"Ralph is the furnace, or rather, the boiler. It's failing, and I've discovered the cost of replacing it is superexpensive. Since I can't let the pipes freeze, I had to schedule the work. They're coming tomorrow."

"Is that why it's so cold in here?"

A dimple in Ami's left cheek winked. "You noticed?"

"I can see my breath."

Ami grinned. "I thought I could work the days I'm not at the bakery, which would be Tuesday, Wednesday, and Thursday. Depending on what you pay me, the money I earned could make a big dent in my furnace bill."

The fact that she was willing to work a second job told him she must be desperate. Beck wished he could help her out. He admired her work ethic, the way she identified a problem and attacked it head-on. Unfortunately, the days she proposed to help weren't when he needed someone.

"I'd love to help you." When he paused, Beck saw the light in her eyes fade.

She squeezed her eyes shut briefly, then let out a long breath. "I hear *but* in your voice."

"I can handle the middle of the week with the current staff." He held up his hands when he saw her mouth open. "What I need is a cook for the Twelve Nights celebrations. But those Fridays, Saturdays, and Sundays are the same days your bakery will be swamped."

"Are you saying you won't hire me?"

The look of despair on her face was quickly masked, but not before he'd seen it. Beck would willingly lend her the money, but he sensed she wouldn't accept if he offered. His short time on the peninsula had taught him the people here were a proud lot. So far, in their short acquaintance, Ami appeared to be no exception.

As Beck gazed into those worried green eyes, something inside him stirred. *Sympathy*, he told himself, *for her plight*.

But even Beck had trouble believing the heat radiating through his body was a surge of sympathy. Before he could do anything foolish, or even fully contemplate doing anything foolish, he surged to his feet.

To his surprise, she jumped up and took his hands in hers. "Don't go, Beck."

He gently disengaged his hands from hers, the movement at odds with the strong desire to pull her into his arms.

It could have been a perfect match. He needed an accomplished cook and was prepared to pay well for the right person. It was easy to visualize Ami in his kitchen. The staff would love having her there. And so, Beck realized, would he.

Not meant to be.

"Beckett, please."

The soft plea in her voice wrapped around his heart.

"I don't know what else to say." But when her eyes remained fixed on his and she didn't step aside, he softened the refusal. "If you can find a way to work Twelve Nights, the job is yours."

Her entire face brightened. "Seriously?"

"Absolutely."

"Oh, Beck." She flung her arms around him. "I'll figure something out. Just you wait and see."

Ami waved to Beck from the doorway of the shop and watched him disappear into the wintery whiteness. She pulled the door shut against the cold and slowly climbed the steps.

Hugging him had definitely been a mistake. Though her arms had only been around him for a heartbeat, it had jumbled her head so much she'd found it impossible to think, much less come up with a solution to their dilemma. Her impulsive action had also made him uncomfortable, as evidenced by his hasty retreat.

Ami glanced at the clock as she reentered her apartment. As it took up most of the wall, it was difficult to miss. The words "Time Spent With Family . . . Is Worth Every Second" were stenciled on the navy paint in silver letters above and below the clockworks. Instead of numbers, there were framed pictures.

Just looking at the faces of her loved ones eased the tightness in her chest. A picture of her father's parents taken on their fiftieth wedding anniversary four years ago was on top. They'd moved to Arizona last year because the cold winter air made her grandmother's arthritis worse.

A portrait of her mother's parents held the six o'clock spot. The smiling couple had been killed in a car accident when her mother was away at college. Ami had never fully understood how hard getting that news by phone had been for her mom until her parents had been called to the hospital for her.

Ami's heart gave a painful lurch. She shifted her gaze to the pictures of her and her sisters individually and then ones where they were together. They'd always been so close. Little stair steps, her parents had called them.

She'd been the oldest, but only by a year over Delphinium. Delphinium's name had been too much of a mouthful, so her sister had become Fin almost instantly. While she and Fin had once been close, they were different personalities.

From a young age, Ami's interest had been focused in the kitchen, while Fin loved parties and being in the center of any action. Ami meandered while her sister sped through life at breakneck speed. Primrose came next, then Marigold.

At this point Prim was the only one of the four girls who'd married and produced grandchildren. While Ami and her dad wished Prim and her twin boys would move back to Good Hope, a terrific job with exceptional benefits in Milwaukee had kept her tethered there, even after the death of her husband.

Ami wiped a hand across her eyes and plopped down on the one spot on the sofa not covered with gifts. This year the entire family would be back for Christmas. Not just to celebrate the holiday but for the open house Ami had planned for her father.

January would mark Steve Bloom's thirty-fifth year with the school district. Since everyone was coming for Christmas, she and her sisters had decided it made sense to have the celebration while they were in town.

Of course, if she didn't get Beck's job, she wouldn't have money to pay for the furnace *or* her share of the party. Not to mention there was a good chance she'd be kicked out of the Cherries unless she got Beck to agree to the tour of homes pronto.

She'd made no further progress in coming up with a solution

to her dilemma when the phone rang that afternoon. By the time she hung up with effusive thanks ringing in her ears, a chill that had nothing to do with the lack of heat filled every inch of her body.

Ami knew she could have turned down the assignment, a drop-off of items in another part of town. But Calvin Koontz, the rotarian who scheduled such drop-offs, had told her before he even made the request that she was the fifth person he'd called. He'd have taken on the task himself except he'd fallen on the ice last week and seriously injured his ankle.

For a second Ami considered asking her father to come with her, but immediately dismissed the notion. He wouldn't be able to take time away from the classroom so close to holiday break.

There *had* to be someone in Good Hope she could get to accompany her tomorrow morning. Or she'd just have to figure out another way to accomplish the task.

Chapter Five

When Ami had thinking to do, she baked. Today, she had much on her mind. Beck. The furnace. Beck. The Cherries. Beck. Her likely encounter tomorrow with Clint Gourley. And, last but not least, her father's growing "friendship" with Anita "I Need A Man" Fishback.

In between overseeing the furnace installation and baking, she'd spoken with all three of her sisters. Not one of them believed Anita posed a real threat.

Her sisters were intelligent women, and Ami might have been reassured, except for one fact. They hadn't been around Anita in years. Even if they had, the woman was a chameleon. She could be sweet and charming one second and manipulative as all get-out the next.

Unfortunately her father, a man who only saw the good in people, appeared to be taking the woman at face value.

His naïveté scared Ami to death.

She saw no choice but to remain calm and observe. If Ami wasn't careful, there was the possibility she could end up pushing her dad further into Anita's grasping arms. She worried she may have done that already when her father commented on the drive home from the fundraiser that Anita worried Ami didn't like her.

When she mentioned she didn't know Anita well enough to dislike her, she'd seen a flash of irritation in her dad's eyes. When he'd asked her to take every opportunity to become better acquainted with the woman, Ami felt forced to agree.

The way Ami saw it, the promise meant she could keep a close eye on the woman. Once her sisters were home and had time to assess the situation, they'd come up with a plan.

By seven o'clock that evening Ami was still searching for someone to accompany her on her mission of mercy in the morning. While awaiting callbacks from several possibilities, she decided to drop off a lemon pound cake at her father's house.

Hopefully a nice visit with him would calm her fears. It felt good to pull out the Schwinn. With her fleece-lined jeans, silky thermal top under her sweater, and arctic-rated coat, Ami barely noticed the cold.

The streets were snow packed but well maintained. The residential streets were well lit, not only from the decorative street lamps but also the brightly colored Christmas lights on every home. Ami found herself singing a variety of carols on her journey.

By the time she reached the familiar block of her childhood, her mood was upbeat. Hopping off the bike, she rolled it up the walkway and parked the Schwinn on her father's porch. In the window, a perfectly shaped tree with multicolored lights twinkled.

The Christmas spirit extended to the exterior. Though definitely more subdued than when four girls had their hands into the decorations, the house still had a festive edge. Outside, white lights wove through a swath of greenery edging the heavy wooden front door. A dark green wreath with the same white lights hung on the door.

The low-pitched story-and-a-half was an attractive home. Built new in the eighties, the bungalow had the appearance of a 1920s Craftsman-style home. Ami loved everything about it, from its taupe hardwood siding with cream-colored trim to the landscaped yard, which reflected her father's love of plants and bushes.

When all the girls had been home, the house had been a cozy haven. She couldn't imagine her father ever leaving this place that held so many happy memories. Recently, though, he'd mentioned several times the place was too big for one.

Once her sisters and nephews arrived, the home would once again be filled with activity and laughter. Ami expelled a happy sigh at the thought and slipped the box containing the pound cake from her basket.

Ami didn't bother to lock the bike. The area was safe. *Neighbors looking after neighbors*, she thought with a smile.

The wind, which had been nonexistent, suddenly picked up speed. Ami was sorely tempted to forego knocking and just walk inside. Only the knowledge that while this might be the house where she'd grown up, it was no longer her home had her hesitating.

Turning her back to the wind, Ami hunched her shoulders, clutched the box against her body, and rang the bell. She waited several seconds and was about to hit the buzzer again when the door finally opened.

Surprise briefly skittered across her father's face before his lips curved into a broad smile of welcome. He stepped aside and motioned her inside.

"I didn't expect to see you this evening," her father began.

"I went on a baking frenzy today. I made you a pound cake." Ami suddenly noticed he wore khakis and a cotton shirt with his navy cardigan, rather than his normal evening attire of well-worn jeans and a sweatshirt. "You look nice, Dad. Did you have a school function this evening?"

"No." Looking uncomfortable, he shifted from one foot to the other. "Actually—"

"I made him dinner."

The feminine voice came from the living room, where a fire blazed in the hearth. Ami turned toward the voice and froze.

Anita sat on the sofa, a glass of wine in her hand. Thick, dark hair waved gently around an angular face with large hazel eyes. Although the shirt Anita wore was long-sleeved, Ami was surprised the woman wasn't visibly shivering in the thin gold silk pants and shirt.

"Anita made a wonderful meal," Steve Bloom said proudly. "Her lasagna is the best I've ever tasted."

Ami tried not to take offense. She'd dropped off a pan of lasagna for her dad just last week.

"I love to cook, but it's no fun just for one." Anita bestowed a sweet smile on Steve before turning her attention to Ami.

"We had lemon meringue pie for dessert," her dad added.

The pie was her father's favorite.

"The pound cake will keep." Ami kept her smile firmly in place.

Anita lifted her wineglass. "Join us."

Ami stiffened. *Join us?* The woman acted as if this was *her* home.

"Yes, please join us," her father echoed.

Though Ami had initially planned to simply drop off the cake, chat with her dad for a few minutes, and then head home, she decided leaving now might appear rude. "Thanks."

While her father left the room to pour her a glass of wine, Ami stepped into the cozy living room with its dove-gray walls and massive stone fireplace. She chose the chintz-covered chair her mother had always favored, directly across from the piranha.

It gave Ami great satisfaction to know evidence of her mother filled every corner of the room. The upright piano against one wall had been hers. She'd insisted all her girls take lessons, but only Fin had shown talent. On the side table, special picture frames, carefully chosen by Sarah Bloom, held photos of the family.

"I was surprised when the buzzer sounded. I didn't hear a car outside." Anita paused, then her gaze narrowed. "That's right, you don't drive."

Ami crossed her legs and hoped her father would return quickly.

"I can't imagine imposing on my friends for rides." Anita gazed at Ami over the rim of her glass. "But not driving is better than hurting someone."

Ami's cheeks burned as if she'd been slapped.

"It's a beautiful evening for a bike ride." Ami lifted her chin and smiled her thanks as her father returned and handed her a glass of red. "I spend so much time indoors this time of year, it's nice to be out in the fresh air."

"I'm afraid I don't share your love of the cold." Anita gave a little shiver. "Even now I'm a bit chilled."

"I can turn up the heat." Her father had begun to rise when Anita's fingers closed around his hand, pulling him down.

"I'll be fine if you just move a little closer," Anita purred.

If you'd just put on some decent clothes, you'd be fine.

Ami swallowed the words on the tip of her tongue.

Steve scooted closer with a pleased smile, even going so far as to put an arm around Anita's shoulder. Ami noticed her father staring with an expectant expression.

"Sounds as if you two had a nice dinner." Ami feigned a look of interest. "Lasagna and pie. Very nice. I love the meal, but it does take a lot of pots and pans."

"It sure does." Anita expelled a melodramatic sigh. "I should get up now and tend to the mess."

Though the woman made no attempt to move, Steve took her hand. "I told you not to worry about that, Cookie. Your back is bothering you, yet you slaved over a hot stove in order to make me a fine meal. I'm certainly not going to let you do the cleanup, too."

The warmth in his voice had red flags popping up so fast it made Ami's head spin. And *Cookie?* Her father had a pet name for Anita Fishback?

This was worse than she'd imagined.

"Your father is a true gentleman." Anita covered Ami's father's hand with hers. She gave it a squeeze before slanting a faux smile in Ami's direction. "He's so good to me."

At that moment, Ami wished she were Marigold. Growing up, the youngest Bloom sister had perfected a number of gagging sounds.

"Why don't I take care of the dishes?" her dad offered. "It'll give you two girls a chance to talk and get better acquainted."

Was that a warning glance her father shot in her direction? Sure as heck looked like one. Ami felt herself stiffen.

"Don't go, Honey Bear. Stay here with me."

Honey Bear?

Ami covered her snort with a cough.

When her father's eyes narrowed, she coughed again just for effect.

"That cold air must have gotten to my lungs more than I realized," she added.

The tight set of her father's jaw told her he wasn't convinced.

"I have an idea," Anita began, then waved a dismissive hand, the diamond tennis bracelet around her wrist catching the fireplace's glow. "No, it would be asking too much. Forget I said anything."

Anita lowered her gaze, looking all innocent and contrite, but not before Ami saw the calculating look in her eyes.

Like a piranha, Ami thought. Lurk, then dash out and strike.

"Tell me," Steve urged his *Cookie*. "I'm sure whatever you have in mind isn't too much to ask." Her father shifted his attention to Ami. "Anita always thinks of others first."

Ami had no doubt that was true. Like now, Anita was thinking of how best to hook and reel in Steve Bloom.

"Tell me," Steve repeated when Anita milked the moment by remaining silent.

"Okay, but only because you insist." The apologetic look on the woman's face might not have fooled Ami, but her father's face softened.

"Ami is a whiz in the kitchen. I thought, well, if she doesn't mind, perhaps she could clean up?" Once again the apologetic look made an appearance. "It wouldn't take her long. Since her bakery was closed today, she had a day of leisure."

When Ami didn't immediately respond, Anita demurred. "Forget I said anything."

Ami remained silent, waiting for her father to inform Anita he couldn't possibly ask his daughter to clean up the mess from their dinner.

Those words didn't come. Instead, her father leveled a look at her. "What do you say, Ami?"

After a restless night, Ami woke before dawn. The scene with her father and Anita had made sleep impossible. She still believed she'd been right in politely refusing the request. Her father had been furious. It wasn't like him to get so angry.

Yet, when she'd seen Anita's smug smile, she'd wondered if she'd won the battle but lost the war.

No. Her father was a sensible man. He'd get over his anger. Except she had no doubt that Anita would be tossing kerosene on the smoldering embers to keep the fire burning.

But for now, Ami had other matters demanding her attention. The sun had barely begun to rise when Ami placed a call to Beck.

He answered on the fifth ring. "Ami. This is a pleasant surprise."

The sound of Beck's soft southern drawl steadied her.

She switched the phone to her other hand. If Beck didn't agree, she wasn't sure what she was going to do. She was running out of options and out of time.

"Is something wrong?" His voice sharpened.

"No, no, nothing's wrong." Her now-dry hand fluttered in the air. "I hope I didn't wake you."

His chuckle was as warm and smooth as a glass of her father's Kentucky bourbon. "I've been up for a while now. I was getting ready to step into the shower."

The image that flashed before her—of Beck naked with little rivulets of water streaming down his muscular body—fogged her brain. "You—you can call me back."

"It's okay. Tell me what I can do for you."

Come with me today. Give me the job. Open your house to the tour. Oh, and let me see you naked.

"Ami? Are you still there?"

"I'm here." She told herself Beck wouldn't disappoint her. Until she recalled her father's actions last night and realized you could never predict how someone might respond. "I need a favor."

"The answer is yes, if you toss in a kouign amann." A hint of amusement colored his words.

"You don't even know the question."

"I've tasted the pastry and know I'll come out ahead regardless of what you ask."

"I'll make you a dozen if you agree."

"Tell me what I can do to help."

Ami decided she must not have done a good job of keeping the desperation from her voice. The playfulness had disappeared from his, as if he sensed the tension beneath the lighthearted banter.

"I have to deliver a food basket this morning to a needy family. The man in the household can be somewhat . . . intimidating. I'd like you to go with me. It shouldn't take long." The words tumbled out. "If we leave soon, we could be back for coffee and pastries at the usual time."

"Intimidating how?" An edge of steel ran through the words.

Ami hesitated, hoping she wasn't overreacting. As far as she knew, Clint had never forced himself on any woman. Still, Beck's words the other night about trusting her gut rang in her ears. "I don't like how he looks at me."

There was a long pause.

"What time do you want to leave?"

The acquiescence came so fast, Ami wasn't prepared. She thought quickly. "I can stop by your house at seven. Unless that's too early—"

"I'll be ready."

"Great. Thanks." Embarrassed by the relief she felt, Ami suddenly wanted nothing more than to get off the phone.

"I want you to promise if you're ever faced with a similar situation, you'll tell me."

"This kind of thing doesn't happen all that—"

"Ami." His voice held a warning.

"I promise." Ami clicked off the call and realized something wondrous. She wasn't scared anymore.

Chapter Six

Beck found himself surprisingly eager to accompany Ami to the house of the *intimidating* man. He'd defended his share of clients with anger management issues. He knew how unpredictable they could be, especially around holiday times when emotions and stress tended to be on rapidly rising elevators.

The thought that Ami had even considered walking alone into such a situation made his temper soar.

No one would hurt Ami. Not on his watch.

While he waited for her to arrive, Beck pulled out his cell phone. Hearing the pleasure in his mother's voice made him glad he called. Displaying her usual wit, his mother caught him up on the latest family news. He updated her on the café. He'd barely ended the call when Ami arrived ten minutes ahead of schedule.

In a red, down-filled jacket with a picnic basket in her hand, she looked like the Eskimo version of Little Red Riding Hood.

Beck smiled as he reached for his keys. "I'll warm up the car."

"I thought we'd walk." She glanced down and winced at the sight of the snow dripping from her black UGGs onto the gray Swedish rag rug. "It's a beautiful day."

Beck had retrieved the *Gazette* from the porch earlier, and beautiful wasn't a word he'd use to describe the weather outside. To a southern boy, the air felt positively frigid. "Your nose looks like Rudolph's."

"Thanks for noticing." She grinned, seeming not to take offense. "I admit it may be a bit nippy right now, but the sun is out so it should warm up quickly."

"Are you certain you don't want to drive?" Beck immediately corrected himself. "I mean, I'm happy to drive you."

Within his first week in Good Hope he'd learned Amaryllis Bloom didn't own a vehicle. She went everywhere by riding her bike or walking. Or, when the weather was particularly bad, she caught a ride with friends.

"I love to walk." Ami gazed up at him with a hopeful expression. "C'mon, Beck. It really is a gorgeous day."

"Okay. We'll do it your way." He took the basket from her, hefting the woven wicker up and down in a bicep curl. "I could get a workout with this baby. What's in here?"

"Lots of goodies." Ami smiled her thanks as he held open the door and they stepped onto the porch. "There's a whole ham, courtesy of the Good Hope Market. They also donated vegetables and a can of coffee. The general store tossed in trail mix, packages of crackers, and several varieties of soup-in-a-jar mix. I added several tins filled with cookies and bars. There's also a loaf of fresh-baked bread."

"You should have asked me for something," he told her as they veered off Market Street. "I'd have donated."

"Good to know." Her bright smile told him he'd be contributing to the next food basket. That was okay with him. As far as Beck was concerned, no one should go hungry.

Ami was chattering about all of the services the rotary provided to the community when her foot slipped on an icy patch. She pitched forward.

Beck shot out a hand, wrapping his arm around her waist, steadying her. How good she smelled and how right it felt to hold her close.

The unexpected direction of his thoughts set off alarm bells. When she stepped back, he wasn't ready to let her go.

"Why are you staring at me?" she asked.

"The same reason you're staring at me."

Ami blushed. "I've got my footing. You can let me go now."

Reluctantly, he dropped his hands and they resumed walking. Beck continued to draw her out about her community service and wondered if there was any piece of the Good Hope pie this woman didn't have her fingers in. "Is delivering food baskets another part of your Giving Tree duties?"

She laughed. Though the sun shone bright and the day promised warmth, Ami's cheeks and nose were red with cold. "I've got my hands full overseeing the Christmas gifts."

"Yet here you are, delivering a basket."

"I couldn't say no." Her eyes turned soft. "Calvin Koontz is in charge of baskets. Cal is retired and loves making up the baskets and doing deliveries. But he slipped last week on the ice and injured his ankle."

Beck wasn't surprised that Ami had stepped up. "So you volunteered."

"Not exactly." A dimple made a rare appearance in her cheek before her expression sobered. "Cal was having difficulty finding someone to fill in. He's very dedicated. He had a number of people turn him down. Cal was distraught by the time he reached me. I couldn't say no."

"Can you tell anyone no?"

Ami offered a halfhearted laugh. "I told my father no last night. That didn't work out well at all."

Before he could ask any questions, she gestured to the broad expanse of snow off to her right and changed the subject. "I bet you never saw sights like this where you used to live."

This was as close as Ami had ever come to asking about his past. He appreciated her respect for his privacy, and he'd returned the favor by never asking why she didn't drive or date. But lately he'd begun to wonder why all the secrecy. They were friends. While he didn't want to delve too deeply into his past, he certainly could be more open.

"I don't believe there's a more beautiful place on earth than Good Hope," Ami said with unexpected reverence.

Beck surveyed the area and had to agree. Last night's snowfall had bestowed a fresh layer of white. Ice crystals glittered in the early morning light, making it look as if shards of diamonds had been scattered across the field.

Colored Christmas lights in the distance provided a startling contrast to the white snow and the bright blue sky. No, Beck could honestly say he'd never seen anything like this in the South. "Good Hope is its own world."

If the flash of her smile was any indication, his comment pleased her.

"Do you ever regret moving here?"

Knowing she deserved honesty rather than platitudes, Beck considered the question. "When I first arrived, I wondered if I'd made a mistake."

While Beck had been eager for a change, he hadn't realized what living in a small town on a peninsula meant. Good Hope was an extremely tight-knit community.

"I imagine the welcome you received must have seemed overwhelming." Ami chuckled. "You had instant friends, whether you wanted them or not."

Though he'd told himself it was important to keep it all business between them, the notion that she might have simply been doing another service for the community when she'd stopped by Muddy Boots gnawed at him.

"Was I simply another project for you to cross off some list? Is that why you showed up with your pastries?"

The belligerence in his tone surprised him and startled her, if her widened eyes were any indication. Still, her gaze never wavered.

"Initially," Ami admitted. "But I kept coming because I enjoy having coffee and conversation with you."

Beck exhaled a harsh breath. He shouldn't care this much. It felt like a betrayal to Lisette.

"I enjoy it, too." Despite his reservations, he took a step closer, his gaze firmly fixed on her. "I wouldn't let you in the door every morning if I didn't."

She laughed. "So if I come one morning and the door is locked, I can surmise I'm no longer welcome?"

"That's not going to happen," Beck said gruffly and took a step closer.

The air between them pulsed with so much energy, he was surprised sparks weren't visible.

He'd have wrapped his arms around her and pulled her to him if the honk from a car horn hadn't caused them both to jump. Only then did Beck realize they were standing in the middle of the road.

Beck cupped Ami's elbow in his hand and maneuvered them closer to the curb. The driver in the white Impala gave a friendly wave as he drove past.

Ami returned the wave, then pointed. "The Lohmeiers live down that street. Third house on the left."

For the first time Beck noticed fields of snow on one side had given way to streets lined with ramshackle houses. Because none of the sidewalks had been cleared, they continued to walk in the street. This time they stuck near the curb. Though it was early, the lights were on in the Lohmeier house. Like most of the homes surrounding it, the residence was a white, single-story frame home with a stoop rather than a front porch. The garage, detached from the house, listed visibly to one side.

"What's the situation here?" Though there was no one outside at this hour, Beck kept his voice low.

"Cassie Lohmeier lives here with her three kids. We went to school together. She was several years older than me. Her sister, Lindsay, was in my class."

Something in her voice put Beck on alert. He suspected she had more history with this family than she was saying. "Are you and Cassie well acquainted?"

"I knew her more as a child, not so much as an adult. She got pregnant at fifteen, went on to have two more kids by another guy before they split. Clint Gourley is her latest live-in. He's on disability for his back after a motorcycle crash in October."

Beck filed away the information. "Does Cassie work?"

"She's pregnant with her fourth and has been experiencing complications." Ami's voice betrayed no emotion or judgment. "A neighbor mentioned food was in short supply to Calvin, hence the basket."

"Other than her sister, does she have any other family in the area?" From what he'd observed, most of the families in the area were tight-knit and supportive.

"Anita Fishback is her mother."

Beck stilled as the name registered. "Your father's girlfriend is related to Cassie?"

"Anita isn't his girlfriend." Ami spoke sharply, then immediately appeared to calm herself. "Sorry."

Just when Beck thought he had everything figured out, someone tossed a curveball. "So Anita's pregnant daughter needs a charity food basket."

"The Giving Tree is not charity," Ami reminded him.

"Neighbors helping neighbors, yeah, I remember. But why does she need help? Her mother is a successful business owner and—"

"Anita cut Cassie out of her life," Ami told him. "As far as I know, the two haven't spoken in years."

Beck slowed his steps. "What happened?"

"I'm not sure."

"C'mon, Ami. You know everything that goes on in this community."

From the look of hurt on her face, Beck realized it was the absolutely wrong thing to say.

"I'm not a busybody, Beck." She snapped the words, her face flushed bright red.

"I never said you were." Beck kept his voice matter-of-fact. "But you *are* well connected. And you've lived here your whole life."

"That's true." Appearing somewhat mollified, Ami thought for a moment. "Cassie took her father's death hard. Almost harder than Anita, though that's not fair to say. Everyone grieves in their own way."

Beck knew that to be true. He'd taken his share of hits for remaining dry-eyed at Lisette's funeral.

"Anita jumped back into the dating game barely six months after the funeral," Ami continued. "She appears to be one of those women who has to have a man."

Beck shifted the heavy basket to his other hand. "What does all this have to do with her relationship with Cassie?"

"Cassie believed her mother moving on so quickly meant she hadn't loved her dad. Cass began acting out." Ami exhaled a sigh. "Cassie pushed her mother away. Anita finds Cassie an embarrassment. Both women are headstrong and surprisingly similar in personality."

"Where does the sister fit in?"

"Lindsay is stuck in the middle. She's her mother's pride and joy."

Beck realized they'd nearly reached the house. "What's your history with the live-in guy? I assume he's the intimidating man."

"Clint is a jerk."

The comment had Beck blinking. This was the first time he'd heard Ami speak badly about anyone. With the exception of Anita, of course.

"Clint hit on me hard last summer."

If Beck hadn't been focusing on her face, he might have missed the imperceptible tightening of her jaw.

Though Ami never said she'd rejected the guy's overtures, that fact was obvious. "How'd he take the rejection?"

"He didn't like hearing no."

Beck had more questions. Many more. But by now they'd reached the stoop. Even before Ami pressed the doorbell, several dogs began barking inside.

He watched Ami square her shoulders and paste a smile on her face as the door cracked opened.

Cassie was an older, worn-out version of her younger sister, Lindsay. Same honey-blond hair and gray-blue eyes. Same narrow face that was more angular than beautiful. Same whippet-thin body. Except Cassie's body was now swollen with baby, and the eyes that once sparkled with mischief were dull and weary.

After putting the two rottweilers in a back bedroom—where they continued to bark—Cassie's oldest daughter returned with two mugs of coffee.

"Thank you, Dakota." Ami offered the girl a warm smile. "How old are you now?"

Dakota, a pretty girl with dark hair and amber eyes, wore jeans and a hoodie. "I'm seventeen."

"Wow." Though Cassie had several years on her, Ami found it mind-blowing that anyone she'd played dolls with as a child could have a seventeen-year-old daughter. Of course, most women didn't have their first baby at fifteen.

Clint, who'd been lurking in the doorway since they arrived, moved close and placed his hand proprietarily on Dakota's shoulder. "Like I told Cassie, our little girl is growing up."

Dakota flinched but otherwise remained perfectly still. Her expression went blank.

Something in the way Clint looked at the girl made Ami's skin crawl. Cassie, now munching on cookies with her feet up on a frayed hassock, seemed oblivious to any tension between her daughter and her boyfriend.

Ami cleared her throat. "That makes you a junior in high school?"

"Yes, ma'am." Using the question as a reason to move, Dakota stepped closer to Ami and sat on the arm of her chair.

Beck had remained quiet since she'd performed the initial introductions, but Ami observed his brown eyes taking it all in, including the tattered furniture and the new large-screen television. She was certain his shrewd gaze hadn't missed the worn clothing on Cassie and her daughter and Clint's shiny leather boots.

Ami supposed Clint had been a good-looking guy once upon a time. Though he was only in his midthirties, hard living was starting to show. His body was soft and paunchy. There were lines on his face normally not seen in a man so young. His hair, the same shade as Cassie's, was spiked up with gel. If he was trying to hide the fact that his hairline had done some serious receding, it wasn't working.

The look in his eyes, that predatory gleam with an underlying mean edge, was the same. She remembered the stories she'd heard back in middle school, how he and his friends had beat a possum to death . . . just for fun.

The thought made her stomach roll.

"Isn't there school today?" Beck asked casually.

"Yes, sir. The bus picked up the boys a few minutes ago." Dakota flushed. "I stayed home so I could take Mom to her doctor's appointment."

"'Cause I can't drive." Clint placed a hand on his back and forced a wince. "Back injury."

Ami knew for a fact Clint drove all the time . . . when it suited him.

"These almond bars are delicious." Cassie grabbed another from the tin.

"Thank you. They're very popular." Ami took a sip of coffee and smiled at Dakota. "Next time you're by the shop, stop in. I'll give you some more almond bars to bring home for your mom."

"Dakota don't get into town much." Clint's gaze fixed on the girl. "We like to keep her close."

"Oh, Clint, honey." Cassie gave a nervous laugh. "She's in Good Hope for school every day."

Ami reached over and gave Dakota's hand a squeeze. "Stop by, please."

Chapter Seven

Ami hid a smile as Beck reached for a third kouign amann. The walk back from Cassie's home must have stimulated his appetite.

Though she'd planned to broach the subject of Beck giving her a job on the walk back from the Lohmeier home, the conversation had focused more on the abject poverty of the home and the jerk that was Clint Gourley.

Beck also had concerns over the way the man had leered at Dakota. Ami made herself a promise. If the girl didn't come to her in the next few days, she'd seek her out.

Once she'd made that decision, it was time to get down to business. No more letting the conversation flow like a meandering river.

Eliza had spotted her and Beck when they passed by the general store on their way to Muddy Boots. If Ami didn't call Eliza to report in soon, the executive director of the Cherries would be calling her. The problem was, lately it felt as if all she'd been doing was asking Beck for favors. She certainly didn't want him to get the mistaken impression she was using him.

Ami knew he was concerned about his head cook situation, and she hoped that if she could help with that, he'd be willing to help her complete her Cherries assignment by agreeing to open his house to the tour.

"I've come up with a solution to your need for a cook." Once Ami saw she had Beck's attention, she pressed forward. "I texted Hadley this morning, and she agreed to increase her hours on the weekends. Karin, a college student who worked for me last year, has also agreed to help out. Since you don't serve breakfast, I can get a lot of my baking done before I come over to cook for the lunch crowd."

If Beck was surprised she'd brought up the job again, it didn't show. "You'll pay out more in wages than you'll bring in."

"Not if you pay me what I'm worth."

The figure she named had his jaw dropping open.

Recalling Hadley's admonition, Ami took another sip of coffee. When Beck remained silent, she stuffed a piece of pastry in her mouth so she wouldn't be tempted to fall into nervous chatter . . . and sell herself cheap.

Beck cleared his throat. "That's a lot of money."

Ami lifted her chin and met his chocolate-brown eyes head-on. "I'm worth it."

"The amount you're asking is twice what I'm paying Janey."

"You'd only be paying me that for a month." She took a huge drink of coffee to wash down a chunk of pastry that had lodged in her throat. "Considering all the increased money you'll be making because of the holidays, your budget can handle it."

Ami tried to read his expression but discovered Beckett Cross had a stellar poker face.

She'd shot high but would do it for less. Ami certainly didn't want him to turn her down. Was it really fair to ask him to pay her *twice* what he was paying Janey?

With her heart slamming against her rib cage, Ami placed her cup on the counter. Before she could toss out a lesser amount, Beck smiled.

"You have a deal."

Satisfaction flowed through her veins like warm honey. Who knew she was so good at negotiating?

"When can you start?"

Ami couldn't stop grinning. "How about I do a trial run Thursday evening? That way I can get oriented to the kitchen before the Twelve Nights celebrations begin."

Beck nodded his approval. "That'll work."

Buoyed by her success, Ami decided to go for broke. "I have just one more condition before I accept."

Beck frowned. "I thought you already accepted."

"Not yet." She lifted a hand, let it flutter in the air. "This is such a small thing to ask."

He inclined his head.

"I want you to agree to open your home to the tour."

For a Thursday night, the Muddy Boots café was hopping. Beck hadn't expected much of a crowd since many would be eating out tomorrow because of the tree lighting ceremony. But word must have gotten out that Ami was behind the stove. The place had been packed all evening.

Blackmail. Beck stabbed a bite of potato and shoved the food into his mouth. Ami had seduced him with a sweet smile and the promise of help, then gone in for the kill.

Worse yet, he'd caved.

He chewed and the taste buds in his mouth sighed with pleasure. Who knew plain old meat loaf and potatoes could taste so delicious?

Instead of coupling meat loaf with traditional mashed potatoes and gravy, Ami had taken a baked potato out of its skin, mashed it up, added butter, and covered the potato with creamed corn. The bacon, onions, and peppers that had topped the meat loaf while it cooked were added to the corn.

It looked strange, but the taste was mouthwateringly good. The homemade sourdough bread she'd added for the crunchy texture seemed to be a hit as well.

Though Beck wanted to sit and savor, and perhaps have a piece of the cherry crisp with ice cream for dessert, he cleared the table and went back to work.

Normally the two servers were able to handle the cash register, but tonight the diners just kept coming.

Beck took over the cash register.

The next guy in line looked familiar, but Beck couldn't place him. Tall and rangy with gray hair, silver-rimmed glasses, and hazel eyes. He'd noticed him at a four-top eating with the man and woman who stood beside him now.

"How was your dinner?" Beck asked.

"The food was excellent." The rotund woman with hair coiled in a braid on top of her head spoke before the man could answer. "With Ami at the stove, how could it be anything but fabulous?"

The woman gestured to her dinner companion. "When I heard Steve's daughter was cooking tonight, I told him we simply had to eat at Muddy Boots this evening."

So, the thin guy was Ami's father. In his khaki pants and sweater vest, he reminded Beck of the peninsula's version of Mr. Rogers. While Beck hadn't watched much television as a kid, he remembered the soft-spoken man with an endless supply of cardigans. A man who'd been the antithesis of Beck's workaholic father.

"Ami's cooking lived up to the rave reviews." The other man, tall and athletic-looking in his early thirties, spoke for the first time. He turned back to Steve. "It'd be nice if Ami could come out for a second so I could compliment her personally."

Beck's gaze sharpened. His gaze drifted to the man's left hand. No wedding ring.

"Beck." Ami appeared at his side. "We're going to need to substitute—"

Ami caught sight of her father and Beck saw her tense. She covered it well with a smile.

"Dad." She rounded the counter and gave him a quick hug. "I didn't realize you were here."

"I didn't want to disturb you." Steve seemed hesitant. "I could tell by the crowd you were busy."

Ami eased both of their discomfort by shifting her attention to the woman. "Etta. How nice to see you again."

"Excellent meal, my dear." Etta's smile flashed. "You remember Clay Chapin. He's our new principal."

"Clay. Ohmygoodness." Ami turned and gave the man a hug. "Welcome back."

"It's great to be back home."

Ami glanced at Etta. "I didn't realize Mr. Svensen wasn't returning."

Her dad and Etta exchanged glances.

"Lars's heart sustained considerable damage," her father said.

The news about the principal's heart attack at the last football game of the season had spread like wildfire through Good Hope. Beck had not only heard about it from his patrons but had read about the incident in the *Gazette*. Like Ami, he hadn't heard the man had been replaced.

"I'm sorry to hear that." Ami turned back to the new principal. "But I'm happy to know the high school will be in your hands. Your mother must be thrilled to have you back."

Beck listened as Ami made small talk with the three educators for a few seconds before he interrupted. "What is it we need to substitute?"

"We'll let you get back to work." After slanting a glance at his daughter, Steve paid the bill, then ushered his colleagues out of the café.

Realizing he'd been somewhat abrupt, Beck braced himself for Ami's wrath. Instead she gave his arm a squeeze. "Thanks for that little push. I have a feeling Etta and Clay would have stayed and talked forever."

He found it curious she hadn't included her father. The fact was, Steve Bloom appeared as eager to leave as Ami had been to have him go.

Beck studied Ami. Her face was flushed from the steam table, and a few wisps of hair had escaped the sparkly crocheted hair covering she wore while she cooked. He could see why Clay Chapin hadn't been able to take his eyes off of her.

Ami quickly explained they were almost out of meat loaf but suggested substituting roast beef as the entrée.

After securing his approval, Ami returned to the kitchen while Beck rang up the next customer. It made him happy to know that even if the new principal called Ami for a date, she'd be too busy.

Between the café, the Giving Tree, and helping him get his home ready for the tour, there would be time for only one man in her life this holiday season, and that was Beckett Cross.

———

The café may have closed at nine but it was nearly ten when Ami dropped into bed and a dreamless slumber. Four a.m. came way too soon, but after a second cup of coffee, she felt almost human. First Friday marked the kickoff of the Twelve Nights celebrations. Everyone was looking forward to the lighting of the thirty-foot tree in the town square and caroling led by the high school choral director, Loretta Sharkey.

With the weather projected to be mild—in the midthirties—a large turnout was anticipated. This meant Ami needed to make certain the bakery had lots of cookies and bars on hand. As red, tart cherries were the main crop on the peninsula, the residents of Good Hope held a special affinity for all things cherry.

Tonight, along with the standard decorated sugar cookies, the shop would offer chocolate cherry blossoms, a fancy name for cherry sugar cookies topped with a Hershey's Kiss. There would be chocolate Bing bars and cherry shortbread cookies. Kids of all ages would enjoy pretzels dipped in almond bark and brownies shaped like Christmas trees with candy cane stems.

The baking Ami had done over the past two days had been a labor of love, but not without personal pain. Baking had been something she'd always done with her mother or one of her sisters. This year, it was just her and Hadley.

She slanted a sideways glance in time to see her friend take a pan of kringle from the oven. Despite working until midnight at the Flying Crane, the pretty blond had arrived promptly at four. It had taken Hadley only *one* cup of coffee to be her normal perky self.

Ami rested her back against the counter. "I can't tell you how much I appreciate you working these extra hours."

"I was glad to be asked." With the colorful scarf covering her hair and the royal blue of her shirt making her eyes even bluer, Hadley could have been a model for a "Visit Scandinavia" advertisement. "The extra money will come in handy."

"I'm sure the Flying Crane would have given you more hours." Not only that, Ami knew Hadley would have made more with tips in addition to her wages.

Hadley placed the baking pan on the cooling rack, looked at the golden-brown braids of dough, and rested her back against the counter. "Serving intoxicated college kids isn't my way of getting into the holiday spirit. Besides, baking is my salvation."

As if she'd said too much, Hadley turned and added flour, baking powder, and salt to a bowl. With quick, efficient movements, she put butter in a large bowl and began to stir.

Salvation. The word turned over and over in Ami's brain like a mixer blade slogging through dough.

Ami knew how much it meant to have a supportive person in your corner during dark days. Her mom had once been her salvation.

Since her mother's passing, every Christmas had been bittersweet. Did the holidays bring the same conflicting emotions for Hadley?

"Are you going to be around on Christmas?" Ami spoke in a casual, just-tossing-it-out-there way that probably didn't fool Hadley.

Hadley added sugar to the butter before lifting her gaze. "Where else would I be?"

"I don't know." Ami placed a sheet filled with white chocolate cherry shortbread cookies into the oven. "North Dakota?"

"Why would I go—?" Hadley stopped herself. "Not this year."

"Well, since you're going to be around, I'd love it if you'd join us on Christmas Eve. We'll be celebrating at my dad's house, so there'll be plenty of room."

"The house will be filled with family. I don't—"

"I'd love for you to meet my sisters." Ami's tone turned pleading. "Please say you'll come."

Hadley searched Ami's gaze. Apparently reassured by what she saw, she smiled. "Okay. But I bring the bread."

"Deal."

The door to the shop jingled open. Ami closed the oven door and hurried around to the front. "Can I help—?"

She skidded to a stop and her heart gave a leap.

Beck kicked the door closed with a foot, balancing a cup of coffee in each hand. His hair was mussed from the wind and little bits of snow clung to the tips.

His burgundy houndstooth jacket wasn't one Ami had seen before. Though not up on the latest designers, Ami could spot a quality garment at ten paces. Beck's coat definitely hadn't come off any discount rack.

"Wha-what are you doing here?" Even as she spoke she crossed the room to take one of the cups.

"You didn't come for coffee, so I brought coffee to you." He sniffed the air. "What do you have to go with it?"

"What time is it?"

"Nine fifteen." He looked amused. "Does that make a difference on what I get served?"

"I've been so busy baking I lost track of the time." Ami glanced at the cupcake clock on the wall and grimaced. "I'd have sworn it was seven at the latest."

"Then it's a good thing I decided to stop over."

"Who was at—" Hadley paused in the back doorway and took in the scene.

Despite the fact that there was at least a foot of space between them, Ami was seized with the ridiculous urge to jump back and put more space between her and Beck.

"Hadley." If Beck was off balanced by her assistant's appearance, his warm smile gave no indication. "Good to see you again."

"I didn't mean to interrupt—" Hadley began.

"You didn't." Beck crossed the dining area and handed her the cup of coffee he still held. "You've both been busy this morning. I thought you might enjoy some coffee. It's not a blend you carry. It's chicory and Ami's favorite."

"Thank you." Hadley's curious gaze slid from him to Ami. "Can I get you a piece of kringle?"

"I'm fine." Beck was almost to the door when he turned back and his gaze locked on Ami's. "See you at ten."

Without another word, he strode through the door, the bells jingling as it closed.

"Seriously." Hadley offered an apologetic smile. "I didn't mean to interrupt."

"I usually meet Beck for coffee at nine." Ami started to rake a hand through her hair, remembered the snood, and let her hand drop to her side.

"He likes you."

"He tolerates me."

"Why does the thought that he might be attracted to you make you so uncomfortable?" Hadley took a sip of the coffee Beck had given her. "You're single. He's single."

"Becoming involved could mess with our friendship."

"Oh, so now it's a friendship. A second ago you told me he tolerates you."

"Don't you have some cookies to get out of the oven?"

"What about yours?"

Ami glanced at her watch. "Another five minutes."

They returned to the kitchen and the baking, with Ami resolving to pay closer attention to time. She was also going to pay closer attention to Beck.

The thought that Beck might care for her as more than a friend filled Ami with such sweet longing that her heart began to ache.

Though she wouldn't get her hopes up, she had to admit Hadley had a good eye for such things. Could it possibly be true? Was Beck falling for her?

After placing the cookies on a rack to cool, Ami inhaled the pleasant scent of chocolate and sugar, closed her eyes, and let herself dream.

Chapter Eight

Beck had decreed the café would stick with the standard menu Muddy Boots had been serving since the Twelve Nights celebrations had first begun in Good Hope. Chili and cinnamon rolls might seem an odd combination, but Beck had been told year-round residents and tourists alike stopped at the café on First Friday specifically for that meal.

The simple menu certainly made things easier for Ami. But that didn't mean she wasn't keeping busy. That's why when one of the waitresses came into the kitchen shortly before seven o'clock that evening and said Beck needed to see her out front, she demurred. Until the girl told her she'd stay in the kitchen to help get the food out.

Ami gave the woman her apron and hurried to the dining room. She found Beck waiting by the cash register.

He glanced pointedly at his watch. "We should have just enough time. Grab your coat."

When she hesitated, Beck placed his hands on her shoulders and spun her in the direction of the coatrack. "Hurry."

The second she returned, he took her arm. "Let's go."

Ami pulled back and planted her feet. "Not until you tell me where we're going."

"It's almost time for the tree lighting in the town square." He smiled and tugged her forward. "You don't want to miss it."

"But the café—"

"Business has slowed considerably in the past thirty minutes." Beck opened the door and gestured outside. "Most have already eaten."

Ami stepped into the crisp evening air and breathed deeply. The forecasters had been right. Because of a lack of wind, the night felt almost balmy.

Though the sun had set hours ago, the town square was awash in lights. The lamplights glowed emerald green, and all of the businesses, save Muddy Boots, had been decorated with clear or colored lights.

Shirley Allbright, owner of the Enchanted Florist, had gone for funky this year. She'd replaced her traditional pine garland with plastic poinsettia flowers in blue, yellow, pink, and silver that had been taken apart, then reassembled around clear lights. After stringing the flowers on green wire, Shirley and her daughters had wound the strands around the railing at the front of her building, which resembled an old-fashioned front porch.

Not wanting to be outdone, Ami had encircled her shop window with fairy lights, then added a wreath made out of beads and vintage bulbs in varying shades of pink to the door.

Caught up in the Christmas spirit, Ami had offered to help Beck put up a few lights on the café earlier in the week. But he'd made it clear that while he may have allowed himself to be blackmailed into putting his home on the tour, he drew the line on lights.

Thankfully, the Muddy Boots frontage was cute enough on its own. The fact that it was the only business not decorated wasn't all that obvious. At least not to Ami. But Katie Ruth had told Ami that Eliza had noticed and wasn't pleased.

What the executive director of the Cherries didn't seem to realize was that Beck had made great strides in embracing the Christmas spirit. He'd agreed to the tour. He'd agreed to allow her to store the Giving Tree gifts at his home. The thought reminded her of the items still cluttering her living room. "I'll need to stop by—"

"Shhh, they're about to light the tree."

Mayor Jeremy Rakes, the man who would throw the switch, strode toward the podium. Ami could never see Jeremy without thinking of Fin. The mayor was the same age as Ami's sister, and the two had dated all through high school.

Ami had always liked Jeremy, with his lanky frame, sandy-blond hair, and friendly smile. Since he was the son of one of the community's most prominent families, it had come as no surprise to anyone when the hometown boy had been elected mayor last year.

As Jeremy had grown up in Good Hope and knew practically everyone, the mayor's short trek to the stage was slow going. Every few feet someone stopped him, wanting to shake his hand or exchange a greeting.

Though Ami found herself enjoying the energy of the crowd, she still couldn't figure out why she was here instead of in the Muddy Boots kitchen. She rose on her tiptoes to whisper in Beck's ear to ask him that question.

Too late, she realized her mistake. He smelled so good, a spicy scent mixed with soap. Worse, when she leaned close, he put his hands on her shoulders to steady her.

It didn't matter that she had on her red puffy coat; she could feel the heat of him through the fabric.

"I thought you hated these kinds of things," she managed to stammer.

The heat engulfing her only surged hotter when he turned his face, putting their lips mere inches apart. "Hate is such a strong word."

She forced herself to step back, knowing if she didn't, she might do something crazy . . . like kiss him. "Why are we here, Beck?"

He leaned forward to tuck a strand of hair behind her ear. "I thought you'd like to see the tree all lit up."

It was as if he'd reached up and stroked her heart, sending warmth flowing through every inch of her body.

"Turn now or you'll miss it."

Ami swiveled just in time to see the fir explode in dazzling colors of emerald green, sapphire blue, and flame red. A collective "ah" rose from the crowd, followed by spontaneous applause.

The high school choir launched into "Silent Night," and Mrs. Sharkey motioned for the onlookers to join in. Ami sang loudly, intensely aware of Beck at her side. At first Beck was silent. But as one carol followed another, she finally heard his baritone join with hers.

Impulsively, she slipped her arm through his and leaned close, as if they were sharing a piece of sheet music. He slanted a sideways glance at her and grinned. Happiness bubbled as their voices blended with those of the assembled throng.

By the time the caroling ended with "We Wish You a Merry Christmas," the evening felt like a package that had been wrapped up and topped with a pretty bow just for her.

The crowd began to disperse and Ami cast an anxious glance at the bakery. Both Hadley and Karin were on duty, but were two enough to handle the post-tree-lighting crowd?

"Shall we check out Blooms Bake Shop?" Beck's question must have been rhetorical because he'd already veered in that direction. "I've heard their stuff is pretty good."

"I've heard it's *excellent*," Ami shot back and made him laugh.

"Then we definitely should check it out."

"What about the café? Shouldn't we get back?"

Beck waved a dismissive hand, as if he wasn't at all concerned about the state of his business. "The staff can handle chili and cinnamon rolls."

Ami decided if he wasn't worried, why should she be?

They followed a group of giggling middle school girls into the bakery. The pleasant scent of cinnamon and chocolate permeated the air. The tables were occupied, as were the stools by the window. From what Ami observed, the orders at the counter were being quickly and efficiently filled.

Hadley and Karin were dressed in identical red ski sweaters. The headbands with reindeer antlers they both wore were topped with tiny brass bells that jingled with every movement.

Ami caught Hadley's eyes. When her assistant gave her the thumbs-up, the last bit of worry dogging Ami disappeared. "They've got it under control."

"Looks that way." Beck stared at a gray-haired woman delicately eating a piece of kringle. "What is that?"

"Kringle. It's fabulous. I'll bring you a ring when I stop by tonight."

Beck inclined his head. "When you stop by where?"

"Your house."

Something she couldn't quite identify sparked in those dark brown eyes. "Because?"

He looked so serious and intense Ami had to resist an almost overwhelming urge to touch him.

"Because I have to get all those Giving Tree gifts out of my apartment so I can put up my tree."

"You want to move the gifts tonight?" His brows drew together. "You've been working since four a.m."

"I'll be working long hours every day until Christmas. At this time of year, there is no perfect day or night." She gave him a playful shove. "C'mon, let's get out of here and make room for paying customers."

On her way toward the door, another surge of teenagers drove Ami straight into the arms of Clay Chapin.

"Well, hello." The principal kept his hands on her shoulders a moment longer than necessary. His gray eyes held hers. "I hoped I'd run into you again. I didn't expect it to be this soon."

"I'm not working at the bakery this evening," Ami started to explain, then realized Beck had made it through the juggernaut at the doorway and now stood silently at her side. "You remember Beckett Cross? The new owner of Muddy Boots."

"Of course." Clay held out his hand and shook Beck's. "Steve said Ami is working for you over the holidays."

Beck smiled pleasantly, then turned to Ami. "We best get going. We have a lot to accomplish before you come over tonight."

Before Ami could form a single coherent thought, Clay made some excuse about getting inside before all the kringle was gone.

Ami couldn't believe Beck had been so careless with his words. He'd made it sound as if they were a couple. Actually, he'd made it sound as if they were sleeping together.

Beck raised a brow. "Something funny?"

Ami shook her head. Her smile faded at the sight of a figure in a turquoise coat and thigh-high black boots headed their way.

"Eliza alert." She managed to sputter out the warning before the woman reached them.

"Beckett. Ami." The cool tone could have frosted glass.

"Happy holidays, Eliza." Ami managed to summon a smile. "You look lovely this evening."

Eliza dipped her head as if accepting an accolade from an inferior, then focused on Beck. "I want to personally thank you for agreeing to make the Spencer-Shaw home available for the tour."

Ami held her breath, praying Beck didn't say anything that could be misconstrued. Nothing about a deal between them, nothing about her visiting his home later, just . . . nothing. Yes, saying nothing would be best.

"Amaryllis explained the situation to me. I saw the importance and agreed to open *my home* to the public for that one evening."

It was clear—at least to Ami—Beck didn't appreciate Eliza referring to his house as the Spencer-Shaw home. Ami mentally filed that piece of information away so she wouldn't make the same mistake.

"*I* had already explained the situation to you, Mr. Cross," Eliza said pointedly.

"Did you?" Beck looked bored with the conversation. "If you'll excuse us, we need to get back to the café."

Eliza directed a pitying smile in Ami's direction. "I heard you'd taken a second job. Obviously the bakery business isn't all you hoped it would be."

Ami's blood did a slow boil. She gestured toward the shop, which was standing room only. "As you can see, Blooms Bake Shop is doing quite well."

"Then why—?"

"Neighbors helping neighbors. That's the Good Hope way." Beck lifted a brow and fixed his gaze on Eliza. "Or do I have that wrong?"

If the flush riding up her neck was any indication, Eliza Shaw was doing her own slow burn. "It's been nice chatting, but I need to move on."

Beck watched her leave, then took Ami's arm and turned in the direction of the town square. "I need a drink."

"We used to be friends." Ami couldn't quite keep a note of sadness from her voice. "Now she barely tolerates me."

"What happened?" Beck purchased two cups of hot chocolate from a vendor set up in the square.

Several years ago, the city had installed industrial parabolic heaters in the overhang of the gazebo. Between her down coat, the heaters, and now the hot cocoa, Ami barely noticed the cold.

"What happened between you and Eliza?" Beck repeated.

"Nothing, really. We were casual friends in high school. That was a long time ago." Ami told herself it wasn't as if she had to give him the full story, only enough to staunch his curiosity. "She was always more a friend of a friend. Now everything I do irritates her."

Beck took a sip of cocoa, his gaze never leaving her face. "Why do you think that is?"

"Um, I don't really know for sure." Her laugh sounded a bit desperate. She stared into her cup and changed the subject. "I bet everyone has someone in their past who dislikes them or who they dislike."

Beck's expression darkened. "Often with good reason."

"Well," Ami forced a bright tone. "Let's talk about tonight. Will you be helping me move the gifts to your house? Or will I have to do it myself?"

Beck parked his Land Rover directly in front of the bakery. Thankfully, it was late enough that the Friday-night revelers had moved to the bars near the waterfront.

He expected to transfer most of the presents himself. But Ami must not have gotten the bulletin that lifting heavy objects was a man's job. She worked as hard as he did, carrying items down the stairs and packing the SUV with the skill of a seasoned professional. It took four trips to clear all the gifts from her apartment.

At his house, Beck dropped an armful of blankets, each in a plastic wrapper, on top of several large boxes of kitchenware on the floor of a back bedroom. Ami relegated a box of Bristle Blocks to an open spot just inside the doorway. Other than leaving a walkway to the wrapping table—two sawhorses topped with a piece of plywood—he and Ami had decided all open spaces were fair game.

"Time to head home." Ami pushed back a strand of hair and heaved a weary sigh. "Four a.m. will come all too soon."

At first Beck didn't understand. Until he remembered that tomorrow was another big day. Not just for the bakery. He'd been warned the Snow Blade Parade was a crowd favorite and to make sure the café had plenty of food on hand.

Tomorrow Ami would get up early to bake before rushing to the café to cook for the lunch crowd. Talk about burning the candle at both ends.

"Why don't you take a nap after you finish baking?"

"That's so sweet." Her voice turned as warm as her eyes, telling him she appreciated the offer. But the slight tilt to her chin told him before she even spoke that she wouldn't be taking him up on his offer.

"You and I, Mr. Cross, have a deal," she continued in that sweet, slightly husky voice that he found incredibly arousing. "Once I get through tomorrow, there's just Sunday. It won't be nearly as busy."

Beck hadn't thought that far into the future. "Remind me again what's on the Twelve Nights agenda for Sunday."

"Activities at the Rakes Farm. Sledding, singing around a bonfire, then cider in the big red barn. Oh, and fabulous cookies."

The smug look in her eyes put him on alert. "Who's providing the cookies?"

Ami flashed a triumphant smile. "Why, Blooms Bake Shop, of course."

The Energizer Bunny had nothing on her. "You're an amazing woman, Ami Bloom."

"You're right." Her bright smile flashed. "I am."

He laughed.

Her laughter soon mingled with his.

Then their eyes met. The laughter died in his throat and his heart became a swift, hard beat.

He reached out for her and felt her arms encircle his neck. She was so lovely. Did she have any idea of the power she had over him?

The feel of her soft curves had Beck forgetting his resolve to keep it all business between them. Just this once he would stop thinking and open himself to the moment, to her. He shifted, gathered her closer still, and kissed her temple.

When she gave a pleasure-filled sigh and lifted her face, he lowered his mouth to hers and found it as soft and sweet as he'd imagined.

The kiss started out gentle and tender but quickly morphed into something more, something that felt . . . life altering. When her fingers slid into his hair and she began to kiss him back with equal enthusiasm, Beck knew he was in over his head.

At the moment, he didn't care. A smoldering heat flared through him. The rush of sheer physical awareness that had assailed him as soon as his arms closed around her intensified tenfold. His need for her became a pulsing ache inside him.

From Ami's uninhibited response, it appeared she felt the same pull. But when he flattened his hand against her lower back, drawing her up against the length of him, she stumbled.

Beck reached out to steady her, but she brushed away his hands.

"I—I should go." Though her cheeks were dotted with bright spots of pink, she appeared back in full control.

Which was more than Beck could say for himself. He wanted her. Right now. If she was willing, he'd—

Beck didn't let himself finish the thought. The way she was backing up told him if she'd once been interested, she wasn't anymore.

The relief he felt was tinged with regret. "I'll drive you home."

"I'll walk."

"It's late." His tone brooked no argument.

After a thoughtful second, she shrugged. "Sure."

The drive to the bakery was made in silence. Beck tried to initiate conversation on the short trip, but Ami's monosyllabic responses had him giving up before he even turned off Market Street.

He pulled to the curb, half expecting her to hop out without a word of good-bye. Once again, Ami surprised him. She unbuckled her seat belt and shifted to face him.

"I let things get out of hand," she told him. "It's been a while for me and, well, you're a great kisser. But that's no excuse for throwing myself at you. So . . . I apologize."

Ami was out of the vehicle and inside the bakery before Beck processed her words.

She'd let things get out of hand?

He was the one who hadn't been able to stop from kissing her. She'd responded, but the original kiss had been at his instigation, not hers.

Why would she think otherwise?

Beck pondered the puzzling question the rest of the drive home.

Chapter Nine

"I love the fact that you jumped him." Hadley shot Ami a wink, then pushed off from the crest overlooking a snow-covered meadow.

Ami easily kept up with her friend, gliding down the slight mound—too small to be called a hill—on her cross-country skis, then coming to a stop beside Hadley at the bottom.

After making it through a busy weekend and playing catch-up on Monday, Ami had decided to celebrate her day off from the café by enjoying last night's additional two inches of snow.

This had been Ami's first chance to bring up Saturday night's debacle with her friend. She'd barely pulled her skis on when the story began tumbling from her lips. It took longer than it should have because Hadley wanted every detail.

"*Jumped* isn't entirely accurate." Ami breathed in the cool, clean air and felt some of the tension in her shoulders dissolve. "I kissed him. He kissed me back."

"Do you think if I kissed him, he'd kiss *me* back?"

Ami shot her friend a sharp glance.

"Just kidding." Hadley laughed. "Seriously, if word got out Beckett Cross was serving kisses, Muddy Boots would be swarming with women."

Ami wished now she hadn't brought up the kiss. She didn't have a clue what was happening between her and Beck, so how could she explain it to Hadley?

No, that wasn't entirely true. Ami knew she was falling for the man with the soft southern drawl and gentle eyes. What she didn't know was how to end the free fall.

One thing for certain, the thought of Beck kissing anyone else made her stomach churn. "I don't believe he's looking for a relationship."

"I'm not talking about a relationship." Hadley gave her a wink and pushed off across a pristine white field edged by a coniferous forest. "I'm talking sex."

They continued across the field in companionable silence, the soothing sound of skis sliding across the snow only broken by the loud squawk of a raven. The strong scent of pine from the nearby forest hung heavy in the air.

With each push of her poles, the churning in Ami's stomach became a sharp pain. She shoved past the discomfort of imagining Beck with a faceless female and caught up with Hadley.

"Something else about this Beck thing confuses me." Hadley inclined her head, her expression mild. "Buying a café in a small town is hardly what you do when you want to be left alone."

"True," Ami agreed.

"What brought him here? I mean, what caused him to pick Good Hope as a place to settle?"

"No idea." That, Ami thought, was a big part of her hesitation to get more deeply involved with the man. She didn't even know the most basic information about his life before he arrived in Good Hope.

You know everything important, a tiny voice in her head whispered. *You know he's decent, kind, and honorable.*

"What does he say when you ask?"

"I don't ask."

Hadley skied to a stop beside a large spruce, then studied her friend. "Why not?"

Ami focused on the distance, avoiding Hadley's scrutinizing gaze. "The way I see it, if Beck wants me to know about his past, he'll tell me."

"But—"

"Just like you," Ami continued. "I don't pry into your background."

"You're right, of course." Hadley sighed. "I'm just curious. Have you been able to pinpoint his accent?"

"Southern?"

Hadley laughed. "Have you googled him?"

Ami couldn't help but laugh when her friend wiggled her brows. The mischievous glint in Hadley's blue eyes reminded her of her sister Marigold, who'd always had some scheme up her sleeve.

"I did a little searching when he first arrived." Despite the cool air, heat slid up Ami's neck. The truth was she felt bad about snooping into Beck's private life. Yet the guilt hadn't been strong enough to keep her fingers away from the keyboard. "I plugged in a few different variables and tried again last week."

"I searched yesterday," Hadley admitted with a cheery smile. "What did you find?"

"Big fat zero."

"I came up empty, too. We'll probably never know what brought him here."

Ami lifted one of her ski poles and pointed at Hadley. "No one can keep their past hidden forever."

Hadley made a face.

"I'm serious." Ami spoke with an air of feigned nonchalance even as her heartbeat hitched. "We both know Beck isn't the only one in Good Hope with a few skeletons in the closet."

───────

That night Ami enjoyed a simple dinner of pad thai and a green papaya salad while watching the local five o'clock news. Afterward, she hummed along to the Christmas carols playing on her phone while she brought out her slow cooker. While doing her own version of a jingle-bell boogie, she blended whipping cream, milk, vanilla, and white chocolate chips together.

She set the timer on low and glanced at the clock. Two hours should provide more than enough time to pick out a beautiful fir and bring it home from the rotary club's tree lot.

Her gaze dropped to the large red box covered with white dancing reindeer on the floor, and her excitement surged. In just a couple of hours the ornaments and lights it contained would turn a plain green tree into a thing of holiday splendor.

Ami had a wonderful evening planned for herself. She'd sip snowflake hot cocoa and decorate the tree while listening to the soothing sounds of Norah Jones. Anticipation fueled her steps as she bounded down the stairs and out into the crisp night air. Snow crunched under her boots on the short walk to the Christmas tree lot, located several blocks away. Although most of Ami's friends preferred to cut their own trees at one of the nearby farms, without a vehicle, Ami didn't have that option.

As it was, she was going to have to drag the tree home. Which meant size would be a consideration. Still, Ami had no doubt she'd find the perfect tree of her own.

She passed Beck's house on the way and slowed her steps when she noticed lights on inside. Though she'd seen Beck that morning for coffee, she found herself wishing he was out shoveling so she could stop and talk.

But he didn't appear, and moments later the parking lot edged in Christmas lights came into view. Ami spotted *her* tree the second she stepped onto the lot. Five feet tall with a lush shape, it was everything she wanted. As she started across the lot to claim it, a spindly hand on her arm stopped her.

Gladys Bertholf, Cherries matriarch and treasurer, smiled up at her. Dressed in a furry black hat with a thick white band and a dark, full-length mink coat, the elderly woman looked as if she'd stepped straight out of the pages of *Dr. Zhivago.*

"Merry Christmas, Amaryllis." Gladys's lips were as red as her cheeks. "I used to tell my beloved Henry, God rest his soul, this is why I never leave home without looking my best."

She must have looked confused, because Gladys chuckled. "You never know who you might run across."

Ami resisted the urge to glance down at her fleece-lined jeans and red puffy coat. At least she'd put on mascara that morning. "Have you enjoyed the holidays so far?"

"I have indeed, my dear. It's been hectic. I'm sure you've heard I'm playing the Ghost of Christmas Past in *A Christmas Carol* at the playhouse. Between rehearsals and three performances a week, most days I don't know whether I'm coming or going."

The woman's joyous trill of laughter was infectious.

"The play is getting excellent reviews."

"I'd tell you to stop by and see it, but I've heard you've been keeping busy, too." Gladys's pale blue eyes danced with amusement. "Kudos to you on getting Mr. Cross to open his home to the tour."

Ami waved away the compliment.

"I imagine he was happy to do it. For you, Amaryllis." Gladys gave another hearty laugh. "Not for Eliza."

Ami wasn't about to get into that discussion. "Are you here by yourself? Because if you need help loading the tree, I can—"

"You're so kind, but Frank insisted on coming with me. He's securing the tree in the trunk now. I offered to help, but my son is old-school. He believes physical work is a man's job." Gladys paused as if realizing she'd been rambling. "How about you? Have you found a tree yet?"

"I believe I have." Ami gestured her head in the direction of the fir.

"You were smart to bring man power."

"Pardon me?"

"Your man." Gladys gestured with one hand, the diamond bracelet above the black leather glove catching the light. "I see him right over there."

Ami didn't bother to look. Whomever Gladys was looking at certainly wasn't here with her.

"Well, I'd best scoot. Frank doesn't like to be kept waiting. See you at the next meeting."

"Break a leg," Ami called after Gladys.

The woman lifted a hand in acknowledgment but didn't turn around.

"Did you really just tell an elderly woman to break her leg?" Amusement filled the deep voice.

Ami's heartbeat hitched as every synapse in her body pinged with awareness. She slowly turned.

With rumpled hair that brushed the collar of his shirt and cheeks that held a hint of five o'clock shadow, Beck looked sexy as sin. And he smelled terrific, a spicy scent that made her want to step closer.

Ami couldn't keep the pleasure from her voice. "This is a nice surprise. What are you doing here? I thought your tree was being delivered."

He chuckled, a low, pleasant rumbling sound. "I'm not here for a tree."

"Then why?"

"I saw you walk by my house and thought I'd say hello." When he leaned toward her and lowered his voice, time seemed to stretch and extend. "Hello, Ami."

Her heart skipped a couple of beats. She grinned. "Hello, Beck."

"Now, tell me why you told the old woman to break a leg."

Ami laughed. "Gladys Bertholf is the treasurer of the Cherries. She's also an actor in *A Christmas Carol* at the playhouse."

"Ah, that makes sense." Still looking bemused, Beck shifted his gaze. "Have you found a tree yet?"

"Yes." Ami slanted a glance in the direction of the balsam fir she'd spotted moments before. Her heart sank. "It's the one that family is looking at."

Beck followed her gaze. "You have good taste."

"If they don't take it," she said in a low tone, "I will."

Even from this distance, she could hear the couple arguing. The woman liked it. The man was insisting it was too small.

"How do you propose to get it home?" Beck's gaze turned speculative. "Do they deliver?"

"I plan to carry it."

"Seriously?"

She nodded.

Beck stared at her as if she'd lost her mind. "You propose to carry a five-foot-high tree three blocks. By yourself."

"Easy-peasy." Ami forced an air of confidence. While she had no doubt she had the strength to drag the tree home, she did harbor a few concerns about what shape the needles would be in once she got there.

"What about your dad?"

"What about him?" Ami's heart gave a sudden leap when she noticed the couple and their two children moving toward the bigger trees.

"Couldn't you have asked him to help you?"

With the tree firmly in sight, Ami wove her way toward it.

"My father and I had a little spat the last time I was at his house," she said over her shoulder. "Besides, he's probably busy with Anita."

Beck caught up with her just as she reached the tree. "You could have asked me."

After placing a proprietary hand on one of the limbs to stake her claim, Ami shook her head. "I've already asked too much of you. The last thing I want is for you to think I'm using you. Because I'm not."

"I know that."

She widened her eyes at the surety in his tone. "You do?"

"You're not that type of person."

"Thank you."

"I'll make this easy. You don't have to ask me to help carry the tree to your place, I volunteer."

It was an offer she couldn't refuse. Though he told her he could carry the tree by himself, she was determined that this be a joint effort. Beck took the base while Ami took charge of the top.

Beck didn't even look askance when halfway home she burst into song, singing several popular Christmas carols. Once they reached the bakery, he stabilized the tree as she unlocked the door, then waited at the bottom of the steps while she ran up to make sure the path was clear for the tree.

Only minutes later, the tree stood straight and tall in its stand. Thick and full, the perfectly shaped fir's pleasant wintry smell filled the room.

Ami stepped back, hands on hips, and studied the tree. "It's beautiful."

"Yes." Beck spoke from behind her. "Beautiful."

When she turned, she discovered him staring at her, not the tree.

Heat rose up her neck, and despite the new furnace's warmth, Ami shivered. "Thank you again for helping me."

"It was my pleasure." His gaze settled on the box at his feet. "Are the ornaments in there?"

She nodded. "I thought I'd put on Norah Jones and do it up right."

"Need some help?"

"I don't want to impose—"

"Hey." The touch of his hand on hers stilled the words. "I offered because I'd like to help. It'll be our trial run before we do mine. It's been a very long time since I've decorated a tree."

"Are you saying you've been a scrooge?"

He laughed. "According to Max, I still am. But I'll have you know, until the past couple of years, I always had a tree. A designer was assigned the chore of decorating it."

Ami frowned. "Decorating is fun, not a chore."

He stared at her for a long moment, then smiled. "Tell me what to do."

"Take off your coat and boots and get comfortable." Even as she instructed, she sat on the sofa and slipped off the UGGs. "I'll put on Norah. Then we'll start on the lights."

Although Ami's ornaments were every shape and color, the lights were all a pale pink. When Beck asked why, she told him without a hint of embarrassment that pink was her favorite color. Once the lights were strung, Ami called for a break.

"We just got started," Beck protested.

"The timer went off." Ami hurried over to the counter in the kitchen. "It's snowflake cocoa and candy cane brownie time."

"In that case"—Beck grinned—"I could use a break."

Ami asked him to cut two brownies out of the pan while she garnished the cocoa with whipped cream and shards of candy canes.

While they sat at the tiny table across from each other, the pure tones of mellow piano and acoustic guitar enveloped them and brought an air of Christmas magic to the room.

"What's with the jar?" Beck gestured with his head to where a mason jar sat perched on the counter. Small scraps of green and red paper filled the glass interior.

Ami sipped her cocoa. "It's my gratitude jar."

The corner of Beck's mouth twitched. "A *gratitude* jar?"

"That's right. Each day I write down things I'm thankful for on those little pieces of paper. At the end of the month, I open up the jar, read them, and reflect on the blessings in my life." Ami rose. "I haven't done mine for today. We can each do one."

Beck cleared his throat. "I'm not really into such things."

Ami ignored him, went to a drawer, and pulled out two small strips of paper. After grabbing two pencils, she handed one to Beck and kept one for herself, dropping the strips in front of each of them. "It doesn't have to be real wordy."

For a second she thought he might refuse. Then he bent his head and scribbled something. After carefully folding the paper, he handed it to her. She put hers and his in the jar, then took his hand. "Break time is officially over. We have a tree to decorate."

The next hour passed quickly. Ami couldn't remember the last time she'd laughed so much. Beck was easy to be around and had a sense of humor in sync with her own. Once the ornaments were on, with the star at the top, they stood back and studied their masterpiece. Ami's heart rose to her throat.

This was *their* tree, she realized, not hers.

He took her hand as she walked him to the door, and she savored the moment of closeness.

"Thanks for all your—"

Before she could finish, he shifted, gathered her close against him, and kissed her softly on the mouth. Then he reached up and touched her cheek, one finger trailing slowly along her skin until it reached the line of her jaw.

Her heart galloped in her chest and her eyes grew wide.

"You were right," he murmured, those dark eyes never leaving hers.

"About?"

"Decorating can be fun. With the right person." He lowered his head, and his mouth found hers again. Then he was gone.

Ami listened to his footsteps on the stairs, then heard the door to the shop jingle open, then close. She hurried to the window and watched him until he turned the corner and disappeared from sight.

Love flooded into her, swamping her, leaving her weak and needy. Ami could no longer deny what was happening. She was falling in love with Beck.

Fears and hopes tumbled together in her head. As she cleaned the kitchen, Ami's gaze kept straying to the mason jar. Finally she could withstand the temptation no longer. She opened the lid and pulled out the two strips at the top.

On her green one was the name she'd printed: *Beckett Cross.*

With her heart in her throat, she slowly opened his red one. Her lips curved. In bold, sure strokes he'd also written a name.

Ami Bloom.

Chapter Ten

Wednesday evening, Beck turned his Land Rover down the lane leading to the property known as Rakes Farm. More of an orchard than a farm, with five hundred acres of tart cherries and thirty acres of apples and pears, the land had been in the Rakes family since the 1880s. In addition to fruit trees, the estate held a converted barn and an elegant Victorian home, both popular venues for parties and wedding receptions.

This evening, Mayor Jeremy Rakes was hosting a holiday party for Good Hope business owners. Tonight was but a preview of what was to come Friday evening, when Rakes Farm would once again open its doors to the public for another of the Twelve Nights festivities.

Beck couldn't imagine ever wanting strangers traipsing through his property. The thought of the Victorian home tour, now only ten days away, made Beck flinch. Thankfully, he'd only agreed to open the main level to the public.

Last Friday he'd contacted a vintage furniture store in Sturgeon Bay. The owner had agreed to furnish the main level with period pieces as long as his shop was acknowledged on a prominently displayed placard.

The fact that there would be furniture was reassuring, but as it was a *holiday* tour of homes, a Christmas feel was essential. Ami's offer to assist him with decorations was one he immediately accepted. When she'd mentioned the Cherries were available to lend their expertise, he'd blanched.

Beck would help Ami with the lights and the greenery and whatever else she thought necessary, but he made it clear Eliza and her cohorts were not welcome in his home. He'd softened the refusal by adding that he would find it more enjoyable if it was just the two of them.

The slow smile that widened her lips had warmed him to the core. He'd meant every word. Beck liked her company and felt at ease with her. If Ami were with him tonight, he knew he'd be looking forward to the evening with anticipation rather than dread.

It wasn't as if he didn't like Jeremy or any of the other merchants who were sure to be here. But he was around people all day. He'd quickly discovered that in Good Hope, visiting with patrons was as important as what was on the menu.

Though the regular staff had handled the lunch and dinner crowd without any snags today, it felt to him as if something, *someone*, was missing. He'd found himself going to the kitchen to spend a few minutes with Ami only to remember this was one of her days off.

Beck was still considering turning back when the Rakes farmhouse came into view. It was a massive structure three stories tall with a porch that wrapped halfway around the front. Leaded glass above each window and a turret made out of copper, as well as the exterior colors of salmon, green, and yellow, brought a unique quality and charm to this Victorian-style home.

He found himself curious if the inside was as striking as the exterior. Since he'd come this far, he might as well check it out. Nothing said he had to stay all evening. With that thought in mind, he followed the winding drive to a large gravel lot. The amount of available parking was a clear indication the place was more than a family home.

Beck parked beside a sturdy Subaru. Though the lot was far from full, it appeared there was a good turnout. Max would have been here if he hadn't gone out of town.

Once again he wished Ami had come with him. He'd mentioned the event, but she made it sound as if she wouldn't be attending, so he hadn't brought it up again. Lately there'd been something different in the air whenever they were together. It would be easy to label the change as unease, but that wasn't the right word.

It was more of a watchful waiting, a simmering tension as if neither of them could decide how to deal with whatever there was between them.

That's why he'd kissed her again last night, to put to bed any awkwardness between them. Oh, who was he kidding? He'd kissed her because he couldn't keep his hands off her, didn't want to keep his hands off her.

He understood moving on was natural, and he knew Lisette wouldn't want him to be alone forever. But a part of him feared it was too soon and meant he hadn't loved his wife as much as he'd thought.

Still, Ami was a beautiful, fascinating woman, and he couldn't believe another guy hadn't snatched her up. When he was around her, he was starting to feel happy and content in a way that he hadn't been in years.

Tossing the troubling thoughts aside, Beck started up a recently shoveled sidewalk toward the farmhouse. If the swaths of evergreen looped on the porch rail and secured every few feet with red ribbon hadn't alerted him, the huge wreath on the front door made it obvious this home was ready for Christmas.

He was greeted at the door by a young woman wearing a red skirt, crisp white shirt, and a Santa hat topped with a fluffy white pom-pom. Even if her name hadn't been embroidered in red script on her hat, Beck would have recognized her instantly.

"Dakota, what a pleasant surprise. I didn't expect to see you tonight."

"My counselor recommended a couple of us for jobs this evening." She lowered her voice to a confidential whisper. "We're getting ten dollars an hour."

"Good for you," he said. "How's your mother?"

The teenager glanced at an older woman—a supervisor, perhaps?—watching from several feet away. "She's good. May I take your coat?"

Beck slipped off his jacket and handed it to her. He spoke as softly as she had only moments before. "Don't forget to stop by the bakery."

She gave a tiny nod, draped the coat carefully over her arm, and handed him a claim ticket. "Have a wonderful evening and a merry Christmas."

"Merry Christmas to you."

The girl's dark eyes widened at the size of the bill he handed her. "Thank you very much, Mr. Cross."

She hurried off, and Beck wandered into the large living room off to his right. His eyes were drawn to the corner where the star atop a perfectly shaped Christmas tree nearly brushed the ceiling. Beck stepped closer for a better look at the massive fir.

Decorated in shades of red and green with plaid accents, the thick base of the tree sat in a galvanized pan filled with sand. Small nets made from colored construction paper and filled with candied fruit, sugar-covered nuts, and sticks of candy hung from branches.

Little dolls, remarkably human-like, hung from branches along with walnuts and apples. At least a hundred unlit candles in red and green were anchored to the limbs.

"It's the way they used to decorate in Victorian times," a soft, feminine voice spoke from behind him. "Quite lovely."

Beck smiled and turned. The evening was definitely looking up. "I thought you weren't coming."

"I'm a woman." Ami shrugged good-naturedly. "I changed my mind."

"I'm happy you did."

As the event was casual, he'd pulled on a pair of khakis and a dark brown sweater his sister had gotten him for his birthday last year. Ami was decked out for a party. The green wrap dress enhanced her gentle curves, and heels gave her at least another three inches of height.

She looked happy, festive, and good enough to eat.

"The candies in these little nets were called sweetmeats." She leaned forward and touched one of the paper cones. "Back in the day they held pastries, bonbons, stuff like that."

"You seem to know a lot about such customs."

"Baking is my business." She brushed a piece of lint from his sweater. "In case you've forgotten."

"How could I?" He smiled. "I smell those delicious aromas each time I step out of the café. And every time you step close."

The look of startled surprise skittering across her face made him smile.

"You always smell like something sweet," he added.

Two tiny lines appeared between her brows. "I'm not sure that's good."

"Trust me." Beck took a step forward. "It's very go—"

"There you are." Clay Chapin pushed through the crowd, never taking his gaze from Ami. "Jeremy told me you were here. I'm glad I found you."

Only when Clay stood directly in front of her did he appear to notice she wasn't alone. The principal shifted his gaze to Beck and smiled.

The two men shook hands.

Ami's brow pulled together in puzzlement. "I'm surprised to see you here, Clay."

"The times they are a-changing." Clay grinned. "Besides, a party isn't complete without a token educator."

Ami laughed. "Well, I'm glad of it."

Beck stiffened as the two chatted easily for several minutes about people and high school events unfamiliar to him.

Finally, Ami glanced at the bar, then at Beck. "I believe I'm ready for that glass of wine."

Though there hadn't been time to discuss refreshments before Clay showed up, Beck played along. He placed his palm against the small of Ami's back. "Let's get you one."

After saying good-bye to Clay, Ami waited to speak until the principal was out of earshot. "Seeing him here is quite a shock."

"Because he's an educator, not a business owner?"

"No. There's a little bit of everything here this evening."

"Then why the surprise?"

"He's a Chapin," she said, as if that explained it all.

Before he could ask what she meant, they reached the bar. Once they had their glasses of wine in hand, she and Beck spent the next hour mingling.

"I'm impressed." He waited until the mayor had stepped away. "You really do know everyone."

"No big surprise." She took a tiny sip from the crystal flute. He noticed she hadn't made an appreciable dent in the liquid. "I've lived here all my life."

"Did you ever leave?"

"I got my Bachelors in business administration from the University of Wisconsin in Madison," Ami told him. "I didn't want to leave, but when it came time for me to go to college, my mom was doing better. Education was superimportant to both my parents. I knew it would stress them both out if I insisted on staying."

"A BBA." Beck stroked his chin. "That surprises me."

She lifted a brow and took a sip of wine.

"I thought you'd have gone to culinary school."

"My talent is homegrown. Some people sing or dance or have an aptitude for sports. My gift lies in the culinary arts." She gave a little laugh. "I don't mean to brag."

He found it all fascinating and was about to tell her so when she moved to the large stone fireplace, her slender fingers traveling over the vintage stockings hanging from the mantel.

Beck's mouth suddenly went dry as he imagined the feel of those fingertips against his skin. He cleared his throat and tried to remember what they'd been discussing. Ah, yes, her education. "Did you enjoy your business classes?"

"At the time not so much, but now I'm grateful. Everything I learned helps me run my business."

"So you graduated, came back, and opened the bakery."

"Not quite that quickly. Or easily. I worked for the previous owner. When she was ready to sell, I had enough money for a down payment to buy the business. The rest, as they say, is history." She took a sip, studied him over the rim of her glass. "Where did you go to school?"

For a second Beck was tempted to slip behind the wall he'd erected when he'd left Georgia. Until he recalled his resolution to be more open with Ami.

"I received my undergraduate degree from Vanderbilt. I majored in political science." Beck paused, then frowned. "She's drunk."

"Who's drunk?"

"Eliza. She's over by the tree, speaking with Katie Ruth."

Ami casually glanced in that direction. She narrowed her gaze. "How can you tell?"

"She's unsteady on her feet. A second ago she nearly fell into the gingerbread house display." A muscle in Beck's jaw jumped. "She's laughing too loudly."

As if on cue, Eliza emitted a peal of laughter that echoed through the big room.

Ami's expression turned puzzled. "She's certainly acting strangely. I don't ever recall seeing her so . . . so uninhibited."

"Did she drive here?" Beck thought of the dark, winding roads leading back into town. "Or did she come with someone?"

"I have no idea." Ami frowned when Eliza stumbled. She'd have fallen if not for Katie Ruth.

"She shouldn't drive home." He gave Ami's arm a quick squeeze. "I'll be right back."

When Beck returned, he found Ami sampling cookies at the dessert table. The unfamiliar colors and shapes told him these weren't from her bakery. "Are they as good as yours?"

Ami answered before she'd even taken a bite of the candy-striped cookie in her hand. "Not even close."

The bold assertion made Beck chuckle. "I thought you told me you were providing the cookies."

"That was for the Twelve Nights event held here last Sunday," she clarified. "Jeremy thought he should spread the business around, so he gave the contract for tonight's open house to Crumb and Cake."

Beck lifted a brow. "Anita Fishback's bakery?"

"That's the one." When Beck picked up an almond bar and took a bite, she watched him intently.

"What do you think?" she asked once he'd finished the bar.

He briefly considered teasing her but chose honesty instead. "Not even close."

"Ding. Ding. Ding." She rose on her tiptoes and plopped a noisy kiss on his cheek. "Right answer."

Beck laughed.

Ami finished off her cookie. "What did Jeremy say about Eliza?"

"She came alone, but he promised he'd make sure someone drove her home."

"I'm glad."

Ami sounded sincere, but Beck knew there was no love lost between her and the executive director of the Cherries.

"Are you?"

"Absolutely." Ami punctuated her answer with a nod. "Eliza and I might have our differences, but I'd never want her to hurt herself or anyone else because of a careless decision."

The emotion reverberating in her voice surprised him. He wondered if she knew someone who'd been hurt by a drunk driver. Concern gripped his gut. Beck opened his mouth to ask when Jeremy announced the band was starting off the evening dance set with tunes from the sixties.

A melody filtered into the room from a large parlor at the back of the house. Ami's lips curved upward.

"You like this song?" Beck asked, unable to tear his gaze away from those full, red lips that only moments before had been pressed against his cheek.

"'My Girl' by the Temptations was a favorite of my parents'." Ami moved slowly back and forth, her eyes half-closed, as if lost in the memory. "They used to hold each other and sway to the tune in our kitchen."

"Dance with me." Beck knew he was playing with fire. Merely standing this close and breathing in the sweet scent of vanilla and sugar had his body remembering just how good it had felt to hold her, to kiss her.

Yes, he realized, dancing with her was a disaster waiting to happen. Beck held out his hand.

Chapter Eleven

Standing this close to Beck and breathing in the spicy scent of his cologne had Ami's insides jittering. The knowledge she'd soon be in his arms again, just like when they'd kissed, had her steps quickening with anticipation.

As she strolled beside him under the colonnade separating the two large living areas, Ami caught Beck staring.

A slow smile spread across his face. When his gaze dropped and lingered on the V of her dress, the desire in his dark eyes had her stumbling.

His hands grasped her shoulders, steadying her. "Whoa. Careful now."

"Thank you." Ami shot him a quick smile. "I'm not usually so clumsy."

"Well, I'm not usually demanding, so I guess we're even."

Ami looked startled. "Demanding?"

"I didn't *ask* you to dance." Beck's gaze remained intense. "I commanded."

"If it makes you feel better, I command you to dance with me. Now we're even."

His warm laughter wrapped around Ami like a soft, comfortable sweater. She wanted to dance with Beck, wanted to *be* with him. Though she'd played it cool earlier in the week when he'd asked her if she was coming to the party—not wanting him to think she expected him to escort her—she'd secretly hoped to see him here.

As they approached the crowded makeshift dance floor, Ami realized just how many people she knew were in attendance. Eliza, stunning as usual in a simple black sheath, was hanging on Jeremy, who didn't appear to mind. The sparkly bracelets on the arm she'd looped around his neck glittered in the light.

Looking festive in a red sweaterdress with an oversize cowl neck, Katie Ruth Crewes danced with Clay Chapin. Most of the other couples, attired in their Sunday best, fell into her parents' age group.

Steve and Sarah Bloom should still be dancing.

Ami could visualize it now: the pearls her father had given his wife for their twenty-fifth anniversary looped around her mother's neck . . .

A sharp stab of pain, strong enough to draw blood, lanced Ami's heart.

But it faded quickly when Beck pulled her to him and executed an intricate spin that left her breathless.

"You've got some nice moves, Mr. Cross," she told him when she caught her breath. "Who taught you to dance?"

"Would it surprise you if I said I taught myself?"

"Not really." She threaded her fingers through his soft hair and her heart did a little flip-flop. "You seem like the kind of man who could do anything you set your mind to doing."

"What a nice compliment." His sexy southern drawl sent a hot riff of sensation up her spine.

"You smell terrific," she said, slightly flustered.

"Two compliments from a beautiful woman," he murmured, his eyes twinkling with humor. "I'd say this evening is off to a stellar start."

As they danced to the familiar melody, his palm splayed against her back. Ami felt the heat all the way through the silky fabric of her dress. When Beck began to slide his hand up and down her spine in slow, sensual strokes, she couldn't help but wonder what it would feel like if there was bare skin beneath his fingers and—

"What shall we talk about?" Beck's breath was warm against her ear. "Politics? Religion? Whether or not a merchant should be blackmailed into opening his home to the tour?"

At the last suggestion, she couldn't help but chuckle. The laughter died in her throat at the sight of the dark-haired woman in the clingy black dress.

"What's the problem?" Beck brushed a strand of hair back from her face with the tip of his finger, his gaze completely focused on her.

"Anita Fishback." Ami pushed the words past lips that felt frozen.

"There's so many people here," he said in a reassuring tone. "We won't have to interact with her."

"I'm afraid ignoring her isn't possible."

His gaze searching her face, Beck held her out at arm's length.

Ami answered the question in his eyes. "She's dancing with my dad."

Beck spun them around so quickly it made Ami's head spin. The move had him now facing the couple instead of her. Though Ami wanted to protest, she quickly realized not seeing Anita cossetted in her father's arms was making it easier for her to steady herself.

"I take it this comes as a surprise."

"Great deduction, Sherlock," Ami muttered, then was instantly contrite. "I'm sorry. It's not fair to take this out on you. To answer your question, no, I didn't realize my dad would be her date."

"Or that you'd see them dancing to your parents' favorite song." Though Beck spoke casually, his eyes remained dark.

"Icing on the cake. A maraschino cherry atop the sundae." Ami gave a humorless laugh but found talking with Beck to be a calming experience.

"Tell me more about Anita. Help me understand why you feel she's wrong for your father."

Ami had never been one for gossip. She had better things to do with her time. The truth was, she pretty much liked everyone. And they usually liked her. But Anita had always been a predator. While Ami wanted to believe the woman had changed, her gut told her otherwise.

"Several months ago, my great-aunt Lil passed away." Ami absently slid her fingers into the hair at the back of Beck's neck. "Once her estate in Minneapolis is settled, my father will inherit a tidy sum. I find it interesting that shortly after the rumor of my father's newfound 'wealth' began circulating, Anita started showing interest in a widowed schoolteacher."

"It could be a coincidence."

Ami shot Beck a dour glance. "Yes, and Santa is real."

"Isn't he?" Beck grinned.

"Be serious." She swatted him on the arm even as her lips lifted in a smile. "It's not simply men she likes, but men with money."

"There are lots of women like that out there." Beck exhaled a breath. "My brother Anders dated one a few years ago."

"You have a brother?" Ami wasn't sure what surprised her most, that he had a brother or that he'd volunteered the information without her asking.

"I have two, actually." He smiled at her surprise. "Elliott is my twin. Anders is eight years younger."

The fondness in his voice when he mentioned the two men told her that whatever had caused him to move to Good Hope didn't involve any trouble between him and his brothers.

"You're a twin." She tried to wrap her mind around a second Beck. "Identical?"

"Yes."

"Did you ever find it weird to have another person always around who looked so much like you?"

"Not really."

"Fin is a year younger than I am. People who don't know think we're twins."

"I don't believe it." Beck shook his head slowly. "There simply can't be another woman on this planet as beautiful as you."

While Ami couldn't stop the rush of pleasure at the over-the-top compliment, everyone knew her personality paled in comparison to her vibrant sister's. "Wait until you see Fin. She'll blow you away. She has that effect on everyone."

"Where is she at now?"

"Living life fast and furious in LA." Ami's voice filled with pride. "She's an advertising exec. Smart. Funny. Everyone adores Fin."

"They're leaving the dance floor."

Ami blinked. For a few seconds she'd forgotten all about her father and the piranha.

"Do you want to go over and say hello?"

"I don't want to drag you into the middle of my family drama." Ami took a deep, steadying breath. "You do business with Anita and—"

"I do business with Blooms Bake Shop, not Crumb and Cake."

"Right now, yes, but she could come up with a sweet deal tomorrow and steal you away."

"The woman could offer me a lifetime of free desserts and I'd still turn her down."

"That wouldn't make good business sense," she chided.

"Money isn't everything." His husky voice became a caress. "I'm on *your* side, Ami, not hers. That's not going to change."

"Thank you." She gazed at him through lowered lashes. "Then I believe it's time to speak with my father and 'I-Need-a-Man.'"

A startled look crossed Beck's face. "'I-Need-a-Man?'"

"Fin's nickname for Anita."

Beck threw back his head and laughed.

Beck reached out for Ami's hand as they crossed the second living room, but she gently refused the gesture. Still, he was glad she'd allowed him to come with her for moral support.

Steve and Anita stood in front of the tree with their backs to them. Whatever story Anita was telling was making Ami's father laugh.

Ami squared her shoulders and fixed a surprisingly natural-looking smile on her lips. Beck was impressed. If he didn't know her true feelings, he'd have bought the act.

"Dad," Ami called out in a cheery voice when they were several feet away.

Steve whirled. He looked wary, Beck thought, but hope leaped into his eyes at the sight of his daughter. It appeared their recent disagreement had been as hard on him as it had been on her.

"Ami. Beck," Steve said in an overly hearty tone as his gaze hungrily searched Ami's face. "We didn't expect to see you here."

We.

By the barely perceptible widening of Ami's eyes, Beck knew the word had registered and didn't sit well, nor did the fact that Steve's palm rested familiarly against Anita's back.

Going on instinct, Beck grasped Ami's hand and gave it a squeeze. This time she didn't pull away.

"I don't know why you're surprised." Ami's voice remained as pleasant as her smile. "Jeremy invited all the merchants to his open house."

Her father flushed. "I simply meant that when I mentioned the event to you last week, you said you didn't think you'd be attending."

Beck wondered if Steve had accepted Anita's invitation thinking his daughter wouldn't be here. From the thoughtful look in Ami's eyes, the same notion had crossed her mind.

"Your father came as my plus one." Anita's sharp-eyed gaze shifted to Beck and lingered on their joined hands. "Are you two here together?"

Beck let Ami answer.

"I came with Katie Ruth." Ami shifted her attention to the tree. "It's lovely, isn't it?"

They spent five excruciating minutes discussing the tree, the party, and the Twelve Nights festivities before Ami brought up Anita's granddaughter.

"Dakota looks pretty this evening."

Beck chimed in. "Apparently her counselor at school recommended a couple of students to work the open house."

"Dakota is here?" Steve shifted his gaze to Anita. "Cassie's oldest?"

"She was taking coats at the door," Ami told her father.

"A young man took ours when we arrived." Steve turned to Anita.

"We'll have to say hello before we leave. I had Dakota in my English literature class last year. She's a lovely girl and very bright."

"Yes." Anita flashed a smile that seemed overly bright. "It's been a while since I've seen her. Cassie knows I don't approve of her lifestyle and has made it very clear she doesn't want me in her—or her children's—life."

"Give it time." Steve's arm slipped around the woman's shoulder and gave it a squeeze. "You and Cassie will find common ground."

His gaze shifted to his daughter. "Because when all is said and done, family sticks together."

An hour later Ami settled into the passenger seat of Beck's Land Rover. "Thanks for the lift. I don't know what happened to Katie Ruth. One minute she was there, the next she was nowhere to be found."

Beck had an idea where Katie Ruth was, or rather with whom, but he didn't speculate. He'd noticed the vivacious blond plastered against Clay Chapin on the dance floor, then later saw them having an intense conversation by the fireplace.

"Taking a beautiful woman home is never a hardship." Beck slipped the key into the ignition and the engine roared to life.

"I like parties—correction—I enjoy socializing." She gave a self-conscious-sounding laugh. "But I'm a fan of smaller, more intimate affairs."

"I used to enjoy both." Beck turned out of the gravel lot. "Now that I've been away from the society scene, I realize I don't miss it."

"I've never been a part of Good Hope society." Ami lifted a shoulder, let it fall. "That's why it took so long for me to be invited to join the Cherries."

His brows pulled together. "I don't understand."

The highway stretched before them like a thin gray ribbon, the instrumental music from the sound system soothing and the seat warm beneath her. Ami felt herself fully relax. "Most of the members—or their husbands—are prominent in Good Hope. Many are descended from families who settled here in the mid eighteen hundreds."

Something in her voice put him on alert. "I had the impression your family was deeply entrenched in the community."

"The Bloom family settled here at the turn of the twentieth century," she informed him. "My grandfather was a fisherman. My dad is a teacher. My mother, a secretary who became a stay-at-home mom once the children started coming."

"Your family isn't prominent."

It was a statement of fact, not a question.

Ami chuckled. "Not at all."

Beck's lips tightened. "Why do you even want to be part of such an elitist group?"

"The Cherries do a lot of good. Their efforts benefit local businesses like yours and mine." The answer rolled off her tongue with such ease, Beck could tell it was her go-to response.

"I feel as if I'm supporting my community by being a Cherrie," she added, apparently sensing his continued disapproval. "They're a great group of women. Truly."

"You're a rotarian." He turned the vehicle in the direction of Good Hope. "Why even bother with another group?"

She grew quiet for a moment and didn't immediately answer.

The light from the dash bathed her face in a golden glow, and Beck was seized with a sudden urge to do whatever was necessary to protect her from those blasted Cherries.

"My mother was very civic-minded," Ami spoke at last. "She hoped to be part of the Cherries but was never invited to join. I believe it would please her to know that a Bloom has finally stormed the bastion."

Her lips quirked up and Beck couldn't help but smile.

"Ami, the rabble-rouser," he teased, just as the lights of Good Hope came into view. "Though I admit I have difficulty seeing you in that role."

Her gaze dropped to her hands. "Actually, there was a time long, long ago when I went rogue."

The ridiculous assertion made him laugh. "What did you do? Skip gym class?"

"I got a tattoo."

The admission popped out so quickly Beck wasn't sure which of them was more surprised. Sweet Ami Bloom with a tattoo simply didn't compute. "You're joking."

"I got it my senior year in high school. I was, ah, having a difficult time coping with the fact that my mother had been diagnosed with cancer. At the time, they gave her three months to live."

Even though more than a full decade had passed since that diagnosis, pain still filled her voice.

Would it be the same for him? Years from now when he spoke of Lisette, would others still hear the grief in his voice? See it in his eyes?

Shoving the thoughts aside, Beck focused on the woman beside him. "Your mother beat those odds."

"She lived ten more years." Ami sighed. "Yet in the end, there was no happily ever after."

Beck had discovered how capricious life could be. His bright and sunny future had been decimated in five seconds. He took a deep breath, deliberately refocused. "You really have a tattoo?"

She ducked her head and nodded.

As he'd never seen that tat, it had to be hidden somewhere beneath

her clothes. His body stirred as his mind considered all the possibilities. "What is it? *Where* is it?"

"That's for me to know and you to find out." She paused,
appearing to rethink the response. "I mean—"

"I accept the challenge."

Her eyes widened. "I didn't issue any challenge."

"We can talk about it more at my place. Come home with me,
Ami."

Chapter Twelve

Startled surprise rippled through Ami at Beck's suggestion. "G-go home with you?"

Beck stopped at the light two blocks from his house and turned to face her, offering a persuasive smile. "For wine and conversation."

"We've been talking all night." She feigned a yawn even as her heart began tripping over itself in anticipation. "I should probably get some sleep."

"Sleep is highly overrated." Beck made the ridiculous claim as if it were fact. "Besides, I never did get a chance to finish telling you about my brothers. And we didn't even speak of the rest of your sisters."

Ami caught her lower lip between her teeth and considered. "I would like to hear more about your family."

Beck looked pleased and a bit smug. "Then it's settled."

He kept the conversation focused on the party while he parked the SUV in the carriage house. Once inside, they shed their coats and climbed the steps to the sitting area off his bedroom.

He gestured to the furniture facing the fireplace. "Sit wherever you want."

Ami noticed Beck smiled in approval when she picked the settee. She wondered if he was picturing himself sitting beside her.

"I love the yellow stone with the blue veins." Ami admired his masculine form as he crouched in front of the hearth. "It's quite striking."

"Siena marble from northern Italy," Beck said absently, focused on getting the fire started. "Fits nicely with the decor."

Ami thought the entire sitting area had much to recommend it. She loved the richly woven blue Persian rug over the shiny oak floors with walnut inlay. The Victorian loveseat settee with its navy-and-cream-striped pattern added to the charm and the feeling of elegant warmth.

Beck's earlier claim that the fireplace wasn't in his bedroom hadn't been entirely accurate. The sitting area with its impressive walnut-and-burl woodwork flowed into the bedroom. If she turned around, she could see the large four-poster bed with the navy duvet from where she sat.

While the downstairs needed much work, Kate had remodeled this part of the house several years earlier. The wallpaper with robust colors of burgundy and blue looked authentic, but anyone seeing it would know the paper was in too fine a shape to be original to the house.

Beck kept the conversation going while he stoked the fire into a cheery blaze. When he went downstairs to retrieve the wine, it gave Ami a few minutes alone.

Instead of getting up to explore, she kicked off her heels and let the warmth radiating from the fire stoke a feeling of contentment.

She'd been going ninety miles an hour since Twelve Nights had begun last week. The sense of overload she was experiencing was no one's fault but her own. From the time she could walk, she'd wanted to have her fingers in a whole lot of everything.

Like today. She could have slept late and enjoyed a leisurely morning off. Yet what had she done? She'd gotten up early to have coffee with Beck, then worked on bakery business all day.

Beck returned with a bottle of red wine, two glasses, and news that snow had begun to fall.

"I can't stay too long." She took a sip of the merlot he'd handed her and gestured with her glass. "What with the snow and all."

"You only live a few blocks away." Beck took a seat beside her, resting an arm across the top of the settee. "And I believe we've already determined that it's always snowing in Wisconsin."

"True enough." Ami couldn't keep from laughing. She shifted in her seat to face him and leaned forward. "Tell me about your brothers."

"Ladies first." He offered a sardonic smile. "I want to hear about you and your other sisters."

"Me? There's not much to tell."

"Any old boyfriends or ex-husbands still pining for you?"

"I've never been married. Or engaged." Ami shrugged. "Any old boyfriends are so far in the past I find it difficult to picture their faces."

"A sign you've moved on." Beck felt a stab at the thought. Lately he'd been having difficulty bringing Lisette's features into focus.

Ami thought of the two men—boys, really—she'd dated in college. "I never loved either of them."

"Tell me about your sisters."

Ami pinned him with her gaze. "As long as you understand I'm not leaving until I hear more about your brothers."

Beck appeared unconcerned by the threat. "We have all night."

"I agreed to wine and conversation, not a sleepover."

He flashed a smile. "Who said anything about sleeping?"

Ami chuckled and rolled her eyes.

"As I could talk about my sisters all night, I'll give you the condensed version. I'm the oldest. Fin—Delphinium, the one I mentioned earlier—is the next stair step."

He lifted one brow. "Stair step?"

"The first three girls in our family were born a year apart. There's eighteen months between Primrose and Marigold, the baby."

"Let me see if I've got this straight." He held up a hand and counted off on his fingers. "There's you, Delphinium, Primrose, and Marigold."

"That's correct."

"You're the only one in Good Hope."

She nodded.

"Where do the others live?"

Ami went with the least-complicated sister first. "Marigold lives in Chicago. She works in a hair salon on the Gold Coast."

"Upscale area."

The comment told her he was familiar with the neighborhood located north of downtown Chicago. "It's very nice."

"Does Marigold get home much?"

During the discussion his hand began to knead her shoulder. It should have been relaxing. But not when the tips of his fingers seemed determined to dip inside the edges of her dress.

"Marigold," he prompted. "How often does she come back to Good Hope?"

"Twice a year." Ami cleared her throat. "Ah, she came last May and will be here for Christmas."

"You must be looking forward to seeing her."

"I am." Ami shifted slightly, hoping to encourage those fingers to delve a little farther inside the silky fabric . . .

Amusement lit Beck's eyes. "You were about to tell me about Primrose."

Ami blinked. "I was?"

"As you began with the baby of the family, I assume you were going in reverse order." To her chagrin, he lifted his hand from her neckline to twine her hair loosely around his fingers.

"Yes, yes, I was." Ami tried to ignore the heat that continued to course through her body. "Prim is the only Bloom who is married. Or rather, she *was* married. Her husband died a little over two years ago. Their boys, twins, are almost six now."

His fingers stilled on her hair. "I'm sorry to hear about her husband. How did he die?"

"Rory had CF—cystic fibrosis—but that's not what killed him," Ami added when Beck began to nod, obviously drawing the same conclusion most in Good Hope made when they heard of Rory's death. "My brother-in-law was an adrenaline junkie. He died in a rock-climbing accident."

"That had to have been difficult for her." Sympathy shimmered in his dark eyes. "Where do she and her sons live?"

"In Milwaukee. She has this great job as an actuary for a large insurance company. She considered moving back, but the twins are happy and she has this—"

"—great job," he finished the sentence. "And last, but not least, the magnificent Fin. You said she's currently living in LA."

"That's correct. And yes, she is magnificent."

Beck would see that for himself once her charismatic sister arrived in Good Hope. Ami forced the nip of jealousy aside by reminding herself she didn't have any claim on Beck or his affections.

If he did prefer Fin, it would be a repeat of what had happened with Kyle, the boy she'd dated her freshman year in college. When she'd brought him home that summer, he'd been dazzled by her sister.

Ami had overheard him hitting on Fin at a fish boil. Of course, her sister had shut him down immediately. Before Fin could even tell her what happened, Ami had broken it off with Kyle and sent him scurrying back to Madison.

Beck cleared his throat.

She blinked and found him staring, concern in his eyes. He took her hand. "Is something wrong?"

"Nope. I'm done." Ami smiled brightly. "Your turn."

"It's getting late—"

"We have all night." She found great pleasure in tossing his earlier words back at him. "I want to hear all about your brothers."

As if realizing protesting was pointless, Beck settled back against the settee. "Elliott is an investment banker in Atlanta. He and his wife, Suellen, have one child, Jefferson. Elliott is extremely disciplined. His life has followed a traditional path—college, marriage, and now a child. Anders, on the other hand, is more of an adventurer."

Clearly intrigued, Ami leaned forward. "How so?"

Beck poured more wine into her now-empty glass before answering.

"After he graduated from Cornell he spent three years in a large PR and advertising firm, steadily moving up the corporate ladder. Then, out of the blue, he quit. For the last year he's been crisscrossing the country working odd jobs."

There was no censure in Beck's tone when he spoke of his younger brother, only fondness and admiration.

"Where is he now?" Ami asked. "Or do you know?"

"We stay in contact by text." Beck gazed into the burgundy liquid, then up at her. "Right now he's a ski instructor in Aspen. Before that he was putting up hay in Wyoming. Who knows where he'll be next."

"You sound as if you envy him."

"Anders is his own man. I respect someone who follows their own path."

"What about you, Beck? What did you do after you graduated from college? Did you follow Elliott's traditional path?"

"I did. I graduated from Vanderbilt, attended law school at Duke, then married."

"You're m-married?" The word stuck in her throat.

"I was married. I'm not anymore." Beck took a sip of wine and stared into the fire for a long, quiet moment. "My wife died in a car accident eighteen months ago."

"Oh, Beck." Ami slipped an arm through his and squeezed. "I'm so sorry."

Though he didn't push her away, his bicep was stiff and unyielding. She stroked his arm with a gentle hand.

His eyes had taken on a faraway look. "One minute she was there, the next she was gone."

"Were you in the car with her?" Ami spoke quietly.

"No. I wasn't in the vehicle."

Relief surged through Ami. She continued to stroke his arm. "Tell me about her."

"Lisette was a physician, a beautiful, accomplished woman with her whole life ahead of her."

"She sounds amazing." A *doctor*. A *beauty*. Ami sighed. What kind of person was jealous of a dead woman? "I take it you didn't have children."

He hesitated for a fraction of a second before answering. "No children."

A heaviness now hung in the air, a pall Ami was determined to lift.

"You may be a twin, but from your description of the two men, you appear to have more in common with Anders."

Puzzlement furrowed Beck's brow. "What makes you say that?"

"Think about it. Anders chucked it all to bale hay in Wyoming. You chucked it all to flip burgers in Wisconsin." She tapped a finger against her lips. "It might appear to some that Elliott is the only sane one in the family."

He chuckled. "You'll think I'm really crazy if I tell you how I decided to move here."

Ami was pleased to see the haunted look in his brown eyes had disappeared. "Tell me."

"I opened a map of the United States, shut my eyes, and let my finger drop. It landed on Good Hope."

"Seriously?"

"Told you it was crazy."

"Actually, it seems to be more 'meant to be' than 'crazy.'" Ami tilted her head. "Are you really an attorney?"

"I am."

"What type of law did you practice?"

"I was a criminal defense attorney in Athens, Georgia."

Ami pulled her brows together. "Why did you stop practicing?"

"I started to see the people I'd kept out of jail killing again, hurting others again. While I believe everyone is entitled to a defense, I no longer wanted to be the one getting them off."

Ami mulled over his words. "Did you ever think about changing sides? You know, become a prosecutor?"

"No."

No other explanation. Just no. Ami was curious, but not once had Beck interrogated her about her decision not to drive. She would afford him the same respect.

"I'm happy that your finger landed on Good Hope." With her arm still looped through his, Ami snuggled up against him. "Though I'm sure your family misses you."

"I stay in touch." Unexpectedly, he leaned forward and gently stroked the side of her cheek. "Tell me about the tattoo."

"When my mother was diagnosed, I was so angry. At the situation. At the unfairness of it all." Even now Ami remembered the rage and overwhelming despair. She took a long drink of wine and stared into the fire. "I not only got a tattoo, I started staying out past curfew and talking back. My grades dropped. I was a mess. I wanted to scream or to chuck it all. I don't know if you can under—"

"I understand all about rage and despair."

"I feel bad that I added to my parents' stress at a time when they were already overloaded." Ami often thought of those months with a sense of shame.

"What made you finally stop?"

There were any number of things she could tell him, but Ami wanted to be straight with Beck. Of course, that didn't mean confessing all. "I was in an accident. My friend, a passenger in the car I was driving, was badly injured. Blasted Bambi."

Beck paused in the act of refilling her wineglass. "What did you say?"

"A deer. It was in the road. I swerved to avoid it, lost control, and hit a tree." Ami was able to keep her tone even but couldn't stop her hands from trembling. She placed her wineglass on the table next to the loveseat, sensing Beck's sympathetic gaze. "It was an old car, no air bags. I was wearing my seat belt but Lindsay was not. She hit the windshield."

Ami wasn't sure when it happened but Beck's arms were now around her. He pulled her close and held her, resting his head against hers.

"Lindsay Lohmeier?" he asked after a long moment.

Ami nodded. "She had facial lacerations, a closed-head injury, and a badly broken leg. The doctors worried she might have permanent mental impairment. Thankfully, she made a full recovery. If not for the scar on her face, you'd never know she'd been so seriously injured."

"Is that why you don't drive?" The rich baritone soothed as it probed.

"I've tried numerous times," she admitted. "I get panic attacks."

She waited for him to tell her that she needed to be strong and soldier through her anxiety. Instead he continued to hold her. The closeness of his body and the warmth of his acceptance comforted her.

"Since this seems to be confession time." She toyed with the buttons on his shirtfront. "I must confess that I know your secret."

His brown eyes turned razor sharp. The intensity of that gaze left no doubt he'd been a force to be reckoned with in the courtroom. But Ami was equally strong and ready to be direct.

"You didn't bring me here to talk. Or to drink wine."

Beck blinked, nonplussed. "I didn't?"

"No." She trailed a finger up the front of his shirt. "You have nefarious motives."

A smile cracked that stern expression. "Think so?"

"Absolutely. You bring me up to your bedroom—"

"Sitting room."

Ami glanced pointedly behind them at the bed. "You ply me with alcohol."

"Wine. And you haven't finished one glass."

"You made it clear you want to see my tattoo."

He finally caught on and his smile widened.

"Bedroom. Wine. Tattoo search. If that doesn't qualify as nefarious, I don't know what does." She gave Beck a self-satisfied smile. "I rest my case."

He chuckled. "For the sake of argument, let's say you're right."

Ami felt a stir of excitement. "Am I?"

"About some, but not all."

"Clarify, please."

"I brought you to the *sitting* room," he overemphasized the word, "and offered you wine because I thought it'd be nice, not because I wanted to get you drunk and take advantage of you."

"Disappointing, but continue."

A quicksilver smile flashed. "You are right, however, about one thing."

She leaned closer, which was next to impossible, considering she was practically in his lap now. "What is that?"

"I want you to show me that tattoo."

Chapter Thirteen

Beck kissed Ami under her jaw. "So, tell me, my little sugar nymph, will you stay and play?"

Anticipation fluttered through her as Ami gazed at his handsome eyes, so warm and sparkling with just a hint of mischief. After the tiniest hesitation, she smiled.

"I'd like to stay and play . . ." Ami spoke in a light tone, then sobered. "But one question first, do you have protection?"

His expression turned equally serious. "Yes."

She took a breath, let it out. "Well, then . . ."

With his gaze firmly locked on hers, Beck rose to his feet and extended his hand. When they reached the bed, he kicked off his shoes and hopped fully clothed on top of the navy duvet. He sat up, propping the pillows behind his back, then stared expectantly at her.

Intrigued and curious, Ami sat on the edge of the bed.

"Come closer, please."

She met his gaze and their eye contact turned into something more, a tangible connection between the two of them. A smoldering heat flared through Ami, a sensation she didn't bother to fight.

"What do I get if I do?" Her sultry whisper appeared to surprise him as much as her.

He grinned. "Me."

"In that case . . ." With a chuckle, Ami hiked up her dress and scooted over to him.

His arm slid around her shoulders and he pulled her close. With a contented sigh, Ami rested her head against him. Her head fit perfectly just under his chin. Having him so close was a dream come true.

She loved the way he smelled, a woodsy mixture of cologne and soap and maleness that brought a tingle to her lips and heat percolating low in her belly.

"This has been a good evening." His voice was a gruff rasp.

"You sound surprised."

As he stroked her arm and played with her hair, it struck her that he was getting her used to his touch.

"I went to the party at the Rakes Farm out of a sense of duty." His brown eyes resembled pools of rich chocolate in the soft light. "Jeremy is a good guy."

"I like him, too." Ami sighed with pleasure as Beck nuzzled her neck. "A lot."

When he lifted his head, she grinned. "Not in that way. He and my sister, Fin, were inseparable back in high school. If such a thing as a golden couple existed at Good Hope High, it was Delphinium Bloom and Jeremy Rakes."

Beck appeared to absorb the words as he took her earlobe between his teeth and nibbled.

Shivers rippled across her skin. "Jeremy, he . . . he was so supportive and good to Fin when our mom got sick."

"You really want to talk about Jeremy?" Beck asked as he licked the sensitive skin behind her ear.

"I thought you did." She gasped the words as Beck's fingers slipped inside the neckline of her dress. Ami arched her head back to give him better access.

He chuckled, a low, pleasant, rumbling sound. "What happened between him and your sister?"

Ami's breath caught, then began again. Beck's fingers reached the edge of the lacy bra. What had he asked? Oh, yes, about Fin and Jeremy. "She—she broke up with him before they left for college. They wanted different things out of life."

It took Ami a heartbeat to realize that while she'd been dishing on her sister's dating history, Beck had used his free hand to unzip the back of her dress and was now pushing the garment down.

Though the air in the room had been cool only minutes earlier, Ami's skin now burned as if on fire.

His hands spanned her waist. Beck ran his palms up along her sides, skimming the curves of her breasts before the edges of his fingers brushed the tips through the lacy fabric.

"Enough about them." Beck's voice sounded low and strained. "Let's talk about you."

It took Ami several erratic heartbeats to find her voice. "Me-e?"

Then he unfastened the hook on her bra and her breasts spilled out into his waiting hands, and rational thought became impossible.

She felt a shivery kind of ache all over.

"Oh, Ami." Wonder filled his voice. "Your body is exquisite. The color of your nipples reminds me of a . . . fully ripe peach."

He cupped the soft curves in his hands, his thumbs brushing across the tight points of her nipples.

The stroking fingers sent shock waves of feeling through her body.

"I can't help wanting a taste."

Ami arched back and closed her eyes. Her need was a stark, carnal hunger she hadn't known she was capable of feeling. "Yes, please."

Beck gave a strained chuckle. "Always so polite."

He lowered his head and his mouth replaced his fingers. His tongue circled each tip before bringing one nipple into his mouth.

Ami surged against the pleasure swelling like a tide inside her. Her body ached with desire so intense she thought she might burst into flames. When he finally lifted his head, Ami grasped his face in her hands and gave him a ferocious kiss. He tasted like wine, and she wanted to drink him in until she was drunk.

As the kisses and touches continued, Ami wasn't conscious of exactly when they'd shed the rest of their clothes. She only knew he'd been as eager as she was to have nothing between them.

Beck had an athlete's body with broad shoulders, narrow hips, and large, clever hands. She found herself overcome with the desire to run her fingers over his body, to feel the corded strength of skin and muscle sliding under her fingers. She wanted to feel the weight of his body on hers. Wanted to feel him inside her.

The flames from the firelight cast a golden glow to the room, which was unlit save for a floor lamp in a far corner. It felt as if she and Beck had been transported to a world made up of just the two of them, one filled with warmth and caring and incredible need.

His lips returned to her mouth for a long, deep kiss that had her head spinning. She slid her fingers through his hair.

When his warm mouth moved down her neck, scattering kisses everywhere, she arched her back and begged him not to stop. With a smile and a murmur of reassurance, he continued to taste and touch until her whole body ached with a need she hadn't known she possessed.

Ami had never experienced anything like the emotions and feelings Beck stirred in her. After tracing the small broken-heart tattoo on her left hip with one finger, Beck placed a kiss in the center.

As their lovemaking continued, Ami grew more confident, becoming bolder. She was determined to give pleasure as well as receive. If Beck's moans were any indication, he appreciated her effort.

Her pleasure began to build; Ami desperately wanted—no, *needed*—him to be even closer. Beck held off, kissing and touching her in ways that made her squirm and writhe beneath him in pleasure. Finally, when his breath came in short puffs and she was ready to explode, he sheathed himself and entered her slowly.

She was ready.

Beck took it slow until she arched toward him and began to rock her hips in a pattern as old as time. She dug her nails into his back, determined not to have him stop.

Her passion soared like the rockets that exploded over Green Bay on the Fourth of July. She tossed her head from side to side, tried to catch her breath, then gave up the effort as her release claimed her.

She cried out Beck's name and clung to him. She hadn't known, she thought hazily as her body released and muscles contracted, that this much pleasure existed in the world. That she could feel so good, so right, so everything.

Beck continued to stroke, to caress, until he'd wrung every last drop of pleasure from her before he took his own release, plunging deep once more and crying out.

When he shuddered and collapsed onto her, his heart beating hard against her chest, it pleased Ami to know she hadn't been the only one affected.

Ami wasn't sure how long they remained there. When he finally rolled off of her, she felt cold and lonely and more than a little apprehensive. She wasn't experienced, and she desperately hoped it really had been as good for him as it had been for her.

Then he made everything so easy and right by simply pulling her close. "You about killed me, Ami darlin'."

She saw warmth and amazement in his eyes. His lips curved up. "You did pretty good."

"Pretty good?" he said in a teasing growl.

"Okay, excellent." She chuckled, so languid and relaxed any concerns she'd harbored had nowhere to hide. "I wonder if it would be as good in a different setting."

Puzzlement filled his gaze.

She leaned over and planted a kiss at the base of his neck, his skin salty beneath her lips. "Like in the shower."

"Ami Bloom, you are a surprise and a delight." Beck grinned and grabbed her hand. "Let's find out."

───────

Instead of having coffee and pastries at his café the next morning, Beck whipped up a breakfast of bacon and eggs and lots of black coffee at his house. Then he insisted on walking her home. They held hands on the way to her bakery.

When they reached the front door to the shop, Beck folded her into his arms, anchoring her against his chest as his mouth covered hers in a deep, compelling kiss. Dreamily, Ami stroked his thick hair.

"I'd like to see you—and your tattoo—again," he murmured against her neck.

Love for him blew through her. She'd never felt such a connection to any man. Ami wasn't just falling in love with Beck. She was already there.

Her lips curved. "I think that could be arranged."

"Later, darlin'." He stepped back, but his arms remained around her, as if reluctant to give up the intimacy.

She cast him a flirtatious glance. "You know where to find me."

But when he turned to go, she went with impulse, grabbing the lapels of his jacket and, raising herself on her tiptoes, kissed once more.

She heard him whistling as he strolled away. Ami knew just how he felt, as she was ready to burst into song. Once inside her shop she decided to enjoy a cup of tea while her heartbeat steadied.

Ami hummed as she heated water for the tea in the back. Despite her hearty breakfast, a lemon curd scone seemed to be calling her name, so she dropped it onto a pretty floral plate. As she sank into a chair, Ami realized she couldn't remember the last time she'd felt so happy.

Darlin'.

It might be sophomoric, but she loved the way the endearment rolled off Beck's tongue.

She'd devoured half the scone when a tapping sounded at the door. Though the Closed sign was facing the street, out-of-towners often knocked, hoping the sign was a mistake. Ami shifted her gaze and saw Dakota at the door, a thin jacket the girl's only protection against a stiff wind.

Quickly unlocking the door, Ami motioned the teenager inside. "Come and warm up." Ami noticed but didn't comment on the girl's red-rimmed eyes. "You're just in time for tea and scones."

"Thanks, but I'm not hungry." Dakota pushed a straggly strand of hair back from her eyes with a jerky gesture.

"You might be when you taste my lemon curd scones. They're fabulous." Ami kept her voice light and casual. "The tea will warm you up. You have to be cold. The wind is brutal today."

"Okay, yes." Dakota's eyes darted around the shop.

"We're alone," Ami told her as she crossed the room, made a cup of Earl Grey, and plated another scone. "I'm glad you stopped by."

"I didn't know where else to go." Dakota took the floral cup and saucer with a hand that visibly trembled.

"A bakery is always a good choice." Ami offered an easy smile.

Dakota bit into the scone, chewed. "This is good."

"Told you." Ami winked and sipped her tea.

The teen kept casting furtive glances at the front window, as if worried someone walking by might see her. "You're probably wondering why I'm here."

"I invited you." Ami picked up her plate and cup. "On second thought, why don't we go upstairs to my apartment? We can talk more comfortably there."

Relief rippled across Dakota's face. She jumped to her feet so quickly her knees bumped against the table.

Inside her apartment, Ami gestured to the small dinette table in the kitchen. "Why don't we sit over there? The sun is coming in so fiercely this morning, as long as we don't look outside and see the snow, we can pretend that it's summer."

Ami kept talking as she made her way across the living room. It wasn't until she reached the kitchen that she realized Dakota hadn't followed her. "Is something wrong?"

"It's so clean. Not cluttered with junk." Dakota seemed embarrassed by the admission, yet added, "And your tree is beautiful. Those pink lights are supercool."

"Thank you, Dakota." Ami motioned the girl forward. "I wanted something that felt like home."

Dakota's face darkened. "I wouldn't want anything like my home."

The fear in the girl's eyes had Ami's heart twisting. "Sweetie, come and sit down. Tell me what's troubling you."

"I shouldn't have come here." The teen glanced at the door behind her and appeared ready to bolt. "You can't help me. No one can."

Ami crossed the room. She placed her hand on Dakota's shoulder and gazed into troubled hazel eyes. "I want to help you. I *will* help you."

Uncertainty crossed Dakota's face, but she released her grip on the doorknob and finally took a seat at the table.

They spent a minute sipping tea and eating. Ami chattered about the various scones they made at the bakery, hoping to put the girl at ease.

Not until Ami returned to the table after putting the teakettle on for more water did Dakota bring up the reason for her visit.

"You know Clint."

A sick feeling took up residence in the pit of Ami's stomach. "Yes."

Dakota continued to nibble on her scone but kept her gaze on Ami. "What do you think of him?"

"I don't like him." Ami spoke bluntly, seeing no need to sugarcoat. "And I certainly wouldn't trust him."

"You shouldn't trust him," Dakota warned. "He has a mean streak. And he's determined. Once he wants something, he's going to have it. Like me."

Ami inhaled sharply. "Has he—"

"Not yet," Dakota hastened to reassure her. "But it's just a matter of time."

"Tell me what's going on."

"My skin crawls every time he looks at my chest, every time his hand touches my shoulder." Though it was warm in the apartment—thanks to the new furnace—Dakota wrapped her arms around herself as if she was suddenly freezing. "He makes comments about how nice I look. Nothing you could pin him on, but I know what he's really saying and what he wants. I'm not stupid."

"Is it just you? Or your brothers, too?"

Dakota looked confused. "Kaiden and Braxton?"

Ami nodded.

"He ignores them." A light of understanding filled her eyes. "Clint only likes women."

Or girls, Ami thought to herself. Still, knowing Dakota's younger brothers were safe remaining in the household was a blessing.

"So, it's only you that he's focused on."

A muscle jumped in Dakota's tightly clenched jaw. She gave a jerky nod. "I overheard him telling a friend that as soon as he gets the chance he's going to—"

Dakota whispered the rest of the sentence. The words were shocking but not unexpected. Ami had seen that predatory gleam in Clint's eyes.

"What does your mom say?"

"According to her, Clint is a stand-up guy. She made it clear I better not screw it up for her with my lies." Dakota gave a bitter-sounding laugh. "Oh, and I need to quit flirting with him."

For one of the few times in her life, Ami was struck speechless.

"I don't flirt with him." Dakota spoke quickly, as if worried Ami might believe her mother. "I avoid him as much as possible."

"Do you have a school counselor you could speak with—?"

Dakota gave a dismissive snort. "Apparently being a perv isn't a crime unless you actually do something. The counselor did speak with my mother, who told her I was jealous of the coming baby and making up stories."

The girl closed her eyes against the pain. A second later her lids popped open and the eyes were ice.

"We could go to the sheriff." Leonard Swarts had held that position for twenty years, and Ami knew him to be a good guy.

"It'll be the same thing that happened with the counselor." Dakota heaved a resigned sigh. "When he asks what Clint has done, I'd have to say nothing yet. But sure as heck going to the sheriff will piss Clint off."

"Maybe he'd be afraid to do anything if he knew Sheriff Swarts had been alerted?"

"If you know Clint at all, you know it'd only make him more determined to get away with it. He'll figure a way to discredit whatever I say against him, and my mother will back him." Dakota raked a hand through her hair. "I didn't know where to go."

"What about your grandmother?"

"No." Dakota dismissed the suggestion without an explanation.

"Lindsay would take you in." Ami knew Dakota and her aunt were close. Lindsay wasn't a pushover like her sister, and Ami felt confident she'd do whatever was necessary to protect her niece.

"I know she'd let me live with her if I asked," Dakota admitted. "But Aunt Lindsay is the only real support my mom and brothers have right now. If she sided with me, Mom would cut off all contact with her. I can't let that happen."

"Which is why you came to me." Ami finally understood.

"It was stupid." Dakota nervously crumbled the rest of her scone on her plate. "I don't know why I thought you could help. It was just when you told me to stop by, I got the feeling you saw through Clint. I was hoping I wouldn't have to leave town. But right now I don't see any other choice."

"You could speak with an attorney." Ami reached out a hand to stop her when Dakota rose to leave.

Dakota plopped back in the chair. "What about?"

"You could become an emancipated minor." The words popped out of her mouth, dredged up from the past. Years ago, Ami's father had told her about a kid at the high school who went out on his own. "Be responsible for yourself. Get a place to live here in Good Hope. Finish school. Maybe get a scholarship to college. Lindsay is always bragging how smart you are."

"I'm in the top five of my class," Dakota admitted with a hint of pride. "But that's a legal thing, right? You have to go to court and everything?"

"I'm not sure what's involved. But I know court is part of it."

Dakota's shoulders slumped. "I've got enough money for a bus ticket, but that's all."

"One of the attorneys in Sturgeon Bay might be willing—"

"I need someone to help me now. With Christmas coming, no one is going to take the time. Especially when they find out I don't have any money."

The girl made a good point. But Ami wasn't about to give up.

"Could you figure out some excuse to stay with your aunt for a few days or so?" Ami asked.

"Maybe. Why?"

"I want you safe while I contact an attorney. I'll try Sturgeon Bay, and if we can't get an appointment, I know one here in Good Hope."

"There isn't an attorney in Good Hope," Dakota told her.

"We didn't have one before," Ami told her, "but we do now. He moved here last summer."

Chapter Fourteen

Feeling as nervous as a sixteen-year-old boy, Beck pulled out his phone. While he didn't need an excuse to call Ami, he was glad to have one.

He'd just gotten off the phone with Cory White. The young teacher and his wife were celebrating their tenth anniversary. His parents had given them a gift certificate to Muddy Boots. Cory wanted to know the best time for them to come in that evening.

Since it wasn't yet the weekend, Beck didn't expect a large crowd. Tom and his helper would handle the dinner rush with ease. The food would be good, but not anything special. Knowing Cory and Jackie's history, Beck wanted the evening to be memorable.

Ami answered on the first ring. "What a coincidence. I was just about to call you."

The warmth and ease in her voice had his grip relaxing around his phone. "I missed you, too."

Beck heard her startled intake of air. He hadn't meant to say what was on his mind, but neither was he going to apologize for it. Leaning back against the wall, he blocked the sounds of the early lunch crowd and focused on the conversation.

"We need to talk about something." Her voice had turned serious, and he pictured a little pucker of a frown forming between her brows.

Beck hesitated. Did she want to talk about where they went from here? If that was the case, he wasn't prepared. He was still trying to sort out his feelings.

There was no denying what had happened between them had been about more than sex. There was a connection between him and Ami that transcended physical need and pleasure.

As if she'd read his thoughts, Ami gave a nervous-sounding laugh. "It's nothing concerning us. Not that there is any *us*."

From the comment it appeared she was equally unsure and tentatively trying to find firm footing. But she was wrong about one thing; there was very much an *us*.

Beck decided to play it cool for now. "What's up, Ami? What can I do to help?"

"Dakota stopped by this morning."

Whatever he'd expected her to say, it wasn't this. He frowned. "Didn't she have school?"

"She skipped. But truancy is the least of her problems." Ami blew out a breath. "Would you have a few minutes to talk about her situation this evening?"

"Sure." From his vantage point, Beck could see that everything in the café was running smoothly. "Or we can discuss it now. I have time."

"I prefer to make a few phone calls first," she demurred. "See if I can get this resolved on my own before involving you."

Something in her voice pricked his curiosity. "Are you certain you want to wait?"

"Yes. Later will be best. Good-bye, Be—"

"Wait. Don't hang up. I have something to ask you."

Silence filled the air for several heartbeats.

"Ah, what is it?"

He'd flustered her, which amused him. Probably because he was feeling a bit flustered and unsure himself. "I know how hard you work and I don't want to add to your overflowing plate." Beck hesitated, recalling her propensity to agree to most requests. He didn't want to take advantage of her. Yet he was aware of her fondness for Cory and Jackie.

"Spit it out, Cross."

"It concerns Cory and Jackie."

"I'm listening."

Beck went on to explain about the call he'd received from the teacher. In the end, he didn't need to ask. Before he could, Ami volunteered.

"I'd love to make a special anniversary dinner for them. Maybe whip up a cheesecake for dessert. Cory told me at the last fundraiser that's his favorite—and Jackie's, too."

"Do you have time?"

Ami ignored the question as if it were inconsequential. "I'm going to call Jackie right now and ask what meal they'd like served. Surprises are nice, but I want the dinner to be filled with their favorite dishes."

She actually sounded excited at the prospect of spending her free time creating a meal for a couple she only knew casually.

The thought humbled him. Back in Georgia, Beck had known many who gave generously to charities but would never personally offer assistance. Before moving to Good Hope, before Ami, he had to admit he'd been one of them.

"You're a gem, Ami."

"Neighbors helping neighbors is the Good Hope way." She spoke in a light tone, deflecting the praise. "Well, I'll see you—"

"Soon, darlin'. We'll see each other very soon."

Smiling broadly, Beck pocketed the phone.

———

Ami arrived promptly at five, but any talk of Dakota was put on hold when Tom burned his forearm badly enough to necessitate a trip to urgent care.

Though the crowd wasn't huge, it was still more than Tom's assistant, a culinary student home for the holidays, could manage. Ami stepped in and took charge.

That left Beck to greet Cory and Jackie when they arrived at six. He'd reserved one of the tables in a corner for them.

Cory was younger than Beck had thought he'd be for a man with three children. If he was thirty-five, Beck would be surprised. The teacher wore a stocking cap, and when he took it off his sandy-brown hair stood straight up, short and fuzzy. His wife, a pretty strawberry blond with freckles, walked with an unsteady gait.

Chatting amiably, Beck ushered them to their table. Cory pulled out the chair for his wife before Beck could, and she blushed prettily.

"This feels like a real date." Jackie reached across the table and squeezed her husband's hand. "Thank you for planning such a wonderful evening."

Beck knew many of his former colleagues would consider a meal of chicken and dumplings served in a diner as slumming it. Of course, none of them had tasted Ami's cooking.

"Do you have any plans after you finish your meal?"

"My parents are watching the children tonight." Cory smiled at his wife. "Life has been so hectic, the thought of just going home and sitting in front of the fire sounds like heaven."

"I'm sure that must sound incredibly boring." Jackie's fingers tightened around her husband's hand.

Beck thought of last night. The fire. The wine. Ami. "I can't think of anything better."

"Hey, you two." Ami appeared tableside and bent over to give Jackie, then Cory, a hug. "Happy anniversary. How many years has it been?"

"Ten." Cory lifted Jackie's hand to his lips and kissed it. "Ten amazing years."

"We've been blessed," Jackie said.

The comment stuck in Beck's head as he and Ami headed back to the kitchen.

"Did you hear Jackie say they've been blessed?" Beck asked when they were out of earshot.

Ami's lips lifted in a soft smile. "They are such a happy couple."

"He has leukemia," Beck reminded her. "She has MS."

"And they're about to lose their house." Ami lifted a shoulder in a tiny shrug. "But they're happy, Beck. They love each other and their kids. They have more friends than they can count. In all the ways that count, they're very blessed."

Beck followed her into the kitchen, his mind reeling. "Are they really going to lose their home?"

"Looks that way." Ami kept her voice low so the staff couldn't overhear. "They got behind when Cory was off work. I believe they only need three or four thousand dollars to get the loan up to date, but it might as well be a million. His paycheck barely covers their day-to-day needs."

Beck pondered what he'd been told while Ami returned to the stove. When Ami had learned chicken and dumplings was their favorite meal, she'd asked Beck if they could just make it the café's evening special. Of course he'd said yes.

It proved the right decision. The dish, coupled with green beans, coleslaw, and a yeast roll, had been flying out of the kitchen.

As he watched Ami personally plate Cory and Jackie's food on the china dishes she'd brought with her, Beck couldn't stop thinking of the couple in the dining area.

Once the server picked up the food and left the kitchen, he pulled Ami aside. "Couldn't the Giving Tree help them out?"

Ami shook her head. "There has been a lot of need in the community in recent months. There isn't enough money left to fund a donation that large."

"Where do the donations come from?" Beck asked.

"There's an account at the BayShore Bank. People in the community donate to the fund. We also do fundraisers throughout the year." She leaned back against the commercial refrigeration unit, her brow furrowed. "I wish there were something more we could do. Anyway, you should be set for the evening. The rush is over. The cheesecakes are in the refrigerator."

"Do you have to hurry off?"

She winked. "I'm a busy gal this time of year."

Beck shoved his hands into his pockets. "What's on your agenda for tonight?"

"A hot date."

Beck froze. "Really?"

"With paper and ribbon and tape. I'm headed over to your house to wrap gifts." The dimple in her left cheek flashed. "I should be there most of the evening. If you see a light on in the back room when you finally head for home, please don't call the sheriff."

As Beck's body began to recover from the shock of her potential "hot date," he glanced around the kitchen. Right now it was running like a well-oiled machine. It didn't seem fair to have Ami in his home working while he was just standing around. "Need some help?"

"I was hoping you'd offer." She reached for her coat.

Beck proved faster. He lifted it off the hook, then helped her on with it.

"You're quite the gentleman."

He shot her a sardonic grin. "Sometimes."

The flash in her eyes told him she was remembering bits of last night when he'd been not quite so gentlemanly.

"Are you leaving now?" she asked. "Or coming later?"

"Now," Beck decided impulsively and grabbed his own coat. "Why should you have all the fun?"

Out of the corner of her eye, Ami watched Beck efficiently wrap another package. She had expected to have to show him how to wrap, but to her surprise, he was quite proficient.

They quickly settled into a routine, working side by side at the makeshift table in companionable silence. After several minutes she broached the subject that had momentarily slipped her mind. "Dakota is in trouble."

Beck paused, a striped red-and-silver bow in one hand. "What kind of trouble?"

"Things have gotten worse at home."

Ami recounted what Dakota had told her. As she continued to explain, Beck's eyes darkened. By the time she finished, his lips formed a hard line.

She met his gaze. "Do you think she's right? Can the sheriff really do nothing?"

"I'm not sure how they handle such things here, but back where I come from, they'd probably get the entire family together and gather all the facts." Beck paused for a moment. "Has Clint ever done anything inappropriate?"

"No." Ami picked up another package and set it on the table. "That's the blessing. So far, Dakota has made sure she's never alone with him. But she's convinced he'll get to her sooner or later."

"Seeing the way he looks at her, coupled with what he said to his friend, I'd say she's right to be worried." Beck dropped the bow and rubbed his chin. "You mentioned she doesn't want to stay with her aunt."

"She'd like to stay with Lindsay, and I know Lin would take her in, but Dakota is right. If Lindsay sides with her, Cassie will cut off all contact with her sister. Which leaves Cass and the boys at Clint's mercy."

"Do you think the boys are in danger?"

"According to Dakota, Clint pretty much ignores them." Ami rubbed the bridge of her nose, trying to ease the tension. "I suggested we see one of the attorneys in Sturgeon Bay about her becoming an emancipated minor. I called a couple of the family law offices there earlier today, but I can't get an appointment at either firm until after the first of the year."

"She might not have that much time." A muscle in his jaw jumped. "When Cassie has the baby, Dakota will be alone in the house with him."

"I think Dakota will run before that happens."

A startled look crossed Beck's face. "Run away?"

Ami unraveled a bow between her fingers. "She was close to doing that this morning."

"That would be disastrous."

"Perhaps you could speak with her about emancipation. Walk her through the steps to see if it's even feasible."

A long silence filled the air. With each passing second, Ami's hopes plummeted further.

"I'd have to research state statutes."

Ami's excitement must have shown, because he raised a hand and shot her a warning look.

"Look. It can be difficult to get a judge to agree, especially if the mother is opposed." That thoughtful look was back on his face. "Does Dakota have a job?"

Ami shook her head.

"The judge will want to know how she can support herself, where she would live. Those questions will need to be addressed." Beck stared, unseeing, at the mass of paper and ribbon before him, and Ami could almost see the wheels turning. "I left the law behind when I moved here."

There was something in his voice that caused Ami, who'd been about to push harder, to hesitate. "If you don't want to do it, I understand. I simply thought because she knows you and you've met Clint and because the other attorneys are busy and—"

"Ami." He offered a reassuring smile. "I'll look into the emancipation possibility, but I believe there may be another solution. How close are you and Lindsay?"

Ami's heart tightened. "We were once best friends."

"Good."

She cocked her head. "What are you thinking?"

"I'd like the four of us to get together and discuss all options." His gaze met hers. "Could you arrange that?"

"Absolutely." Ami closed her eyes for a second as relief surged. "When would you like me to schedule this meeting?"

"Tomorrow. As soon as Dakota gets out of school."

"Tomorrow is Friday."

"So?"

She smiled at his blank look. "One of the Twelve Nights celebrations? Gingerbread house competition in the town hall?"

"It will be crazy, but if what you're saying is true, Dakota is running out of time."

"Where shall we meet?"

"Have them come here. As early in the afternoon as they can make it."

"Aye, aye, sir." Ami gave a mock salute and, for the first time since Dakota had appeared at her door, believed everything would work out . . . thanks to Beck.

Chapter Fifteen

The impromptu hug Lindsay gave Ami as she stepped across the threshold into Beck's home startled him. When Ami had mentioned that she and Lindsay were no longer *best* friends, he'd jumped to the conclusion that the accident back in high school had severed their friendship. Based on his false assumption, he'd expected this meeting to be strained and awkward.

"I didn't realize the two of you were such good friends." Beck kept his tone casual as he showed them to the parlor.

"Oh, Ami and I have been friends since grade school." Lindsay's bright smile seemed to dim as she continued. "We haven't seen each other as much in recent years. But that's going to change."

She gave Ami's arm a squeeze before taking a seat.

Lindsay, a floral designer at the Enchanted Florist, bore a striking resemblance to her sister. Same honey-blond hair and gray-blue eyes. Same narrow face that was pretty rather than beautiful. Same whippet-thin body. Except a little younger and fresh and full of life, rather than beaten down and worn-out.

While it was impossible not to notice the scar on Lindsay's cheek, in Beck's estimation it didn't detract from her attractiveness.

Dakota remained quiet and took a seat next to her aunt on the sectional, leaving Beck and Ami to sit in the two ornate—and very uncomfortable—Queen Victoria high-backed chairs. The furniture obtained from an antique store in Sturgeon Bay had been delivered on schedule. A lavish red-and-gold tapestry rug covered much of the scarred floor. A large, gilt-edged mirror graced the mantel, while pastoral scenes typical of the period hung on the wall, covering the worst of the peeling paper.

Beck thought the scarlet velvet sectional was a bit ostentatious, as was the rosewood parlor armchair in gold satin floral. Still, the rich colors of the period furniture brought needed warmth to the old house.

"I'm not sure why I'm even here." Lindsay cast a quizzical glance at her niece. "Dakota just said it was important I come."

Ami decided to be blunt. "Dakota is concerned about Clint's interest in her."

Lindsay froze for a second. Then her blue eyes flashed. She shifted her gaze to her niece. "If he's touched you, I'm going to murder him."

"Chill, Aunt Lindsay," Dakota said in a slightly bored tone, but the look in her eyes said she was pleased by her aunt's passionate defense. "I've been able to keep my distance so far. But he's starting to talk more about sex stuff. If I don't get away, he'll get me alone and . . ."

There was no need to clarify what would happen; they all understood.

Lindsay's brow furrowed. "Have you told your mom? What does she say about his behavior?"

"She laughs and acts as if it's cute, as if he's joking."

Lindsay closed her eyes for a second and swore under her breath.

"Lindsay." Ami's soft-spoken words had the woman opening her eyes and shifting her attention. "Dakota came to me because she sees leaving Good Hope as her only option."

Lindsay whirled in her seat to face her niece. "Is that true?"

"I can't stay in the same house with him anymore." Dakota's lower lip trembled before she firmed it. "I'm afraid to fall asleep at night."

"Oh, baby." Lindsay wrapped an arm around her niece's shoulder. "You can come live with me."

"That's what I suggested." Ami's gaze slid to Beck.

Beck was glad to see Lindsay so supportive of her niece. For his plan to have any chance of success, it was essential she be willing to stand for the girl.

"I can't move in with you, Aunt Lindsay." Dakota folded her hands in her lap, stared down at them for a long moment. With her hair pulled back and her face bare of any makeup, the girl looked even younger than seventeen. "I want to, but I can't."

"Of course you can," Lindsay protested. "There's a futon in my living room with your name on it."

The girl shook her head. "Mom would be furious. You know how she can be."

"It's true my sister has a temper." Lindsay blew out a breath. "Don't you worry, I'll handle her."

"Remember what happened with Grandma Anita? She'll cut you out of her life if you get in her business. Then she'll have no one. She'll be at his mercy."

Lindsay's face took on a mulish expression. "I guess that's her choice."

"Mom needs you, Aunt Lindsay. You're the only one she can count on. If she doesn't have you or me, she won't have anyone."

The look of indecision on Lindsay's face told Beck that Dakota had raised a valid point. It was a good thing he had another option to offer.

"Let's talk possibilities." Beck leaned forward. "I have concerns about pursuing emancipation. Frankly, I don't believe it would be approved. Dakota doesn't have a job, and with attending school, it would be difficult for her to support herself."

Dakota's shoulders slumped. "I have to leave. That's all there is to it."

"You're not leaving," Lindsay snapped. "That's final."

"I think we all agree it's important not to jump into any action without thinking it through fully." Beck kept his voice calm and focused on Lindsay. "Here's another option. We speak with your sister together. You bring up that Dakota wants to pursue emancipation. You've tried to talk her out of it, but she's already enlisted my help and I'm ready to file the papers."

"File the papers?" Lindsay's brow furrowed. "But you own a café."

"Beck is also an attorney," Ami explained.

Lindsay smiled apologetically. "Oh, I didn't know."

Beck continued as if there'd been no interruption. "I'll mention that such a petition will necessitate the involvement of social services. The caseworker will come out and look at a variety of things, including what support Cassie is getting from the state and the fact that Clint is in the home."

Dakota laughed. "She'll be big-time pissed at you."

"Dakota. Watch your language."

The motherly censure in Lindsay's no-nonsense tone had Beck smiling.

"I'll be the bad cop," he told Dakota. "Your aunt will be the good one."

"How will I do that?" Lindsay appeared amenable but puzzled.

"You'll tell your sister that Dakota can live with you. But only after making it very clear that you really don't have room and having a teenager in your home will put a serious crimp in your social life. Still, Cassie is family and you don't want social services breathing down her neck and causing trouble."

Lindsay's eyes lit up. "That might work."

"If it does, I can stay in Good Hope and graduate." Dakota turned to Beck, and he saw tears shimmering in her eyes. "Thank you."

"Don't thank me yet. I—"

"It's going to work." Ami, who'd been relatively silent, punctuated the pronouncement with a decisive nod.

The look on Dakota's face brought an odd tightness to Beck's chest.

"It might be a good idea for you to start looking for a part-time job after school." Though Beck was also confident the plan would work, it didn't hurt to have a backup. "If we end up needing to pursue emancipation, you'll have some income we can report."

Dakota's hopeful gaze shifted to Ami.

"I'd like to help you, sweetie, but I'm full up on staff." Ami turned to Beck. "Weren't you talking about hiring an extra waitress for weekends?"

The girl's eager gaze shifted to Beck. "I've never waited tables before but I'm a quick learner."

Beck found himself smiling. "Once we've talked to your mother and you've moved in with Lindsay, we'll get some hours scheduled."

Without any warning, Dakota propelled herself into Beck's arms. "Thank you so much. I didn't want to leave but—"

Tears streamed down Dakota's face and onto Beck's shirt. He patted the girl's back. As he murmured soothing words, his and Ami's gazes connected.

The look of admiration in her eyes made him feel like a hero. While Beck didn't consider himself to be one, for the first time in his life he understood how good it felt to help someone truly in need.

———

After Lindsay and Dakota left, Ami returned to the café to prepare for the evening rush while Beck remained at home. Once his Christmas tree was delivered, he would meet Lindsay at Cassie's house.

With Tom taking an additional night off to give his burned arm another day to heal, Ami and her assistant were kept so busy, her shift at the café was over before she could blink. She'd just finished closing down the kitchen when the bells on the front door jingled.

Ami hurried into the dining room just as her father walked through the door. Relief surged when she saw Anita wasn't with him.

Wearing a stylish navy wool coat she hadn't seen before, he strolled into the café. His lips creased into a smile the instant his gaze landed on her.

"If you're here for dinner, I'm afraid we just shut down the kitchen." She returned his smile with a friendly one of her own. "But we have pie or—"

Her father waved a gloved hand. "I didn't come to eat, though I wouldn't say no to a cup of coffee."

"How about we have a cup together."

"Do you have time?"

She glanced sharply back at him, but it appeared to be just what it was: a simple question rather than a snide commentary on the fact she hadn't called him in nearly ten days. Granted, their paths had crossed a couple of times when he'd been with Anita, but other than that, they hadn't spoken.

Ami answered the question in his eyes. "I always have time for you."

After filling two ceramic mugs, she placed them at a table by the window, well out of earshot of the last two customers lingering over dessert.

Her father followed her, removing his gloves and coat as he walked. He pulled out her chair and took a seat opposite her, his hazel eyes solemn.

"I thought you might be with Beck." Steve glanced around the café. "Is he here tonight?"

"He was, but he left about an hour ago. The Victorian home tour is next week and his house hasn't yet embraced the Christmas spirit." Ami took a sip of the coffee she didn't really want. "I'm helping him decorate his tree this evening."

"It's almost ten o'clock," her father protested. "Much too late—"

"Dad." She reached over and covered his hand with hers, finding comfort in the touch. "It's a weekend night. I'm a big girl. Will it make you feel better if I promise to be in bed by midnight?"

The quick flash of his smile warmed her like one of the thermal blankets he'd covered her with as a child. Her father turned his hand over and held hers for several seconds. "I love you, Amaryllis. I don't tell you that nearly often enough. I'm sorry for what happened last week at the house. I should never have expected you—"

"I'm sorry, too, Dad." She swiped at tears that appeared out of nowhere to slip down her cheeks.

His hand tightened around hers. "Don't cry, honey."

"I don't like us being angry at each other." Ami sniffled. "I don't know what I'd do without you."

"You don't have to ever worry about that." He handed her a thin paper napkin. "We're family. Family sticks together."

Ami dabbed at her eyes and thought of Anita. "No matter what?"

"No matter what," her dad said firmly.

The tension that had sat like a leaden weight on Ami's shoulders since that night at his house began to ease.

"When your mom was alive, she always knew the right thing to say and do. After three years without her, well, I'm still finding my way. And I have to admit this dating thing"—he paused, then shook his head in bewilderment—"has me all discombobulated. I guess what I'm saying is, don't give up on me, Ami."

Ami thought of the unwavering support she'd received from her entire family, not only the night of her accident but every night before and since. If she had one regret, it was that she didn't often say what was in her heart.

"You never gave up on me." She covered her father's hand with hers and gazed into his hazel eyes. "I'll never give up on you."

———

Ami held the promise tight to her heart on the walk to Beck's home. While he had the lights, ornaments, and garland out in readiness, they never got around to decorating the tree. The second she walked through the door, Beck enfolded her in his arms.

He kissed her as if it had been years, instead of only hours, since he'd last seen her. Now, two hours later, she was snuggled against him in his four-poster bed under a mountain of blankets while the wind whistled outside. Ami smiled against his shoulder as her father's words flooded back.

"What's so amusing?" Beck's voice was warm and smooth as a glass of honeyed tea.

She shifted so she could look into his face. "My father stopped by the café."

"You settled your differences?"

"Anita is really our only difference," Ami said wryly. "And we didn't speak of her. But we cleared the air and everything is good between us now."

"I'm glad you're happy." He brushed a kiss across her forehead. "I know how much your father means to you."

"That wasn't the reason I smiled."

He cocked his head.

"I think he's worried I'm not getting enough sleep. I promised to be in bed by midnight." Ami's fingers took a stroll down his bare chest.

"Well, it *is* midnight and you *are* in bed . . . just not your own." He gave a deep chuckle. "And you never promised you'd be sleeping."

"You, sir, are so perceptive." She planted a kiss on his warm chest. "It's just one of the things I admire about you."

"Thank you, darlin'." He tightened his hold and tugged her even closer.

Ami emitted a sigh of pleasure. "I'm glad your meeting with Clint and Cassie went so well."

They'd spoken only briefly about his visit to the Lohmeier home that afternoon. When he'd arrived at the café, she'd been swamped with the supper rush. Then, when she'd arrived at his door . . . well, her current position told that story.

"It went well." He propped himself up on one elbow. "Clint was there when Lindsay and I arrived. Thankfully, Dakota's brothers weren't around."

"That's good." Ami's gaze searched his. "Did it play out the way you planned?"

"Other than I thought Clint was going to punch me when I mentioned I was ready to file the emancipation papers." Beck gave a little laugh. "The man could benefit from some anger-control classes." Concern flooded Ami. "But he didn't hurt you?"

Beck brushed his palm against her silky hair. "No. As you saw tonight, I'm unharmed."

She wasn't sure who was more surprised when she flung herself at him, knocking him backward, her body plastered against his.

"I don't want anything to happen to you." Her voice shook as her body trembled.

"Shhh. Nothing happened." He spoke in a soothing whisper, then chuckled. "Though when I mentioned the possible social services involvement, it was as if I'd struck a match to a powder keg. Both of them exploded. But Lindsay, well, she timed it perfectly. She heaved this melodramatic sigh worthy of any Hollywood actor. When she reluctantly said she'd take Dakota, they immediately calmed down and agreed."

Beck continued to stroke her bare back. She hoped she wouldn't have to move anytime soon. "It was satisfying to use my legal knowledge for good. Though I believe it was the social service mention that sealed the deal."

"Cassie is so desperate to have a man in her life that she refuses to see the guy is a predator." Ami sighed. "It's a darn shame."

"It's more than that." Beck's voice took on a hard edge. "It's unforgivable."

Ami's heart skipped several beats.

"Do you really believe that some actions are unforgivable?" She forced the words past suddenly frozen lips.

Beck didn't appear to hear the question. He was too busy planting kisses along her collarbone while one hand curved around her breast.

The shivers of need urged her to simply enjoy the moment, the closeness. But Ami couldn't let the topic drop. This was too important.

"You said her actions are unforgivable."

He lifted his head, his passion-filled eyes now puzzled. "What's this about?"

"Well, I-I've always liked Cassie. I know that she hasn't made good choices in her life, but she's not a bad person."

She thought Beck might say something, but the scrutiny in his eyes only deepened, and Ami was seized with an almost overwhelming desire to confess all. She bet he'd been very successful in the courtroom.

"Let's say Cassie finally comes to her senses. She looks back on this time and realizes what a mistake she made in not seeing Clint for what he really was and she's sorry. Very sorry. Are her actions—or lack of action in this case—really unforgivable?"

"Nothing happened because Dakota looked out for herself." Beck narrowed his gaze. "What if Clint had raped Dakota? If that had happened, would you be so willing to overlook, to forgive?"

His voice rose with each word. His chest, already hard as granite beneath her fingertips, flexed and tensed.

Before Ami could respond, Beck continued, like a locomotive picking up steam. "Do you really believe that a person only has to say they're sorry for all to be forgiven?"

Ami opened her mouth, closed it without speaking.

Beck swore. "The way I see it, people who act irresponsibly don't deserve forgiveness. They sure as heck aren't getting mine."

His chest heaved as if he'd just run a long race. His eyes weren't brown anymore but a hard, glassy obsidian.

Ami's insides vibrated. Beck wasn't the only one having difficulty catching his breath.

"I-I'm sorry," she stammered once she found her voice. "It just makes me sad to see how far Cassie has fallen. I remember her as Lindsay's big sister, one who never complained about us tagging after her, the girl who once went down into the storm sewer after my kitten."

After closing his eyes for a second, Beck appeared to regain control. "I don't know why I went off like that, other than to say you hit a nerve. I'm sure that fact was obvious."

Ami smiled wanly. "Being a defense attorney, you probably handled a lot of cases where people did hurtful things, then walked away, free of punishment."

Beck gave a humorless laugh. "Even worse, I was the one who got them off. I sent them back on their merry way to decimate other people's lives."

"You couldn't have known . . ."

"Couldn't I?" He rubbed his temples.

"Enough of this talk." Although she wanted to weep, Ami forced a light tone.

She tried to tell herself Beck was tired and that's likely what had caused him to react so strongly. But something told her it was more than just fatigue. It could be that the intensity of his reaction had something to do with his wife's accident.

Or perhaps his mood had been fueled by a recent uproar in the local media about two teenage boys who'd been given probation. After shoplifting some cigarettes, they'd knocked down an older man in their rush to get out of the store. The octogenarian had sustained a broken hip and was now using a walker.

The boys had each apologized to the man at their sentencing hearing and the judge had taken their remorse into consideration.

"You're right." Beck buried his face in her hair while his fingers teased her nipple. "We have much better things to do than talk."

As he enfolded her in his arms, Ami shoved aside her fears and gazed into Beck's dark eyes. "Are you referring to sleep?"

"Hardly." Beck offered a wicked laugh and gave her nipple a little pinch.

Heat shot straight to her core.

Just for tonight, Ami told herself. Just for tonight she'd forget her worries and enjoy being with the man she loved.

As his lips closed over hers and his tongue slipped into her mouth, Ami kissed him with all the love in her heart, knowing that one day at a time was all she was guaranteed.

Chapter Sixteen

Instead of immediately hopping out of bed the next morning, Beck propped himself up on one elbow and let his gaze linger on the woman sleeping beside him. How had Ami become so important to him? When he'd left Georgia to build a new life for himself in Door County, the last thing on his mind had been forging a new relationship.

After losing his wife, Beck was determined that hard work would be his only love. But he hadn't counted on meeting Ami Bloom.

The talented baker didn't gaze at him in that sympathetic, pitying way that had become so difficult to endure back home. Instead she brightened his days with her smile and sunny attitude.

She'd made his transition to this unfamiliar part of the country easy. Now she'd trusted him with her body. He knew Ami well enough to know she didn't hop into bed easily. Even though her capacity to give and receive pleasure astounded him, it was obvious it had been a long time since she'd been with a man.

Beck would cut off his right hand rather than hurt her. Which meant he needed to proceed carefully and figure out where they went from here. The knowledge that he had come to care so deeply for someone other than Lisette still troubled him. But it was becoming increasingly difficult to imagine his life without Ami in it.

He brushed a kiss across her cheek, then pulled the comforter up so she wouldn't get cold. With utmost stealth he tugged on jeans and an old Vandy sweatshirt, then headed down the hall to the bedroom he'd turned into an office.

He had some accounts to settle, and this seemed as good a time as any to get them out of the way.

While Beck waited for his computer to power up, his gaze dropped to the unopened letter that had come in the mail yesterday. He didn't need to look at the name and return address on the pale yellow envelope to know who it was from and what he'd find in it.

The instant he'd seen the envelope in his batch of mail, he'd almost tossed it unopened into the trash. But he'd set it aside, knowing that in the end he'd read the enclosed letter, just as he had the other three. The first had arrived shortly before Nina Holbrook's sentencing on vehicular manslaughter charges. The others had shown up every six months since.

Beck gritted his teeth so hard his jaw ached as he recalled the sentence the marketing executive had received. *Probation.*

Two years probation for two lives forever lost.

This woman actually expected him to forgive her?

Just seeing her handwriting had put him on edge and brought all the feelings of anger and loss bubbling up. He knew that was part of the reason he'd been more abrupt with Ami than he should have last night when she'd brought up forgiveness.

Thankfully, her good, pure heart had melted his anger.

But Beck felt his rage build again as he tore open the envelope and pulled out the single sheet of paper. His lips tightened as he read the words. She'd now been sober eighteen months. Her last drink had been at lunch on the day of the crash.

Though her blood alcohol hadn't been above the legal limit on the day she'd killed Lisette, the fact that it was one point below impaired at two o'clock in the afternoon told him Nina had a problem. Especially when coupled with her previous DUI charge.

His gaze dropped once again to the letter.

Forgive me, she pleaded in her perfect penmanship. The missive ended as it always did, with *I'm so very sorry for the loss of your wife and son*.

Beck ended the reading as he always did, by wadding up the thin sheet of vellum and tossing it into the trash.

On Sunday, the draw of the Christmas Stroll and Holiday Market, coupled with mild weather, brought residents and visitors out in droves. All businesses stayed open late and served special goodies and treats.

After handling the dinner rush, Ami left Muddy Boots to check in at the bakery, only to discover Hadley and Karin had everything under control. She was deciding how to spend the rest of the evening when Lindsay walked through the door.

Her friend had stopped by to see if she was interested in checking out some of the shops before they closed. In the past, Ami had always declined Lindsay's friendly overtures.

This time there'd been such hope in her old friend's eyes that Ami had found herself agreeing. Maybe she'd said yes because it was Christmas. Or maybe because lately she'd started wondering just who she was punishing by keeping Lindsay at arm's length.

The air was crisp and the sky dotted with a thousand stars. The sidewalks were crowded with shoppers in high spirits.

The first business on their stroll was the Enchanted Florist, the shop where Lindsay worked as a floral designer. With charming smiles, the teenage daughters of the owner offered them cookies shaped like pretty spring flowers.

Lindsay chose one resembling a daffodil. After dropping a donation in the Giving Tree jar, her friend held up the perfectly formed creation. "This looks like your work."

"Guilty." Ami picked up a lavender cookie on a stick and sank her teeth in the buttery sweetness. "Your boss insisted on flowers in pastels instead of traditional Christmas cookies. They stand out, so it seems to have been a smart move."

"Shirley has a good sense for what works and what doesn't," Lindsay said.

Ami added her own donation to the jar before they wandered outside. When she complained of being chilled, Lindsay insisted on buying them both cups of steaming cocoa from a vendor in the town square.

"Christmas Stroll brings back such good memories. Remember how we used to meet at the general store, then make the rounds chowing down food and lusting after the hot guys?" Lindsay's eyes filled with a look of bemused remembrance. "I practically stalked

Jeremy Rakes. Of course that was a wasted effort. Back then he only had eyes for your sister. How is Fin, by the way?"

"She's still working in Los Angeles for that advertising agency." Ami was proud of the success her sister had achieved. She only wished Fin lived closer and could visit more often. "She'll be back for Christmas this year. She's coming early for my dad's open house."

"I appreciated the invitation." Lindsay took a sip of cocoa and popped the last piece of the daffodil cookie into her mouth. "I can't wait to see your family again."

Ami had debated whether to invite Lindsay, but growing up she'd been close to all of Ami's sisters. Besides, barring a miracle, Lindsay's mother would be there. No doubt hanging all over Ami's father. She pressed her lips together and shoved the disturbing image aside.

"It'll be a hectic time. Speaking of hectic." Ami shot a curious glance in Lindsay's direction. "What's it like having a teenager in the house?"

"It's . . . different but good. My apartment isn't all that big, but we're making it work." Lindsay grasped Ami's hand and gave it a squeeze. "I can't thank you and Beck enough for what you did for our family."

"I didn't do anything," Ami protested.

"You hooked us up with Beck." Lindsay's eyes turned misty. "When I think of what might have happened to Dakota . . ."

"Hey." Ami met Lindsay's gaze. "It's all good now."

"Beck was magnificent. You should have seen Cassie's face when he mentioned social services. And Clint, well, that guy is a loose cannon anyway. They practically threw Dakota at me. Neither of them wants a social worker getting in their business." The smile on Lindsay's face disappeared. "I still believe Cassie will eventually come to her senses and kick that loser to the curb. Until that happens, Dakota will live with me. I'll keep her safe."

Ami exhaled a sigh. "It's still difficult for me to reconcile the current Cassie with the girl I knew all those years ago. Your sister was always so kind and gentle. It wasn't until after your father died that she began to change."

"They were very close. When he had the heart attack and died, it hit her hard. She and Mom were always at odds. That's because they're so much alike."

Ami knew Anita would go ballistic if she heard anyone comparing her to her wayward daughter. The twinkle in her friend's eyes told Ami that was her thought as well.

The shared understanding reminded Ami how it had once been between her and Lindsay. Back in high school they were so in sync they often finished each other's thoughts. The night when Ami thought she'd killed her best friend had been the worst one of her life.

Lindsay's eyes softened, correctly interpreting Ami's expression. "We need to move on from that night."

"I haven't always made the best choices."

"I haven't, either. That's part of growing up." Lindsay's voice was matter-of-fact. "How many of us are the same as we were at seventeen? Or even at twenty-five? We learn, we grow, and hopefully become better and wiser women. That's not something to regret. It's something to celebrate."

"Yes, but—"

"Stop. No more guilt. I don't blame you for my injuries, Ami. I chose not to buckle my seat belt." Lindsay's voice now trembled with emotion. "I'm tired of waiting for you to forgive yourself for something that wasn't your fault. I want my friend back."

Ami stilled the apology on her tongue. Perhaps Lindsay was right. Perhaps it was time to move on. She took a breath, let it out slowly. "Tonight has been fun. Let's do it again."

Lindsay nodded. No other words were necessary.

"Dakota is worried about her mom." Her friend circled back to their earlier discussion. "I assured her I'll make sure Cassie and the boys have what they need and she just needs to focus on getting good grades. I have to tell you, she's superexcited about the part-time job. That was nice of Beck."

Ami's lips curved. "He's a good guy."

With each step they took toward the general store, the scent of spicy brats grew stronger. They were almost to the front porch of the clapboard structure when Lindsay elbowed Ami. "You and Beck seem to get on well."

"We do." Ami kept her tone offhand. "Considering his shop is right next door to mine, that's fortunate."

"That's not what I meant." Lindsay shot her a teasing smile, which made the scar on her cheek more prominent. "Are you two exclusive?"

While her own feelings were strong and true, Ami wasn't sure what was going on in Beck's head. Though she felt certain he cared for her, that's all she knew for sure. Heck, she didn't even know if they were really dating, much less if they were exclusive.

"Beck and I are good friends." Ami waved a careless hand in the air. "We hang out every now and then."

"Are you saying he's available?" Lindsay asked as they stepped onto the porch of the general store. "Because Greer Chapin asked me about him."

Greer was Clay's younger sister. She'd been in Marigold's class in school. Like all the Chapin brood, she'd left Good Hope for college. The pretty brunette had returned to the peninsula several years after graduation to work in one of the family's many banks on the peninsula.

Ami hesitated. She certainly didn't want to lie and say that she and Beck were "together" just because they'd made love. But she also didn't want to give Greer the green light. "I wouldn't exactly say Beck and I are together—"

"We're together," a familiar, deep voice insisted as a hand slid around her waist and warm lips brushed across her cheek. "Hello, Lindsay. How's Dakota?"

Ami tried to put a little distance between her and Beck as Lindsay brought him up to speed on the teen. Beck would have none of it, keeping his arm firmly anchored around her waist.

His smile widened to include both of them. "Have you been tasting all the treats?"

"You bet. That's why we stroll." Lindsay smiled at Ami. "We were just talking about our high school days. We religiously visited all the shops. Except for our senior year when I—"

Ami braced herself, but before Lindsay could say more, Eliza walked up. The stylish shop owner was dressed all in black, including a midlength boiled wool coat Ami didn't recall having seen before.

Lindsay got a warm hug.

Ami received a cool smile.

"I texted you." Eliza focused on Lindsay. "When you didn't answer, I assumed you were out strolling."

But not with Ami in tow, Eliza's look seemed to say.

"It feels like old times. Especially now, having you with us." Seeming oblivious to the tension, Lindsay hooked her arm through Eliza's and flashed Ami a sunny smile. "The three of us always had such fun together."

Beck's eyes met Ami's and she saw the puzzlement in his gaze.

"Yes, well." Eliza shifted from one polished boot to the other. "That was a long time ago."

"I'll let you ladies—" Beck began, but Eliza didn't let him finish.

"How's the main floor coming?" The dark-haired beauty narrowed her gaze. "You realize the Victorian home tour is this Friday."

"Is it?" Beck's mild tone had Eliza's eyes flashing.

"People will expect to see the inside decorated for the holidays," Eliza pressed. "I don't recall seeing Christmas lights on a tree."

Beck flicked a glance at his wrist. "Actually, I'm headed home now to trim the tree. It was delivered Friday afternoon."

Eliza's gaze shifted to Ami. "You should help him. You know the level of decorating the community expects."

Ami opened her mouth but Beck beat her to it. "She's out with her friend this evening."

"I'll keep Lindsay entertained." Eliza glanced at her friend. "Okay with you, Lin?"

"Sure." Lindsay smiled amiably and gave Ami a little push in Beck's direction. "You two *friends* have fun."

"I know you've put in long hours today, so," Beck said to Ami, shooting a censuring glance in Eliza's direction, "there's no obligation."

Based on the pointed look Eliza sent her, Ami knew that the executive director of the Cherries considered helping Beck get his house ready for the tour very much an obligation.

"I'd love to help," she told Beck, then turned and gave Lindsay a hug. She held her friend tight for an extra second, vowing to hold this precious gift of friendship equally tight. "It's been fun."

"We'll do it again." Lindsay smiled at Eliza. "Next time with the three of us."

"That was strange," Beck remarked moments later as they climbed the steps leading to his front porch.

Ami could feel Eliza's eyes on them. She was seized with the unladylike urge to turn around and stick out her tongue as Beck unlocked the door. What kind of luck was it that Eliza's store was directly across the street from Beck's house?

Keeping her tongue inside her mouth, she stepped inside.

Beck pulled the door shut behind them. "I didn't realize you three were such good friends."

Ami caught the curiosity in his tone.

"Lindsay and I were once pretty close." Even as she said the words, Ami felt a stab of guilt. If anyone had pushed back from their friendship, it had been her. "Eliza was always more Lindsay's friend than mine."

Which, while also true, didn't negate the fact that she and Eliza had once laughed and talked and enjoyed each other's company. Now that they were both Cherries and business owners they should have had a lot in common. Yet they'd never been further apart.

Lindsay's acceptance had shown her it was possible to move on. While Ami would never stop regretting her actions of that long-ago night, she didn't have to let the past define her present and future. But first she needed to come clean with Beck about her past.

Then, depending on his reaction, they could move on. Or not. At least there would be no more lies between them.

She was deciding how to best broach the subject when Beck paused in the foyer and held out his hand.

As she gazed at those outstretched fingers, erotic memories rushed forward, swamping her.

"May I take your coat?" he asked when she only continued to stare.

She handed him her jacket and gave a husky chuckle. "The last time you held out your hand to me, you wanted to take me to bed."

A look she couldn't quite interpret flared in those dark eyes. "It would be presumptuous to assume just because we did it once—"

"Once?" Ami arched a brow. "I seem to recall a time in the shower. And then in the kitchen . . . And that just covers Wednesday night."

"Good point." His lips twitched. "There's another factor to consider. Eliza will be keeping a keen eye on my front window, waiting to see when the Christmas tree lights turn on." He hung her coat next to his. "If she sees—"

"—your bedroom light go on instead, she'll know the decorating plans likely got sidetracked." Ami grinned. "She'd be right."

"I know you'll say you don't care what she thinks." His voice lowered and he brushed a wisp of hair back from her cheek with gentle fingers. "I don't want her spreading gossip about you."

"I don't care." Ami stepped forward and wrapped her arms around his neck. "I want you."

A pleased smile lifted his lips. "I want you, too."

His low voice brushed against her heart like a caress.

Beck kissed her softly, then stepped back, forcing her to release him. "I believe it's possible to have the evening we want and appease Eliza at the same time."

After flicking on the parlor lights, he strolled to the tree, a beautifully shaped fir that nearly touched the ceiling.

Reaching into a box, he pulled out a string of lights. With quick, deft movements, Beck untangled them, then wrapped the tiny bulbs around the middle part of the tree and plugged them in.

The brightly lit fir sat in front of the window, ensuring the lights would be clearly visible through the lace curtains.

"I'd say we worked long enough on the tree," Beck announced. "It's time for a break."

With her fingers clasped in his warm, comforting grip, they climbed the steps to the second floor. While Beck busied himself lowering the privacy shades in his sitting area and adjacent bedroom, Ami lit candles and kept her gaze fixed on him.

The angular lines of his face seemed softer in the candlelight, and his dark hair shimmered like fine mahogany. In such a short time, he'd grown so familiar, so dear.

It was odd that when she least expected it, Mr. Right—complete with a southern accent and a kind heart hidden under a sometimes gruff demeanor—had dropped into her life.

When Beck motioned her closer, her heart flip-flopped. This man was everything she wanted, and she appeared to be what he wanted, too.

Would he still want her once he knew her secret? Before they made love, she needed to come clean.

Ami was forming the confession in her head when his warm mouth closed over hers, scrambling her thoughts.

He enfolded her more fully in his arms, his tongue sliding across her lips. When she opened her mouth to him and he possessed her fully, all rational thought vanished.

Tonight, she would show him how much she loved him.

Tomorrow would be soon enough to tell him the truth. This time, the whole truth.

Chapter Seventeen

When the doorbell rang Monday evening, Beck knew who'd be on the other side of the door. Max had called earlier that afternoon and asked if he wanted to go to a fundraiser for Cory White at the Flying Crane. Beck offered to meet his friend at the bar, but Max insisted on swinging by the house after he left the office.

"You have a Santa in your yard." Max held the door open and gestured with one gloved hand toward the slope of the snow-covered yard.

Beck ignored the comment. "In or out, Brody. I'm not paying to heat the outside."

With a smirk, Max stepped into the foyer. "Seriously, man, you've been pranked."

"It's not a Santa Claus, it's Father Christmas." Beck reached for his coat and slipped it on. "The antique dealer from Sturgeon Bay tossed him and the reindeer in with the other stuff he loaned me."

"What are you talking about?"

"The furniture, rugs, and pictures for the main level are all on loan," Beck explained. "Which you'd know if you weren't out gallivanting around the country."

"Hey, I had to help Granny get settled in her new retirement home. I even got her tree up before I left."

"Good for you. Mine is up, too."

"*You* put up a tree?"

"It's Christmas, Max. And with the Victorian home tour this weekend—"

"Don't tell me Beckett Scrooge Cross is participating in a community event." Max put a hand over his heart and pretended to stagger back.

"It's good for the economy. The tour brings people into the area." Beck tossed the words over his shoulder as Max followed him onto the porch.

Max grinned. "I recall saying those same words to you and having my head bit off."

"Your big head looks intact to me."

Max laughed and two women walking by the house paused to smile and wave.

Beck didn't know them but nonetheless lifted a hand in greeting.

The second he stepped off the porch, a blast of north wind slapped his face. The schizophrenic weather had gone Nordic, with the pleasant temperatures of the past few weeks only a distant memory. His southern blood recoiled against the cold and Beck shivered.

Walking briskly helped some, but he could have cheered when the bar came into view. As they drew closer to where the Flying

Crane sat overlooking the bay, sounds of music and laughter filled the frigid air.

Max cast an assessing glance in Beck's direction. "You look different."

Beck didn't respond. He'd learned early on that the accountant loved to hear himself talk and that responses to 90 percent of what Max said were optional.

"I can't quite put my finger on what it is." Like Beck, the CPA was dressed casually for the evening in jeans, boots, and a sweater, topped by a coat.

Back in Bogart, most of the fundraisers Beck attended were black tie and held at one of the many country clubs in the area. He already knew this one would involve a live band, lots of beer, and music loud enough to perforate eardrums.

"Seriously, there's something different."

Okay, three times saying the same thing demanded a response. Or else knocking Max out, and that wasn't really an option.

"I recently had my hair trimmed."

Max assessed the hair brushing the top of Beck's collar. He shook his head.

"It's not your physical appearance," Max said finally. "It's . . . you. You seem happier."

"It's Christmas. Ho-ho-ho."

Max grinned at Beck's feeble attempt. "The incidence of depression soars at this time of year."

Beck didn't need Max to remind him of that; he'd lived that statistic last year. His first Christmas without Lisette. His parents had tried to make the holidays nice, but seeing his brother kiss his wife and toss his giggling baby into the air had sliced like a knife to the heart.

"Things are good," Beck said simply. "Business is booming at the café."

"I hear you and Amaryllis Bloom have been seeing each other." Max religiously read the *Open Door* e-newsletter and had his finger on the pulse of the community.

For one moment of horror Beck wondered if he and Ami had been mentioned in the tabloid rag. He immediately dismissed the thought.

"Ami is part of the Cherries. She's been helping me get my home ready for the tour. She's also cooking at the café on the weekends."

"She's an attractive woman."

Beck turned to his friend. "Your point?"

"No point." Max's expression remained bland. "I'm just happy to hear you're becoming more involved . . . in the community."

Beck responded by grunting and jerking open the battered wooden door of the bar. As he'd predicted, the noise was deafening. While a few couples danced, the majority of patrons stood—or sat—with drinks in their hands, trying to be heard above the pulsating bass.

The glossy mahogany bar took up an entire wall. A long mirror made the average-size bar appear huge. High tin ceilings, while aesthetically pleasing, had sound reverberating like a speaker on steroids.

From young college students barely old enough to legally drink to weathered fishermen who'd seen a half century on a boat, the eclectic crowd had one thing in common tonight: red-and-white Santa hats.

"Hey." Max tapped a fisherman with a white beard on the shoulder. "Where'd you get the hat?"

The man raised his voice and gestured with his head toward the back of the bar. "They're selling them to raise money to help one of the teachers at the high school."

"Beck. I didn't expect to see you tonight."

He turned and saw Hadley holding a tray of dirty glasses. She wore the bar's standard uniform, a black T-shirt displaying the Flying

Crane logo in eye-popping red with a black skirt showing miles of toned legs.

"I didn't know you worked here."

"You know what they say about idle hands." The pretty blond laughed. "What can I get you to drink?"

"I'll have a beer; whatever you have on tap," Beck said.

Max stared at Hadley with blatant interest. "You work with Ami at the bakery."

"I do." Her voice was pleasant but distant. "What can I get you?"

"Same." Max offered the woman an engaging smile, but she didn't appear to notice.

As Hadley moved to a nearby table to take another order, she called to Beck over her shoulder. "If you're looking for Ami, she's in the back."

"Does Blondie have a boyfriend?" Max frowned as he watched Hadley toss her long, curly hair and flirt with a man old enough to be her father.

"I don't know." Beck spoke absently, wondering if he'd be able to convince Ami to come home with him tonight. Though he'd seen her this morning, that had been hours ago.

"She doesn't seem interested in me." Max sounded surprised. "Not at all."

"You're right about that." As Beck pushed his way through the crowded bar, he noticed a pack of obviously intoxicated young men in ball caps standing near the bar.

He shot a censuring glance at the bartenders. Didn't they realize they were putting the entire community at risk by serving people who'd already had too much?

Hadley rushed past him and he grabbed her arm.

"Hey, don't touch the—" She stopped when she saw it was him. "You want to change your order?"

"Those guys over there need to be cut off," he said without pre-amble. "Also make sure they're not driving."

The blond followed his gaze. She studied the threesome for a moment, then nodded. "I'll take care of it."

Satisfied, Beck resumed weaving his way to the back of the bar. He lost Max when they ran into a pretty, dark-haired woman with startling gray eyes whom his friend introduced as Greer Chapin, Clay's sister.

While Max stayed behind to speak with the woman, Beck kept walking.

He spotted Cory and Jackie in the corner, speaking with several other couples. The affable teacher raised his hand and smiled when his gaze landed on Beck.

After returning the greeting, Beck settled his gaze on Ami. She stood behind a table with Katie Ruth, fellow Cherrie and editor of the tabloid rag, the *Open Door*.

He couldn't help but smile at their attire. The two were dressed as Santa's elves in tight red shirts, green pants, and hats with a single jaunty feather. The rectangular table they stood behind held sprigs of mistletoe tied with red-and-white-striped ribbon, tins of cookies, and the popular Santa hats.

As there was currently a line, Beck and Max stood back, sipping the beer Hadley had dropped off.

"Good enough to eat," Max murmured.

Beck glanced at the selection of holiday treats displayed. "Ami makes the best cookies."

"I'm not talking cookies, Cross. I'm talking women."

Beck shot Max a dark glance, while privately acknowledging he found the way Ami's stretchy shirt clung to her breasts arousing.

The accountant grinned, apparently noticing the direction of Beck's gaze. "Exactly."

He gave his friend a warning shove. Max could look at Katie Ruth all he wanted, but he best keep his eyes off Ami. At that moment, the line thinned and they stepped to the table.

Beck slipped out his wallet.

"What can I get you?" Katie Ruth asked with a cheery smile.

"I'd like to make a donation."

The tabloid editor pointed to a large jar, and Beck stuffed a handful of twenties into the top.

"Two hats." Max handed Katie Ruth a large bill. "Keep the change."

"You better be buying that second one for someone other than me," Beck told his friend, "because I'm not wearing one."

"That's the Mr. Scrooge we all know and love."

"We also have cookie tins and mistletoe." Ami, who'd finished with another customer, moved to Katie Ruth's side and smiled at Beck.

"Toss in a piece of that mistletoe, too," Max requested.

"I didn't expect to see you tonight," Ami said to Beck while Katie Ruth placed Max's mistletoe in a small, clear bag.

"I hoped our paths would cross." Actually, that was one of the main reasons he'd agreed to come with Max. "I hated having to rush off this morning."

"You didn't have much choice," she said with an understanding smile.

He and Ami had barely gotten out of the shower when Beck had been called to the café. Two boys had egged the front of several businesses, including Muddy Boots. The sheriff needed Beck to fill out a report. Thankfully, Ami's bakery had been spared.

"Max heard about the fundraiser. I wanted to support Cory and Jackie." He glanced in the direction of the couple. "How are they doing?"

Ami shot a glance at Katie Ruth. "Mind if I take a five-minute break?"

Katie Ruth's gaze skipped from Ami to Beck. She grinned. "Go for it."

Ami led Beck to the quietest corner she could find. She slanted a glance in Cory and Jackie's direction and sighed. "They received some bad news today from the mortgage company. If they aren't up to date on their payments by the end of the month, the company will start eviction proceedings."

Beck frowned. "That seems drastic."

Ami lifted her shoulders, let them drop. "The mortgage company has been accommodating, but a company's patience only stretches so far."

"Is there any way Cory and Jackie can come up with the money?"

Ami shook her head, her green eyes somber.

Beck exhaled a harsh breath. "It's Christmas."

"I know. It sucks." Tears suddenly filled Ami's eyes, but she quickly blinked them away and squared her shoulders. "Tonight is about celebrating Cory's return to health and raising enough money to help them pay off the last of their medical bills."

"By selling Santa hats?"

"They're a hot item," Ami protested. "Along with the mistletoe."

"My mistletoe wants to be put to use." Max stepped close and twirled the dark green leaves and berries he'd purchased above Ami's head. "You know what this means."

She glanced up.

Before Ami could respond, Beck plucked the mistletoe from his friend's hands and gave him a little shove. "It means it's time for you to get lost."

The accountant seemed more amused than discouraged. His eyes danced merrily. "I'll buy another bunch and peruse the inventory."

Max swaggered off.

Ami's brows pulled together in puzzlement. "'Peruse the inventory'?"

Beck hesitated. "Single women."

After a second, Ami chuckled. "I like Max."

"I like you." Beck twirled the sprig between his fingers, back and forward. "I like mistletoe."

Ami cleared her throat. "It-it's always fun to see who avoids it and who deliberately steps under it."

"Like this?" Beck raised the sprig and pulled Ami to him under it.

"Beck, everyone thinks we're just business associates," she hissed, even as she let her body meld against his.

"I'd say it's about time they knew differently." The words had barely left his mouth when his lips covered hers.

***

"Beck kissing you under the mistletoe last night is all over town," Hadley told Ami as they added sprinkles to the dozens of cookies that were headed to a Christmas party at the Good Hope Assisted Living Center. "Katie Ruth mentioned it briefly in this morning's *Open Door*."

"Great," Ami muttered. "Now I just need to wait for my father's call."

Hadley lifted her gaze. "Will he be upset?"

"He's my dad and he's old-fashioned. He'll want to know if Beck and I are serious. He'll probably ask me where I see our 'relationship' going. I'm not ready to answer those questions." Her friend's lips twitched as she carefully added more sprinkles. "At least he doesn't know you slept with Beck instead of decorating his tree."

Ami inhaled sharply. "What makes you think I slept with him?"

"Good old deductive reasoning." Hadley tapped her temple with an index finger. "I ran into Eliza and Lindsay at the general store the night of the Christmas Stroll. Eliza mentioned you were helping Beck decorate the tree. When I saw that no more lights were being added to the single string of lights visible through the window, I realized something more than trimming the tree was going on."

"We could have been having tea and talking."

"Do I really look that gullible?"

Ami rolled her eyes. *Welcome to life in a small town.* "I'm heading over there after we finish here. This time we'll get the rest of the decorating done."

"Yeah, right." Hadley drawled out the words. "The way he looks at you tells me decorating isn't at the top of his list for his evening activities."

"It better move to the top. The Victorian home tour is Friday and his house isn't near ready."

"You've got a lot on your plate right now." Hadley suddenly turned serious. "Between the bakery and the café and the fundraisers for Cory. How did that come out, by the way?"

"Two thousand dollars."

"That's amazing. Especially this close to Christmas."

"It's easy for people to identify with Cory and Jackie. Hardworking people who've tried to live a good life and through no fault of their own have experienced a series of setbacks."

"I heard about them possibly losing their home." Hadley met Ami's gaze. "Isn't there anything we can do to help? What about the Giving Tree?"

Ami shook her head. "It's too much money."

"I'm sorry to hear that . . ." With a sigh, Hadley finished the last tray of cookies and straightened. "Speaking of the Giving Tree, Floyd Lawson stopped by looking for you. He'd tried to reach you on your cell but said it went to voice mail. He left you a note."

Floyd, the treasurer of the local rotary club, was a burly man with a booming voice who played Santa Claus every year.

Ami slipped the phone from her pocket and realized with more than a little chagrin she'd turned it off at the bar last night and forgotten to switch it back on. Three recent calls and a message, all from Floyd. "I hope nothing is wrong."

"From the big grin on his face and the way he slapped me on my back and said, 'Ho-ho-ho, merry Christmas,' I seriously doubt it."

Ami snatched the note from the counter and read it quickly. She gasped, read it again to be sure. Sinking onto a nearby chair, she felt tears sting the backs of her eyes.

"What's wrong? Is it bad? It's bad, isn't it?" Hadley crossed the kitchen area in several strides and crouched beside her friend. "What is it? Tell me."

"It's all good." Ami lowered the paper to her lap and realized her hands were trembling. "An anonymous donor gave a large sum to the Giving Tree. The donor specifically designated the money go toward paying Cory and Jackie's mortgage up to date, with whatever is left going into the general fund."

Hadley looked incredulous. "Are you serious?"

"Read it yourself." Ami gave Hadley the note.

Hadley's gaze skimmed the words before she looked up. "Who would do such a wonderful thing?"

"It's a mystery." Ami's gaze dropped to read the wonderful message again. "All I know is the White family will have a very merry Christmas, indeed."

Chapter Eighteen

Ami floated all the way to Beck's home to help him with the last of the decorating. The news about Cory and Jackie's gift from an anonymous benefactor had already made its way around Good Hope by the time she reached her destination.

The *Open Door* even put out a rare afternoon edition with the news, including an interview with the happy couple. The heartwarming feature filled Ami with good cheer and put a bounce in her step.

Once she reached the large home on Market Street, instead of rushing up the steps, Ami stood on the sidewalk and studied the impressive white structure. As a little girl, she'd looked forward to those times when her mother brought her and her sisters along when she visited Katherine Spencer.

Her mom and the older woman would sit in wicker chairs on the porch, sipping lemonade while Ami and her sisters would crowd together on the large swing. Ami had loved that swing. Heck, she loved everything about the nineteenth-century home.

"It's a beautiful home."

Ami jumped—just a little—at the sound of Beck's voice. She turned and smiled. Was there anything sexier than a man holding a sack of groceries?

"I love your house," she said simply as she started up the short walkway to the porch. "Ever since I was a teenager, I dreamed of buying it and turning it into a B and B."

Beck climbed the steps, then shifted the groceries in his arms. He unlocked the door and stepped back to let her enter. "I wouldn't think too many teens dream of opening a bed-and-breakfast."

Once inside, they shrugged off their coats before continuing on to the kitchen.

"When I was in high school, I cleaned for Katherine. The job gave me money for the extras I wanted that my parents couldn't afford. It may sound corny, but while I polished the woodwork and made the windows shine, I'd hum and pretend the house was mine."

But it was only pretend. Even back then she'd known that as a baker—which was her career goal—she'd likely never make enough to afford such a grand home.

"It's not corny," Beck said softly. "I can picture this as your home."

Ami flushed and placed the bottle of milk and carton of eggs he'd taken out of the sack into the refrigerator.

"I was convinced I could never afford it." That was, until the summer after her sophomore year in high school, when her mother had taken her and Fin on a shopping trip to Milwaukee. "A stay in a Milwaukee bed-and-breakfast opened my eyes and gave me hope."

There had been several large conventions in Milwaukee that weekend and the hotels were all booked. Instead of staying downtown as they had on previous occasions, her mother had found two rooms in a bed-and-breakfast.

Fin had groused. She liked staying downtown, surrounded by tall buildings, not in a residential area where the homes sat back from the street, surrounded by flowers and trees and large carpets of green. Ami had been instantly charmed by the three-story brick home.

"How did it open your eyes?" Beck ignored the staples he'd just placed on the counter, keeping those intense brown eyes fully fixed on her.

"I talked with the owner. She took me back into her kitchen." Ami gestured with one hand. "It was like this one, modern but still with that old-time feel. She told me how much she enjoyed meeting new people and welcoming them to her home."

Like Ami, the portly proprietress loved to cook and bake. According to the woman, having a B and B allowed her to do everything she did best—including making guests feel at home.

Ami had returned to Good Hope with a tiny seed planted in her head. Excited about the possibility, she'd told Fin of her plans. While her sister hadn't laughed, she'd been clearly puzzled. Why would she want *strangers* in her home? Not only that, strangers she had to cook for and clean up after?

She looked up to find Beck with his back against the counter, gazing at her. He motioned for her to continue.

"I knew turning this home into a B and B was the only way I'd ever be able to afford it. While I can't explain it, I had this sense that this was where I was meant to live. I told myself there would come a day when Kate would be ready to sell, and I'd be ready."

"Then I bought it out from under you."

"No, you didn't." She shook her head. "Even if Kate would have given me first option, I couldn't have bought it. I'm not yet in the financial position to take that step."

"Seems to me owning and running a B and B would be a lot of work."

"I guess it's all in how you think about it. I love to cook and bake, visit with people, and make new friends."

"What about the bakery?"

Ami blinked at the abrupt change in topic. "It's doing fine. Why do you ask?"

"You own and run a successful business." He inclined his head, his gaze assessing. "Let's say you'd have been able to buy this house. What would you have done with the bakery?"

As he took her arm on their way to the parlor, Ami realized she'd never once considered what she'd do with Blooms Bake Shop. The thought of turning it over to someone else brought a pang to her heart.

"I suppose I'd hire Hadley—or someone else—to run the bakery for me."

"What about family?" She must have looked blank, because he continued, "Husband? Children? Do they have a place in this dream of yours?"

Ami gazed down the hall, imagining a small, dark-haired girl in footie pajamas running toward her with outstretched arms. Beck stood beside her, a baby in a blue blanket cradled in his arms and a toddler, also in blue, gripping his legs.

Her chest swelled with a longing so intense it stole her breath. When Ami finally found her voice, she had to fight to keep out the tremor. "Yes. In my dream, there's a husband and a whole passel of children."

"Passel?"

At Beck's startled look, Ami laughed. "What can I say? Ask me to dream and I dream big."

An odd look appeared on his face, and he stared at her as if seeing her for the first time.

She laughed and waved a dismissive hand, trying not to be embarrassed by her ramblings. After all, he'd asked. Besides, nothing could dampen her mood.

My cup of good cheer runneth over.

"I have fabulous news." She clasped her hands together, and her voice quivered with excitement as he led her into the parlor, where most of the decorating still needed to be done.

He grinned as if finding her excitement contagious. "What is it?"

"The rotary received an anonymous donation to the Giving Tree." Ami still had difficulty believing it was real. "It was a targeted donation."

"Which means?"

"Oh, of course you wouldn't know that." She gave a happy little laugh. "It means the benefactor specified where the money would go."

"They can do that?" Beck picked up a box of carefully packaged ornaments and placed it on the table.

"Yes, absolutely." Ami's hand fluttered. "It doesn't happen often, but we've seen it before."

"Where did they want the money to go?"

"I guess I'm getting ahead of myself. It's just that this is so wonderful." She took a step closer to Beck. "The person gave us enough to pay Cory and Jackie's back payments on their mortgage. They're now current and the bank has halted the foreclosure proceedings."

"That is good news. Any idea who gave the donation?"

Ami shook her head. "I wish I knew so I could thank him or her. It's such a wonderful gift. Cory and Jackie cried when they got the news."

Beck's lips curved. "I'm happy for them."

"Me too."

The news buoyed both their spirits, and they laughed often during the next hour as they added ornaments to the Christmas tree. Not wanting to duplicate the color scheme in the historic Hill House, they agreed to stick with colors that would enhance the furniture's scarlet-and-gold color scheme.

Surreptitiously, Beck watched Ami wind garland around the banister with a concentration worthy of a chess master. The emotion that engulfed him could no longer be brushed aside. In her quiet, gentle way, Ami was slowly filling the hole that Lisette's death had left inside him.

Beck shifted his gaze before she could catch him staring and filled a basket designed for firewood with an assortment of ornaments Ami had selected. She'd been right. The vibrant reds and golds along with the sparkly branches drew one's eye.

He'd always assumed he didn't like decorating and had avoided what he considered to be a chore. But he was enjoying this time with Ami, working side by side, laughing and talking or simply working in companionable silence.

When he'd moved to Good Hope last summer, Beck had been certain if he was ever ready to love again, it would be in the distant future. He hadn't counted on Ami Bloom.

Beck glanced over and found her studying the banister with her hands fisted on her hips.

He cared about this kind and gentle woman. A lot.

"What?" Ami had turned back and obviously caught him frowning. "Don't like the garland? Too pedestrian?"

"It isn't that." He let his gaze linger for several heartbeats. "You look pretty in green. Your eyes shine like emeralds."

"Why, Mr. Cross." She drawled the words in a poor attempt at a southern accent. "I didn't realize you had a poet's soul."

"We all have our secrets." He winked, then turned back to the firebox he was stuffing with oversize ornaments.

———

Secrets. Ami took a deep breath and attempted to steady her nerves. It wasn't fair to have secrets from the one you loved.

Yet, instead of confessing, Ami turned and surveyed the tree. "It needs a star."

"Let's see if they brought us one in the box."

As he peered inside, Ami leaned over to help him search. The ornaments had been extremely well organized, but the tree toppers had been included in a box with some miscellaneous Christmas items.

Their cheeks were almost touching when Beck turned his head and laid his mouth on hers for a brief kiss.

"What was that for?" Ami asked, pleased by the gesture.

"You make this fun."

"I've enjoyed it, too," Ami admitted. "When you live in a small apartment, there isn't much to decorate. Growing up, Christmas decorating was a two-day event."

"Complete with sugar cookies and hot cocoa?"

"Is there any other way?"

"Sounds like fun." There was a wistful quality to his voice.

"What was it like for you growing up?"

"In regard to Christmas?" he clarified.

Always the attorney.

"Yes." Ami kept her smile easy. "Was there a lot of decorating and cookie baking in your household?"

"My parents have an active social life. December is especially busy. It seemed to make good sense to hire a professional to decorate the tree and the house."

Fin often spoke of people who lived that kind of lifestyle, but Ami couldn't imagine a non-hands-on Christmas. "I bet the decorators did a nice job."

"Always looked good." Beck's gaze shifted to the tree. "Not as good as ours."

Ours.

She liked the way that sounded. "Ours is beautiful. But we still need a star."

"An angel won't do?" He held up one with a porcelain face and a diaphanous gown.

Ami shook her head. "A star says you're home."

She felt the heat of Beck's gaze and stared into intense brown eyes.

"We'll find a star," he said.

They found one in the next box, a burnished gold with a hint of sparkle.

When she climbed the ladder to place it at the top, he remained close, steadying her with his hands. In seconds, the star was in place. She turned back to Beck in triumph.

Her breath caught in her throat at the intense emotion in his eyes. Was it her and their tree he was thinking of, or was he thinking of his wife?

The instant she stepped off the ladder, his hands fell away. Disappointed, Ami forced a smile. "How about I make us some dinner, then we finish up the last of the decorating?"

"She cooks, she decorates, she's Wonder Woman," he teased.

Ami simply laughed. "For the record, *we* decorated, and while I may be starting the meal, I expect help."

Beck followed her into the kitchen. "I'm not sure there's much in the cupboards. Though I did pick up milk and eggs."

"I love a challenge."

In the end Ami took the eggs, some Swiss cheese, onions, and spinach and whipped up a frittata.

Beck produced a bottle of pinot blanc and poured them each a glass. They took their food into the parlor.

The fire crackled in the hearth while they ate. Once they finished, Beck insisted on gathering up the dishes. While he took them to the kitchen, Ami kicked off her boots, totally relaxed.

When Beck returned to take a seat beside her and placed an arm around her shoulders, she sighed in contentment.

He sipped the wine and listened to her talk about her day. If he was a kick-off-his-shoes kind of guy, his would have joined Ami's UGGs. He couldn't recall the last time he'd felt this relaxed and content. It had to have been years.

Like his parents, he and Lisette had been busy professionals. They would often joke that they only met when they were coming or going.

She hadn't even slowed down once she became pregnant, and he'd found himself wondering more than once how a baby would fit into their tight schedules.

He had no doubt they'd have made it work. Lisette was very organized and made time for what was important. He was important to her. So was their baby.

"Beck."

He turned to see Ami's gaze on him, those beautiful emerald eyes filled with concern.

"Is everything okay?" Her voice was as rich as one of her cream-filled pastries.

"All good." He sipped his wine.

"I imagine it's difficult to be so far away from your family during the holidays."

"In some ways it's easier." He spoke without thinking. While he missed his parents and siblings, last Christmas had been brutal.

"How so?"

He waved a dismissive hand. "I'm looking forward to serving Christmas lunch at the café."

She went along with the blatant change in topic without missing a beat. "I never asked, are you planning to cook?"

Beck laughed aloud. "Tom will be in charge of the kitchen."

"Perhaps my sisters and I can come over and help—"

"No." Beck placed a hand on hers. "Focus on your family. With all your sisters back, it sounds like this will be a special year."

"If you need extra help, I want you to call me. And I'm baking the pies, no argument."

"You'll get none from me."

She smiled and snuggled back against him.

On Friday, the Twelve Nights celebrations would start up again and the weekend would be hectic. Once Christmas was over, Janey would be back and life would return to normal.

But as he stroked Ami's silky brown hair and his emotions surged, something told Beck that when this Christmas was over, his life would never be the same again.

Chapter Nineteen

The Cross home threw open its doors from six until ten Friday evening. Guests flooded in, oohing and aahing over the decorations. On exiting the house, each person received a brightly colored Christmas cookie wrapped in cellophane and ribbon. Unlike in Victorian times, Ami's green icing didn't contain even a hint of arsenic.

Ami hadn't planned to be there. After all, this wasn't her home. Though she had to admit, it was starting to feel that way. She'd spent more time under these eaves in the last few weeks than in her own apartment.

When Beck had initially asked her to serve as his hostess, Ami gently reminded him that Friday was a workday for her at Muddy Boots. He'd been prepared, informing her the night of the home tour had historically been a light one for the café and Tom was confident he could handle any rush.

With no other barriers, Ami had enthusiastically agreed.

As was customary for the Victorian home tour, she dressed for the period. The gold brocade she'd picked up at a local costume shop perfectly complemented the home's color scheme, though it showed a little too much cleavage for her taste.

Beck didn't appear to agree. His eyes had lit up when she'd descended the stairs after changing out of her sweater and jeans. He raised her hand to his lips for a kiss that lingered a little longer than what would have been considered gentlemanly in Victorian times and pronounced her stunning.

Ami had to admit she felt beautiful tonight, with her hair pinned in a loose mass of curls at the nape of her neck. Though she rarely took the time, thanks to a younger sister who'd been into hair from diaper days, Ami was proficient in fixing her hair in all sorts of styles.

She'd also spent extra time with her makeup, using a shimmering brown shade for her eyes and applying mascara and lip gloss with a heavy hand.

While she felt confident she looked her best, it was the man standing next to her who stole her breath. Resplendent in black trousers, red silk vest, and white tuxedo shirt, Beck looked yummy enough to eat. The fitted tailcoat showed off his lean, muscular form to full advantage.

He fit her image of a gentleman host to perfection as he stood beside her at the front door, welcoming visitors. In the background, a string quartet played music popular in the Victorian era.

Opulent bouquets of tightly massed flowers boasting a heavy concentration of red roses accompanied by lots of foliage added a sweet fragrance to the air.

"Remind me where we're keeping the extra cookies?" Dakota

asked Ami in a low tone, looking as fresh and pretty as any young deb-
utante of the late nineteenth century. The Worth gown, a blue satin
woven with gold threads, suited her fair complexion to perfection.

Beck had hired the teenager to hand out cookies to those exiting the house by way of the kitchen. For a girl who normally lived
in jeans, dressing up had been an extra bonus.

"I'll show you." Excusing herself, Ami moved through the parlor
with Dakota following. She pointed at the room on the left at the far
end of the hall, then reached into the beaded reticule looped around
her wrist and pulled out a key. "This is the same room where we're
storing the Giving Tree gifts."

"Who's going to deliver them?" Dakota asked as the door clicked
open.

"Why, Santa, of course. On Christmas Eve." Ami gave the girl a
wink. "You'll find the bakery boxes on the makeshift table."

While Ami couldn't imagine anyone walking out with any of the
gifts, not everyone coming through tonight was known to her, and
it seemed best to be cautious. "Be sure and lock the door after you."

"Absolutely." The shadows that had darkened Dakota's eyes even
a week ago had disappeared. Living with her aunt had been good
for her.

Ami placed a hand on the girl's arm. "Thanks for helping out."

"This is a blast. And I can use the money," Dakota confided
with the refreshing honesty of youth. "I'm happy you and Beck
asked me."

You and Beck.

How many times this evening had Ami heard those words? *You
and Beck* have done a fabulous job with the home. Do *you and Beck*
have plans for Valentine's Day?

With everything going on, Ami hadn't thought that far ahead.
The day for lovers. Well, based on their numerous encounters of the

physical kind, she and Beck met the criteria. The big question was, would they still be together in February?

That would be up to him, once she told him the whole truth about her accident.

"Ami."

She looked up to find Dakota's worried gaze on her. "What?"

"Are you okay? You have the strangest look on your face."

"It's these shoes." She stuck out the elegant satin shoes with their pointed toes, French heels, and intricate beadwork. "I can't wait to take them off."

"I think they're sexy."

The husky feminine voice had Ami whirling with a smile of delight.

"I'll get the cookies." Dakota hurried off.

Ami barely had time to register the familiar waterfall of blond curls and laughing blue eyes before she pulled the petite dynamo into her arms. "Marigold. Ohmygoodness, I didn't expect you until Tuesday. What a wonderful surprise."

She hugged her sister tightly, breathing in the familiar scent of jasmine as tears stung the backs of her eyes. Oh, how she'd missed her baby sister.

"It's good to be home," Marigold murmured just before she released her.

"Let me look at you." Ami held the youngest of the four sisters at arm's length and studied her.

Long, curly strands of blond hair, artfully disheveled, fell in a tumbled mass past her shoulders. Vivid blue eyes. A perky, upturned nose that made her look like an intriguing sprite or fairy. She was the shortest of the Bloom girls, barely hitting five three, with a lithe figure that still managed to have curves in all the right places.

Tonight she wore the little black dress so popular with urban-ites. Instead of heels, she had on thigh-high boots that added at least three inches of height.

"You're going to kill yourself in those shoes," Ami, ever the big sister, warned. But there was no censure in her tone, only a warm welcome.

"Pot calling the kettle black," Marigold shot back.

"Huh?"

"You forget. I saw the shoes you have on under that heavy dress. They're lethal."

Ami gave a reluctant chuckle. "Yes, but I have sensible ones upstairs."

"Would that be in Mr. Beckett Cross's private quarters?" Marigold cocked her head. Before Ami could answer, she continued, "I saw our delectable host. I totally approve."

"Beck and I are . . ." Ami paused, searching for the right word. Friends? Lovers?

"Well, look who's all grown up and gorgeous."

Her sister whirled, dispensing a zillion-watt smile on the town's mayor. "Jeremy Rakes. I swear you get more handsome every time I see you. My sister had to be crazy to let you get away."

The flash of pain that flitted across Jeremy's face was gone so quickly Ami wondered if she'd imagined it.

"How is Fin?" he asked in an almost too-casual tone.

"You'll be able to see for yourself," Marigold answered. "She's flying in Tuesday."

"Oh, there you are, Jeremy." Eliza rushed up, not appearing to notice the mayor was already engaged in conversation. "I lost track of you in the crush of people."

"Hey, Eliza." Marigold turned a much more subdued smile on

the Cherries' executive director. "For some reason I thought you'd be at Hill House this evening."

Eliza stared at Ami's sister as if she were a stranger she was trying to place.

"Marigold Bloom." With an impish smile, Marigold extended her hand, leaving Eliza no choice but to take it or look like a schmuck.

Ami concluded it had to be the briefest handshake in history.

"I remember." Eliza offered a perfunctory smile. "And, to answer your question, I'm responsible for making sure everything is running smoothly on the tour."

Her sister's speculative gaze shifted between Jeremy and Eliza, who looked stunning—as usual—in a royal-blue sweaterdress and boots. "Are you and Jeremy dating now?"

"Eliza and I are here tonight in an official capacity," Jeremy said smoothly, before Eliza had a chance to respond. "I'm here as mayor. She as executive director of the Cherries."

"Oh." Marigold nodded sagely. "It's strictly business."

Jeremy's lips twitched slightly, as if remembering what a pain in the backside little Marigold had once been. "Eliza and I are also good friends."

As if to illustrate, he looped an arm around the woman's shoulders. A flush of pleasure spread across Eliza's pretty face.

"Jeremy asked about my sister," Marigold told Eliza. "I told him Fin is arriving Tuesday. It's too bad there won't be time for the three of you to get together. Seeing as you and Jeremy are good friends and Fin and he used to be really good friends."

Eliza's lips lifted in a tight smile. "Yes, that is too bad."

Ami punched her sister in the side. While Marigold had disliked Eliza ever since the woman had turned on Ami after the accident, there was no need to be unkind.

Thankfully her sister got the message and shut up about Fin. She took Ami's hands. "I have to leave."

"You just got here."

"Shannon is having a party at her place tonight."

"I forgot you were coming in early for the wedding." The last time Ami had spoken with Marigold, her sister hadn't been certain she could get off work.

Shannon Tracy had been Marigold's childhood buddy. While they hadn't been as close in recent years, they'd stayed in contact through social media and Marigold's occasional visits back to Good Hope.

"Good to see you, Marigold. Ami." Jeremy rested his hand on Eliza's arm. "Let's check out the Chapin house next."

Eliza's expression gave nothing away. "I'll meet you at the Dunleveys'."

Marigold watched through slitted eyes as the two strolled off. "Looks like the Shaw-Chapin feud is alive and well."

"Some things never change." Impulsively, Ami gave her sister another hug. "I can't wait to hear the latest on you and Daniel."

Her sister's boyfriend, Daniel Smithson, worked for the Chicago Board of Trade. Ami had met him briefly when she'd visited the Windy City last spring.

Marigold glanced around the beautifully appointed parlor. "We'll get together before the open house and I'll catch you up. You can do the same."

Ami inclined her head.

"I can't wait to hear all about you and the delectable Mr. Cross." Marigold's smile widened. "The way you're blushing says there's a lot to tell."

By the time ten o'clock approached, Beck realized Ami hadn't exaggerated. The people of Good Hope and the tourists that flocked to the township in droves loved the Victorian tour of homes. There'd been a steady stream through the house since the doors opened at six.

While he enjoyed greeting everyone and especially seeing customers he recognized from Muddy Boots, Beck was ready to reclaim his home. Still, having Ami at his side had made the evening not only bearable, but pleasurable.

A few times during the night, he'd found himself thinking of this as *their* home. That might be because she'd been spending so much time here, but Beck knew the connection went deeper. Somehow, over the course of the past few weeks, they'd become a couple. When he thought of the future, it was becoming increasingly difficult not to imagine her with him.

"The upstairs is clear." Ami offered a tired smile as she descended the staircase, her hand sliding down the banister. "No stragglers."

"It's clear down here, too," Beck reported.

Ami glanced around. "Where's Dakota?"

"Lindsay picked her up a few minutes ago. She gave me the key to the room where we're storing gifts and said she'd catch up with you later." Beck smiled, remembering Dakota's stunned look of pleasure at the fifty-dollar bonus he'd given her.

"I had a good time." Ami's gaze slid around the parlor and lingered on the star at the top of the magnificent tree. Her heart swelled with emotion. *Home.*

"It wasn't nearly as bad as I envisioned," Beck admitted.

Ami pulled her attention back to the man at her side. Her lips quirked in a smile. "Now there's a ringing endorsement for the home tour."

He grinned and she went warm all over.

"Your cookies were a hit."

"They were, weren't they?" She gave a satisfied nod. "We'll—I mean *you'll*—have to consider serving treats again next year."

If he noticed her almost faux pas, it didn't show. He took her hand and tugged her to the parlor, the sweet scent of roses even more apparent with the house empty.

When they reached the sectional, Ami dropped down and slipped off her shoes. She wiggled her toes and sighed with pleasure. "Now the party can really begin."

"Your wish is my command." Beck returned moments later with a bottle of wine and two glasses. "You look comfortable."

"Removing the shoes helped," she told him, taking the glass he offered. "But these dresses are heavier—and more restrictive—than they look."

"I've got the solution. Take it off."

His innocent expression didn't fool her.

She tapped her temple with her index finger. "You're always thinking."

Beck grinned. "About some things, anyway."

After removing his coat and laying it across the top of a nearby chair, he settled beside her on the sofa. "I'm glad the house is ours again."

Ami tamped down the surge of pleasure and reminded herself that, regardless of what he said, they both knew this was *his* house, not *theirs*.

"My sister stopped by." Realizing her throat was parched from so much talking, Ami took another sip of wine. "I didn't get a chance to ask if she'd introduced herself to you."

Beck shook his head. "Which one?"

"Marigold. The youngest."

"The hair stylist. From Chicago."

"That's her. Perky, charming, and gorgeous as ever." Ami smiled. "Things have been so hectic I forgot she was hoping to arrive early."

"Do you need to leave?" Beck asked. "I can easily wrap those last few gifts before Floyd swings by to pick them up tomorrow."

"Marigold won't be around anyway." Ami waved a dismissive hand. "She came early to attend a friend's wedding."

"Was the wedding this evening?"

"It's tomorrow." Ami wiggled her toes a few more times. "The bride is having a party at her home in Egg Harbor tonight. Since she's here, I assume Marigold will be doing the bridal party hair."

"Hopefully I'll have a chance to meet her while she's in town."

Ami shot him a glance under lowered lashes. "If you come for Christmas lunch, you can meet *all* my sisters."

"I appreciate the invitation." Beck pulled her close, and with a contented sigh, Ami rested her head against his chest. "But Christmas dinner at the café is taking on a life of its own. I never realized there were so many people who spent the holidays alone."

"I wish I could join you."

"You have your family."

You feel like my family.

"Then you're just going to have to make time to come to my father's open house on Tuesday."

"I'm not sure I'll be able to get away from the café."

"It's an open house," she said pointedly. "From four to eight. Drop in for five minutes. Cory and Jackie will be there."

Beck smiled. "I saw them tonight."

Ami's eyes turned misty. "That anonymous gift changed their lives, and the lives of their kids."

Beck splashed more wine into his glass, then looked up at her. "That's seems a bit of an exaggeration."

Something in his eyes had Ami's Spidey senses tingling.

"It was you." She straightened so quickly wine in her glass sloshed. "*You* made the donation."

He hesitated. Then, as if realizing it would be pointless to deny it, he shrugged. "It was nothing."

"I disagree." Her voice rose and cracked. "You gave them a second chance."

"I caught them up on their mortgage. That's all."

She took his hand, gave it a squeeze, her heart overflowing with love. "I'm so proud of you."

Beck shook his head, looking baffled by the praise. "I just wanted them to be able to stay in their home."

They sat silently staring into the fire for a long moment, lost in thought.

"Never alone," Ami murmured.

"What did you say?" His soft words lulled her into responding.

"It was something my mother told me once." Ami set her glass of wine aside. "That when you're surrounded by people you love, you have the strength to face anything."

Beck stilled. When Lisette had died, his family and friends had rallied around him. He'd still felt alone, as if he were an island surrounded by stormy seas. Any effort to bring him comfort didn't, couldn't, reach him. "Do you believe that?"

"I do believe it." Ami met his gaze. "But only if you let people in. There was a time when I tried to shut out the support and the love. If you ever met my mother, you'd know no one shuts out Sarah Bloom for long."

"When the pain is intense, it's easy to shut out everything and everyone."

"Is that what you did when your wife died?"

There were a dozen ways Beck could have responded to the

217

question that would answer it without saying anything at all. Ami deserved better than pat answers.

"Lisette's death came out of the blue."

He abruptly straightened, and suddenly his arm was no longer around her. Yet when she reached over and grasped his hand, he didn't pull away.

"You said it was a car accident."

"I was heading into court when I got the call." His fingers tightened around hers. "They said my wife had been in an accident. An ambulance had taken her to the local hospital."

Ami said nothing.

His breathing turned shallow.

"She'd died at the scene but they didn't want to tell me." He gave a humorless laugh. "Didn't want me having that in my head on my way to the hospital. Instead I raced there, hoping to comfort her. She was already dead. She'd been gone when they'd called."

The pain in his voice had her wanting to hold him tight and never let go. Instead, Ami kept her voice calm and her gaze level. "I can't imagine what that was like for you."

"Imagine the worst day of your life, then multiply it by ten." He set down his glass of wine and pinched the bridge of his nose. "I don't know why I'm telling you all this. It's in the past."

"She's part of you. She always will be."

"Lisette was pregnant. I don't think I told you that before. Actually, I know I didn't. Even now, it's painful to speak about."

"How far along was she?"

"Seven months. A baby boy." He swallowed once, then again, his hand gripping hers so tightly it hurt. Then abruptly he released her and picked up the glass, downing the rest of the contents in one gulp. "It was a woman who killed her. She was a marketing exec, heading back to work after downing a couple of margaritas at lunch. Minor injuries for her."

Tears leaked from Ami's eyes and slipped down her cheeks. "I'm so sorry."

"It's not your fault," he said in a flat tone. "It's mine."

Startled, Ami swiped at her eyes. "How do you figure?"

"Because I was the attorney who'd gone all out to make sure she didn't lose her license after a previous DUI."

Chapter Twenty

Ami opened her eyes before the sun had a chance to rise in the sky, her heart overflowing with love for the man who slept beside her. The fact that Beck had shared something so intensely personal with her last night told her he trusted her fully.

His face looked so peaceful in sleep, but her heart ached for the loss he'd suffered and the pain and guilt he still carried. She couldn't imagine what it had been like for him to not only lose his wife but his baby, too; a little boy who would never have the chance to laugh or cry or love the father who'd already loved him.

Ami blinked back sudden tears.

She'd gone numb when she'd heard the driver had been a woman who'd been drinking. It was clear he hadn't forgiven the woman, nor himself for defending her and getting her earlier DUI charge reduced to reckless driving.

Ami wished she could tell Beck how much it had meant to her when Lindsay forgave her. But she'd remained silent, knowing Beck didn't intend to forgive the woman. He'd later admitted she'd written him several times, apologizing and asking for his forgiveness.

What had Beck said . . . sometimes sorry isn't enough?

That one comment told Ami he'd never see himself having a future with someone like her. In fact, he'd probably hate himself for ever getting involved with her.

That thought had been pinging around in her brain when Beck had begun to unbutton her dress with a desperation that told her he wanted to forget everything that had happened in the past and everything he'd just told her and lose himself in the moment.

She could have refused him. Perhaps *should* have refused him. But she loved Beck. If she couldn't have him for eternity, she would give him comfort and hold him close one last time.

Later that morning, after he and Ami had eaten and she'd helped him wrap the last of the presents, Ami announced she needed to get to the café for the Saturday rush. Normally he'd have been disappointed she had to hurry off. This time, Beck felt only relief.

"I'm going to hang around here and catch up on some paperwork." He walked her to the door and couldn't resist brushing a kiss across her lips. "I'll see you soon."

The fact that her smile seemed hesitant didn't surprise him. He'd laid a lot on her last night.

Once he closed the door, Beck returned to the kitchen and poured himself another cup of coffee. He took it with him to the parlor and sat for several minutes in silence, staring at the festively decorated tree.

While Beck hadn't lied—he did have paperwork demanding his attention—the truth was he needed to regroup. He'd bared his soul to Ami last night.

It was no longer possible to deny how important she was to him.

Oddly, sharing what had happened—and his guilt over his part—had been cathartic.

When she'd spoken of her mother, he'd thought of his parents and brothers and the way he'd shut them out. Little doors closing one at a time until he stood alone, isolated, determined to fight his grief alone.

Ami had reminded him it didn't have to be that way.

Beck pulled his phone from his pocket. Before he could change his mind, he pressed a familiar key.

"Cross residence." The feminine voice, with its soft southern drawl, soothed a raw place deep inside him.

"Mom. It's Beck. I wanted to wish you a merry Christmas. I realize it's early, but I know you'll be busy so—"

"JW, your son is on the phone," his mother called out, interrupting him. The joy in her voice had guilt sluicing through his veins. "Pick up the other line."

"I thought Dad would be at the courthouse."

"It's Saturday." His mother gave a little laugh. "But you'll be pleased to know the old workhorse not only took last week off, he's taking the upcoming week as well. Anders is spending two weeks with us. Elliott and his family arrived last night. Jefferson, well, that little boy has his granddad wrapped around his little finger."

His mother's chatter abruptly ceased.

Jefferson and Beck's son had been due within weeks of each

other. Since the accident, the family had tacitly agreed to avoid speaking of the boy in Beck's presence.

"If he's like Elliott, I bet he's into everything." Beck kept his tone light. To his surprise, he found he could speak of his nephew without being overwhelmed by his own grief.

"He's very precocious," Margot said hesitantly, "and extremely active."

"James," his father's voice boomed over the phone. While in the past Beck had reserved James for his professional life, his father insisted on using his legal name at home also. "Good to hear from you, son. How's life in the frozen tundra? Do you have snow on the ground?"

Beck laughed and relaxed his grip around the phone. "It's December. In northern Wisconsin. Of course there's snow on the ground."

"Are you ready to come home?" The hopeful edge to his mother's question came through loud and clear. "Move back to the civilized South?"

"I'm going to stay." Without him knowing exactly when it had happened, this town, this part of the country, had ceased being an escape and become his home.

"How's the restaurant business?" his father asked.

"It's doing well. This is a busy time." He went on to tell them about the Twelve Nights events and the tour of homes. Before he knew it, he was telling them about the Giving Tree and Cory and Jackie. "Neighbors helping neighbors."

"Sounds like a nice place," his mother said.

"You should all come up and visit this summer," Beck urged. "The Fourth of July celebration is huge. You'll be impressed."

"You want us to come?"

Beck understood the hesitation in his mother's voice. He'd made it clear when he relocated that he wanted—no, needed—to be left alone.

"I'd like all of you to come. You and dad, Elliott and his family, and Anders." Saying the words felt right, and he could almost feel Ami beside him, cheering him on. "I have a big house. There's more than enough room for all of you."

"That would be nice. I—" When his mother's voice broke, his father stepped in.

"We'll make it work." His dad spoke in the same authoritative tone he used when rendering judgments from the bench. "My son, the restaurateur. I never thought when you graduated from law school summa cum laude, you'd end up running a café."

Though his father had tried to stay out of the decisions Beck had made after the accident, he knew it bothered the judge that he'd turned away from the practice of law.

"I had the chance the other day to make use of my law degree." Beck briefly explained the situation with Dakota. "I didn't end up doing anything except offering advice. It felt good to help someone."

"I'm so happy, Beck." His mother's voice was thick with emotion.

His father cleared his throat. "I'm proud of you, son."

Beck could have ended the conversation there and everyone would have been happy. Except he had more to say. Now that he could see more clearly what he had done, how he had hurt the ones he loved, he had to address the issue.

"I'm sorry I pushed you away when all you wanted to do was help." This time it was Beck's turn to clear his throat. "We're a family. I realize now that I didn't lose everything when Lisette and the baby died. I still had you."

"You'll always have us." His mother's soft southern drawl was like a caress.

"Darn right," the judge added in a gruff voice. "We'll be up to see your new place in the summer. You can count on it."

He could count on it, he realized, and count on them. They'd always been there and *would* always be there for him.

By the time Beck hung up, the heavy weight he'd been carrying around for nearly two years had lifted. When he pushed back the curtain of the parlor window, it seemed fitting that the gloomy skies had cleared and the sun had started to peek out on a new day.

The Saturday dinner rush at Muddy Boots ended early. After ingesting a quick meal of Salisbury steak with wild mushroom gravy and smashed potatoes with garlic, most patrons headed outside to watch the Snow Blade Parade. Ami and Beck had just finished their meal when Joe Lyle, a local fisherman, entered the café.

He stood just inside the doorway for several seconds, glancing around the near-empty café. He was a tall man with an Abe Lincoln build and a short-cropped beard. His clothes were pure Door County fisherman: coveralls and strap trousers, an insulated jacket as slick as any duck's feathers.

Ami knew Joe through his daughter, who'd been one of Prim's friends back in high school.

"Mr. Lyle." Ami rose from her seat at the table and Beck did the same. "It's good to see you again. How's Emily?"

"Why if it isn't Amaryllis Bloom." Some of the tension in Joe's face eased and he smiled. "Emmy is good, living in Madison, expecting her first baby any day. Wife and I are planning to spend Christmas with her."

"Give her my congratulations. It's too bad she isn't coming here.

Prim will be back for Christmas and I know she'd love to see her." Ami turned. "Do you know Beckett Cross?"

Without pausing for an answer, she introduced Joe to Beck. The two men exchanged greetings.

Ami noticed Joe seemed uncharacteristically nervous, shifting from one foot to the other, his gaze darting around the café.

Joe shoved his hands into his pockets. "Looks like business is slow."

Beck laughed. "We shut down early, figuring most of the patrons who hadn't already been in to eat are probably at the soup supper First Christian is putting on in the town hall."

"I can rustle you up some Salisbury steak if you're hungry," Ami offered, stepping away from her chair.

"Actually." Joe rubbed his chin and, once again, shifted from one foot to the other. "I stopped by hoping to have a few words in private with Mr. Cross."

While surprised, Ami quickly rallied. "Your timing couldn't be more perfect. I was just getting ready to clean up the dining room and shut down the kitchen. You can keep Beck company while he finishes his coffee. May I get you a cup?"

She took the man's noncommittal shrug as assent and moved behind the counter to pour him a mug. "Cream or sugar?"

"Just black."

Once she'd set the cup down, Ami turned and began to slowly bus a nearby table, hoping to discover just what business Joe Lyle had with Beck.

***

Beck waited while Joe sat and took a long drink of his best chicory blend. After stretching out his legs, the older man leveled piercing blue eyes—a striking feature in an otherwise unremarkable weathered face—on him.

"Mr. Cross, I need your help." Joe splayed his hands on the tabletop and leaned forward. "I ain't got much money, but if you let me make payments, I promise you'll get your full fee. I'm up against a wall here."

Puzzled, Beck inclined his head. "I'm not sure what you're asking."

"Dakota told my youngest that you're a lawyer. That so?"

"Yes, but—"

"Well, back in October my boat was being repaired at a place in Sturgeon Bay when another one beside it caught fire. Before they could get the flames under control, the fire spread to mine."

The older man clenched his hands on the table. "My boat has to be replaced before spring. Me and my family depend on the money I make fishing."

Beck carefully placed his cup on the table. "I don't see where I fit in."

"The insurance companies keep wrangling and no one is budging, which means no one is paying." Joe's eyes turned imploring. "I need a professional."

Finally Beck understood. "Have you contacted any of the law firms in Sturgeon Bay?"

"They, ah, don't extend credit on these kinds of cases." A look of embarrassment crossed the man's features. "I told 'em I was good for it, but no go."

When Beck said nothing, Joe pushed back his chair, stood for a second, then sat back down. "Dakota says you're a smart man. And not expensive."

Beck stifled a groan. With Dakota out there pimping his services, the café would be filled with pro bono clients by the first of the year.

"Like I said, I'm not asking for a free ride. I just need someone to write a letter or to do something to let 'em know they can't keep jacking me around." Joe's gaze met his. "You're my last hope, Mr. Cross."

It would be easy for Beck to say he was no longer practicing law. But the truth was, he did have a current license in the state, and this proud, hardworking man had come to him asking for help.

Neighbors helping neighbors.

Beck gestured to the envelope the man had placed on the table when he'd sat down. "Show me what you brought and I'll see what I can do."

A relieved look crossed Joe's face. "You'll help me?"

"I'll do my best."

"How much?"

"Consider it an early Christmas gift, Mr. Lyle."

"I didn't come asking for charity—"

"Not charity." Beck lifted his cup. "This spring when you bring in a good haul of whitefish, just think of me and my café."

Ami took the tub of dirty dishes to the kitchen, placed it on the counter, then did a little happy dance in front of the dishwasher.

Beck was embracing the practice of law again. Okay, perhaps that wasn't quite accurate. He'd agreed to help one man with his insurance claims. Still, it was a start.

While she knew Beck had grown to love Muddy Boots, the practice of law was a part of him, too. Nothing said he couldn't do both. That was the great thing about Good Hope: the opportunities here were endless.

Granted, he might not get rich, but there was more to life than money and prestige. She had a feeling Beck was finally seeing all that Door County had to offer him if he stayed.

His future was looking brighter by the second. She only wished she could be a part of it.

Chapter Twenty-One

Saturday night, after the rush at the café was over, Beck asked Ami to come home with him. Though she wanted to accept the offer, she told him that with the upcoming week being so busy, she had to get some sleep. Her heart swelled remembering how his eyes had softened, the tip of one finger trailing down her face as if memorizing each feature.

Once Christmas was over there would be more time for them, he'd promised. It had taken all of Ami's strength to nod and agree. But she knew that once she confessed all to him on December 26, there would be no more them. She had to set a deadline or else she'd put it off forever. Besides, she didn't want to ruin his Christmas.

In the meantime, she would try her best to enjoy this most blessed time of the year.

Sunday morning she got up early and headed straight downstairs to bake from four to eight. Then, after making a quick phone call, she hopped on her bike and made the seven-mile trek to Egg Harbor. The trip took a little over a half hour but it was well worth her time.

Last night, she'd racked her brain trying to think of what to give Beck for Christmas. She'd awakened this morning to an unseasonably warm day with the perfect gift in mind: a crystal sun catcher she'd spotted last month in the window of an Egg Harbor gift shop. Because it was in the shape of a star, it seemed perfect for Beck, the man who had everything.

It might be silly, but Ami hoped that eventually, given time, he'd be able to look at the star and remember this Christmas—and their time together—with fondness.

As she'd called the gift boutique before leaving home to make sure they still had the item, they had it gift wrapped and waiting for her.

Once she reached Good Hope, Ami swung by Beck's house. After letting herself in with the key he'd given her, she tucked the prettily wrapped present under the tree.

Though she faced a full day of baking and decorating for her father's open house, Ami stood in the parlor for several minutes. This was likely the last time she'd be welcome in the home that held so many of her dreams. The scent of roses in full bloom closed around her in a sweet, final embrace. Her gaze took in the massive fir she'd helped decorate and lingered on the star.

Home.

The day she'd placed the star at the top of the tree, Ami had let herself dream just a little—of a future with Beck, of making a home with him, of having a family.

Those dreams were gone. Or would be as of December 26.

As she locked the outside door, Ami blamed the sudden moisture in her eyes on the brisk north wind. She covered the distance to her bakery in record time and rushed inside, shivering.

Though Ralph II was spewing warmth from numerous vents, it barely touched the cold chill of regret that wrapped like a noose around her heart. Ami was grateful Hadley wasn't scheduled until the special hours later this afternoon, when patrons would stop by to pick up the cookies, bars, and kringle they'd ordered for the holidays.

That gave Ami plenty of time to bring up holiday cheer from deep inside her and do some personal baking.

After putting another batch of kringle in the oven, she sat in the bakery's dining area with her laptop and a cup of strong coffee. Wanting, *needing*, to keep busy, she perused various food sites looking for lavender cookies with rose-water icing recipes.

The cookies had been her mother's favorite and baking them had been a holiday tradition. There was no written recipe. There had never been a need for one. Ami and her mother could toss together a batch of cookies in their sleep.

Until Sarah Bloom passed away.

When Ami had attempted to conjure up the recipe the next Christmas, her mind had gone blank. No matter how she'd tried, she couldn't think of the recipe. She'd resorted to trying recipes she found on the Internet, hoping her memory would be jogged by stirring familiar ingredients.

The plan hadn't worked. Not yet, anyway.

This year, Ami would find another variation and try again. She was considering one that called for vanilla extract when a sharp rap on the door had her lifting her gaze from the screen.

Her father stood on the other side of the door, gloved hands in pockets, shoulders braced against the stiff wind.

Ami hurried across the room. The second he stepped inside, she pushed the door firmly shut, blocking out the cold.

"What are you doing out in this weather?" Ami asked as she held out her hands for his coat. "This is your holiday break. You should be relaxing at home, watching football, not out in the cold."

"There aren't any major bowl games on tap for today. Besides, I wanted to see my girl." Her father sniffed the air. "Is that coffee I smell?"

"I'll get you a cup. Have a seat." She gestured to the table, then hung his jacket on the coat tree on her way to the back.

In a matter of minutes, she faced him across the small table, two mugs of steaming coffee and slices of kringle between them. "Where's Marigold?"

"She's home decorating for the party. She slapped my hands when I tried to help." He chuckled. "It's good to have her back. Though she was so busy hanging out with her friends this weekend, I barely saw her."

"She's a social creature."

"That she is." Her dad took a sip of coffee, then sighed. "I love this chicory blend."

Ami responded without thinking, "It's our favorite."

Steve raised a brow, cast a speculative glance at her. *"Our?"*

"Ah, Beck's . . . and mine." Ami kept her tone casual. "You've probably heard we meet at Muddy Boots most mornings for coffee and Danish."

As he brought the cup to his lips for another drink, his hazel eyes remained firmly focused on her face. "I've heard you've been spending a lot of time at his house."

Ami resisted the almost overwhelming desire to squirm under the direct gaze. "Beck graciously agreed to store gifts for the Giving Tree's Christmas campaign. I've been helping him wrap."

"Is that all?"

"Oh, and I also helped him decorate his house for the Victorian home tour," Ami added, grateful her brain had decided to start firing on all cylinders. "That was part of my duties as a Cherrie. It was well worth my time. There were lots of positive comments received from those who toured the house." Ami paused. "How did I miss seeing you that night?"

A sheepish look blanketed Steve's face, and now it was his turn to squirm. "Anita and I planned to do the tour, but at the last minute we, ah, we got caught up in some things at home and didn't make it."

Something in the way he put together the excuse had her brain recoiling in horror. It almost sounded as if her father and Anita had been busy . . . in the bedroom.

Not knowing exactly how to respond to that comment, Ami popped a piece of kringle in her mouth and chewed.

"I've been really enjoying this Christmas season." He appeared almost embarrassed by the admission.

The warning Ami had been about to issue against the piranha died in her throat. This time of year had been especially hard on her father since her mom had passed. She'd begun to wonder if her dad would ever be truly happy again.

But the man sitting across the table from her looked content and at peace. If being with Anita helped him weather the difficult holiday season, she'd happily keep her mouth shut.

Reaching across the table, she covered his hand with hers and gave it a squeeze. "I'm glad."

Then, because she feared her dad might want to talk more about Anita—or Beck—Ami changed the subject. "I was just about to start a batch of lavender cookies."

"Sarah's favorite." Though he smiled, his eyes turned sad and Ami cursed her insensitivity.

"Once they're in the oven, I'm baking a devil's food cake with vanilla buttercream icing." Ami sipped her coffee and broke off another piece of kringle. "Which, as I recall, is *your* favorite."

When Ami saw him tense, she knew exactly what her superorganized father was thinking. "I'm aware the open house is tomorrow, but never fear, the cake will be done on time, and it will be delicious."

"You haven't started it yet?"

"Not yet. But, again, no need to worry."

"I'm not worried, I'm relieved." Her father expelled a breath. "You don't need to make it."

"Of course I do," Ami insisted. "Thirty-five years with the Good Hope school district is a big deal. You have to have a cake."

"No, I mean *you* don't have to do it now. Anita offered to make it."

Dumbfounded, Ami could only blink at her father.

"She knows how busy you've been and wanted to contribute to my party." His lips curved in a fond smile. "And we both know cakes are her specialty."

Ami couldn't argue that point. The woman's prowess with cakes was one of the reasons she'd renamed the business she purchased after her divorce Crumb and Cake.

Even as Ami's mind conceded the logic, her emotions railed against the thought of Anita Fishback having a part—*any* part—in a Bloom family party. She opened her mouth to tell her father just that, then remembered this was *his* open house.

"That's great, Dad." She made a concerted effort not to sigh. "Be sure and tell Anita thanks."

A few minutes later Ami walked him to the door, then returned to her laptop. She ate the last piece of kringle, then, without looking at the recipe on the screen in front of her, hit the Print key. She wasn't in the mood to search further. Not with so many other thoughts and worries muddying her brain.

Her father and Anita had grown close quickly. Too quickly? She wished she could say yes, but was it really any different than the connection she and Beck had forged?

Prior to December, if she'd been asked how long it took a couple to fall in love, she'd have said a year at least, more likely two. Yet she was already completely and totally in love with Beck.

Thankfully, her father didn't appear to have crossed the line from like to love. Hopefully he never would. The thought that he might fall in love with Anita made Ami's stomach churn.

Think of something else, she told herself. *Anything else.*

She thought of the life Beck had once led in Georgia. A life far different from the one he had now in Good Hope. Why hadn't that life popped up on any of her Internet searches?

Intrigued, Ami moved her fingers to the keyboard. Instead of just his name, she put "Beckett Cross Attorney Athens Georgia" in the search field and hit Enter.

This time plenty of links appeared, along with an interesting revelation. Beck's actual first name appeared to be *James*. Ami pulled her brows together, shook her head. She couldn't imagine calling him by that name.

She brought her gaze back to the screen and checked out the newspaper accounts first. His wife had been a beauty: tall, thin, and blond with a pretty face and an almost shy smile. They'd made an elegant couple in the many society pictures.

The accident reporting tore at her heartstrings. The woman who'd driven the other vehicle looked dazed and confused in her mug shot. The thirty-five-year-old marketing executive had been charged with—and found guilty of—vehicular homicide.

Instead of jail time, she'd received two years of probation. According to the news articles, the woman's blood alcohol level was just below the limit, so she wasn't considered *legally* impaired. The fact that the stop sign had been missing at the intersection where the crash occurred weighed in her favor.

The prosecution argued that the woman, Nina Holbrook, drove that route frequently and knew the street was an arterial, and thus, cars traveling down that road should be given the right of way.

A tragedy.

Those words were repeated in practically every article Ami read. The look of grief and stunned disbelief on the faces of Beck and his family after the sentencing said it all.

Instead of their images, she saw Lindsay, unconscious and bleeding in the seat beside her. Ami's heart shuddered as one word beat against it in an unceasing rhythm:

Unforgivable.

Chapter Twenty-Two

Ami took a hot shower and got her emotions under control. She pulled on a new pair of flannel-lined jeans, a wheat-colored bulky sweater, and her beloved UGGs, then set off to visit her sister. She found Marigold in the living room of the family home, positioning several large poinsettias for maximum effect.

"I see Dad put you right to work."

Her sister plopped down on the sofa, looking adorable in black leggings and a royal-blue sweater. "Actually, he told me to get some sleep. Said the bags under my eyes could double as suitcases."

"He did not say that." Ami couldn't imagine her gentle father ever saying anything that rude.

"Perhaps those weren't his exact words. But he did mention I looked tired."

Ami studied her sister. She'd pulled her mass of curly blond hair back in a tail that managed to look both stylish and comfortable. But even artfully applied makeup couldn't fully disguise the dark circles beneath those huge blue eyes.

"You look tired, but you also have this kind of glow about you." Ami dropped on the sofa beside her sister. "I'm so glad you're here."

"I've missed you." Marigold gave her a quick, hard hug. "You have to catch me up on all the Good Hope gossip."

"Tonight. Once Primrose and Fin get here." Ami felt a surge of anticipation.

"When exactly will they arrive?"

"Fin has a flight that's supposed to touch down in Green Bay around four or four thirty. Prim and the boys are driving from Milwaukee and will pick her up at the airport. I assume they'll grab something to eat, then drive the rest of the way to Good Hope. So I'd say by nine." Ami smiled. "It'll be like old times; all of the Bloom sisters together."

"I miss those days." Marigold's expression turned pensive.

"Well, you'll just have to move back."

Her sister laughed. "I didn't say I missed them all *that* much."

"Still loving life in the big city?"

"Absolutely. Since I became a full-fledged stylist last fall, I've been able to start building my client list. I love the money, and the artistic freedom I've been given has been wonderful."

"I'm happy for you." Ami paused, then gentled her tone. "Now, tell me what's not so good."

"It's nothing, really." Marigold waved a dismissive hand even as her blue eyes darkened. "Steffan has just been a bit snippy lately."

Steffan, Ami knew, was the head stylist and owner of the salon where Marigold was employed. Handsome and talented, the man had taken Chicago by storm five years earlier when he'd relocated his successful Los Angeles salon to the Windy City.

Ami had been impressed when she'd read that the Steffan Oliver Salon had been named Salon of the Year by *Elle* magazine. Yet the honor hadn't surprised her. Marigold often mentioned the important clients who flew in from other states specifically to have her boss cut and color their hair. Even the cream of Chicago society had to book appointments months in advance to get an appointment with him.

Ami had met Steffan. While a bit on the high-strung side, he'd seemed like a genuinely nice guy. It was difficult to fathom him being snippy to her sister.

After all, he'd personally recruited Marigold while she'd still been in her cosmetology program. From the beginning, Marigold's natural talent had created a buzz. Her sister had started her career at his salon as soon as she'd graduated. That was nearly five years ago.

Marigold had never complained about Steffan before. To the contrary, her sister often mentioned how nice it was to work for a man who had become a good friend. "Any idea why he's acting that way?"

Marigold pursed her lips. "He and his partner, Marc, are going through a rough patch. I think the stress from all that drama might be spilling over into his professional life and making him edgy."

Ami tried to recall what Marigold had told her. "He and Marc have been together a long time."

"Yes. In fact, Marc was the reason Steffan relocated to Chicago." Marigold's eyes turned cloudy. "I know he loves Marc, so I hope they kiss and make up soon. I can't take much more of his mood swings."

"Have you considered leaving and opening your own salon?"

"Not really." Marigold yawned hugely, covering her mouth with pink-tipped fingers. "I learn so much from Steffan and the other stylists. Not to mention working for him opens so many doors for me."

"Sounds like a difficult situation."

"It is what it is." Marigold lifted one shoulder in a delicate shrug. "For now, I'm in a holding pattern, waiting and hoping for the best. Does that make sense?"

Ami thought of Beck. "It does."

"But don't think for a minute that I'm letting him walk all over me." A cocky arrogance filled her sister's eyes. "I'm a darned good stylist and I've been getting a lot of good press lately. If Steffan continues to be difficult, I won't stay."

Talking about the salon appeared to be getting her younger sister more worked up by the second, so Ami changed the subject.

"Tell me about you and Daniel." Ami recalled the excitement in her sister's voice several months ago when she'd mentioned some grand soiree they'd be attending. "Don't you two have a big fancy event coming up soon?"

"Actually, that event was this weekend." Marigold swung her feet off the coffee table and onto the floor. "The party was the reason I didn't think I'd be able to come back early for Shannon's wedding."

Ami pulled her brows together in puzzlement. "Why did you change your mind about going?"

"One simple reason. Daniel Smithson is a dickhead." Marigold expelled a harsh breath and jerked to her feet, adding, "I'm starting to believe that at heart all men are jerks."

Ami thought of Beck and silently disagreed. She moved to Marigold's side and placed a sympathetic hand on her arm. "What happened?"

"I caught him with another woman." Pain flashed through Marigold's baby blues like a bolt of lightning and was gone just as quickly. "Apparently his definition of exclusive and mine are vastly different."

Ami's heart ached for her little sister. She knew that beneath Marigold's cool, confident exterior beat an easily bruised heart. "I'm so sorry, sweetie. How about I make us some hot cocoa and you can tell me all about it?"

"Snowflake hot cocoa?" Marigold asked hopefully, following Ami into the kitchen.

"Umm, not today. Snowflake takes hours to prepare. We'll go with the less fancy variety for now, but I guarantee you'll love it." Opening the cupboard, Ami grabbed a can of unsweetened cocoa powder and went to work. While she waited for the ingredients to come to a boil, she glanced over her shoulder at Marigold. "Attending Shannon's wedding must have been hard. All those hearts and flowers coming so soon after your breakup."

"Actually . . ."

Something in her sister's tone had Ami turning from the stovetop, spoon in hand.

Marigold rested her back against the Formica countertop, a sly smile lifting her lips. "I—"

Raising a hand, Ami stilled the words. "Hold the explanation and grab some mugs. I think I'm going to need some chocolate to wash down what you're about to tell me."

The soft laugh that tumbled from Marigold's lips told her one mug might not be enough. In minutes, Ami sat across from her sister at the kitchen table, with two steaming mugs of cocoa topped with whipped cream between them. "Tell me."

Marigold studied her, appearing to enjoy Ami's blatant curiosity. She took a sip of the cocoa and purred. "You're right. This *is* awesome."

Ami waited impatiently as her sister took another drink. "Tell me what happened at the reception."

"I danced. I flirted. I had a fabulous time." Marigold's dimples flashed. "It was after the reception that the night really heated up."

Ami tried to think what her sister could have done after an Egg Harbor wedding reception that would have brought such a smile to her face. She couldn't think of a single thing.

"You can't tell anyone." Marigold's expression turned solemn. "What I'm about to say must remain in the vault."

Her sister drew an imaginary box in the air and met Ami's gaze with an intensity that sent a shiver of trepidation rising up Ami's spine.

Ami lifted three fingers, mimicking the Girl Scout salute. "I swear."

"Swear on our mother's grave."

"Dear God, Marigold, what did you do?"

"Swear."

"Sheesh, I swear."

Apparently satisfied, her sister took a deep breath, let it out slowly.

"First, I want you to know this was something I'd never *ever* done before." Two swaths of pink appeared on Marigold's cheeks. "I hope you won't think less of me."

Ami reached across the table and took her baby sister's hand. "Nothing you've done will make me love you less. I'll always be here for you."

She realized with a start the words she'd just uttered were almost identical to the ones her mother had spoken to her the night of the accident.

"It's not that grim." Marigold flashed a smile. "In fact, it isn't grim at all."

Ami frowned. "I don't like guessing games."

"You'd never guess this one, anyway."

"Marigold Elizabeth."

The use of her sister's middle name had the imp's smile widening. "I had a one-night stand."

Ami sat back, stunned.

Marigold took another sip of her hot chocolate, appearing to enjoy her big sister's shock. "Yep, with one of Shannon's cousins. The man was überhot and we just . . . connected."

Her sister had been right. She'd never have guessed this, not in a million years. Even as a teenager, Marigold had been cautious in her dealings with boys. How could she sleep with a stranger? Unless, perhaps, the man was someone she already knew. "Had you, ah, met Shannon's cousin before?"

Marigold shook her head. "I don't think so. Unless it was when I was a kid and he came to Good Hope with his parents for some family event. He lives in Michigan."

"Are you going to keep in touch?"

"I don't think so. Still, it was fun. We enjoyed ourselves." Marigold glanced down at the steaming chocolate and her lips curved. "The clandestine part definitely upped the spice element of the evening."

"Where did you—?" Ami waved her hand. "No. Don't tell me. I don't want details."

"Too bad." Marigold's eyes danced with barely suppressed amusement. "I was going to give you a blow-by-blow of the entire evening starting with the way he—"

"Nanananananana." Ami set down her mug and covered her ears with her hands. "Don't want to hear it."

Marigold threw back her head and laughed. "Okay, then, let's talk about you and Beckett Cross."

Ami's smile disappeared. She dropped her hands to the table. "Let's not."

"You promised. I distinctly recall you saying we were going to catch up. Well, I caught you up on Daniel, shared my little secret, and even tossed my boss into the mix. Which means it's your turn."

Ami bought herself a little time by slowly lifting her mug to her lips and taking a drink. "I'm afraid that my relationship with Beck will soon be coming to an end."

Her sister's smile disappeared and her gaze turned sharp and assessing. "Why?"

"The vault door remains firmly shut," Marigold assured her when Ami continued to hesitate.

"I love Beck." Just saying the words aloud brought a sharp ache of longing so intense tears sprang to Ami's eyes.

"Why, that's wonder—" Marigold paused. "It's not wonderful?"

Powerless to stop a few tears from slipping down her cheeks, Ami swiped at them before answering. "The summer before last, Beck's wife and unborn baby were killed by a drunk driver."

"Oh, no," Marigold gasped. "How horrible."

Ami wrapped her fingers around the mug. But the heat couldn't penetrate the sudden chill that gripped her.

Her sister waited a beat, then spoke tentatively, as if navigating her way through a darkened room. "Is he still hung up on her? Is that the issue?"

Ami hesitated. While she knew a part of Beck would always love Lisette, she believed he was ready to embrace the future. But not with her. No, never with her.

"The woman who hit her car had been drinking." Ami expelled a ragged breath. "Beck has zero tolerance for those who drink and drive."

"Understandable. But what does that have to do with—" Marigold stopped, her eyes going wide as she made the connection. "You don't think . . ."

"I don't know." Ami's voice quivered. "That's what is driving me crazy. I don't know how he's going to react when I tell him."

"Don't look for trouble where there is none." Obviously seeing Ami's distress, Marigold spoke in a soft, soothing tone. "You've given your heart to this man, so give him some credit. Trust that once you explain the situation fully, he'll understand."

Ami sniffled. "What happened to the woman who only a moment ago said all men are jerks?"

Marigold stared into Ami's eyes. "It will be okay."

When her sister rounded the table and wrapped her arms around her for a hug, Ami hugged her back, burying her tear-streaked face against Marigold's fragrant hair. "It won't be okay. I know what's going to happen. I'm going to lose him."

"You don't know that. You *think* you know." Marigold stepped back and held Ami at arm's length, her expression surprisingly stern. "Take some advice from your baby sister. Keep the faith. And remember, you never know for sure what's around a corner . . . until you take the turn."

Chapter Twenty-Three

Though Beck had never been to Ami's childhood home, he knew her father lived on a tree-lined street high on a hill overlooking the bay. The homes in that area might not be as grand as the one he lived in now, but they were spacious enough to handle four children with ease.

As cars lined both sides of the street, Beck found a spot several blocks away from the Bloom house and pulled to the curb. A bottle of wine lay on the passenger seat, a gift for the man who'd given thirty-five years to the youth of Good Hope. A gift for the man whose eldest daughter made Beck's life richer simply by being a part of it.

Tucking the wine bottle under his arm, he set out in the direction of Steve's house. People driving by honked and waved in greeting. Beck lifted a hand in response, continually amazed by the friendliness of the residents of this peninsula.

He'd been prepared to take his time getting acquainted, but the citizens of Good Hope would tolerate no standoffishness. Especially not Ami Bloom. Beck quickened his step in anticipation.

Forty-eight hours was too long to go without seeing her. The house didn't feel like home without her in it. Beck had considered texting or calling but had forced himself to hold back. Her sisters were in town, and he knew she was busy finalizing arrangements on their dad's open house.

He was looking forward to meeting her family. If things went the way he hoped, they'd one day be his family, too.

Ami made him laugh. She made him want to reach out and lend a helping hand. She warmed his bed, but even more importantly, warmed his heart.

He simply couldn't do without her. Very soon, that's what he was going to tell her in terms of two very special Christmas gifts that came straight from his heart.

One of those gifts was safely hidden away in his carriage house. The other was in a black velvet box sitting on his dresser. He smiled, thinking of the romantic scene he had planned for the twenty-fourth. Of course, that was assuming he could find a way to steal her away from her sisters—and father—for a couple of hours.

Where there was a will . . .

"Beck."

His head jerked at the sound of his name. Max strode toward him from the opposite direction. They met at the walkway leading to Ami's childhood home, a Craftsman-style bungalow.

"What are you doing in the neighborhood?"

"Same as you," the accountant replied.

"You know Ami's father?" Beck wasn't surprised Max was acquainted with Steve, only that he knew the man well enough to be invited to his open house.

"Years ago he was my Big Brother. And we're fishing buddies," Max added.

"Steve's your *brother*?" Beck cocked his head. Why was he only hearing about this now? "You're related to Ami?"

Max laughed. "The organization, Cross. You know, Big Brothers, Big Sisters. They pair kids without moms or dads with mentors. Steve was mine."

The accountant talked so much, Beck assumed he knew everything about the man. "You never mentioned that fact."

"Do you think you can learn a person's life history in six months?"

"I suppose you're right." Beck cocked his head. "With him being your Big Brother, I assume you know Ami's sisters pretty well."

"You'll like them," Max decreed as they stepped onto the porch.

They'd reached the red-painted front door of the two-story home. A brightly painted sign greeted them: Welcome. No Need to Knock. We're Expecting You!

Beck smiled. *Only in Good Hope . . .*

Yet even as he raised his hand to knock, the door opened.

"Good afternoon. Welcome." The woman with the friendly smile had enough of Ami in her to tell him she was a sister.

The hair was different. Instead of brown, this woman's was deep red interspersed with strands of gold. A smattering of freckles dusted her ivory cheeks. Like her father's, her eyes were hazel.

"I'm Primrose. You can call me Prim." She extended a slim hand to Beck, and when Beck leaned forward to take it, he realized she didn't stand alone.

"Beckett Cross." He glanced down at the two redheaded boys at her sides. "Who are these young men?"

She smiled fondly at her sons. "The one with the jam on his shirt is Callum. The one with the marker on his cheek is Connor."

"Pleased to meet you," they intoned together. While they may have been well coached, the mischievous glint told him being mannerly wasn't a natural state.

"It's nice to meet all of you." Beck stepped inside and smiled at Primrose. "My café, Muddy Boots, is next door to Ami's bakery."

Prim's eyes took on a devilish twinkle, much like her sons'. "I've heard all about you from my sister."

"All good, I hope."

"Of course," she said smoothly, then shifted her attention to Max.

Instead of a handshake, the accountant got a quick hug. "It's been a long time, Brody."

Max cleared his throat and appeared uncharacteristically at a loss for words. "Too long. It's not the same in Good Hope without you."

"Yes, well." Her cheeks flamed with color and her hands fluttered. "Let's shut the door and keep the cold outside where it belongs. Callum and Connor, will you please take these gentlemen's coats?"

Beck removed his and Callum snatched it from him just as Ami strolled up. He felt a surge of satisfaction when her eyes lit with pleasure.

"I thought you might be getting thirsty." Ami held out the glass of lemonade to her sister, even as her smile remained directed at Beck. "I see you've met Beck."

Prim took the tumbler from her sister's hands. "He's every bit as gorgeous as you said, Am."

Ami laughed and shook her head. "Sisters."

Beck couldn't keep his gaze off Ami. Two days might as well have been an eternity. She looked even more beautiful than he remembered in a soft-looking sweaterdress of mint green. Instead of her beloved UGGs, she wore heeled boots of dark brown suede.

He took a step closer and placed a hand on her arm, unable to go one more second without touching her. "You look incredible."

The elusive dimple in her cheek winked. "The dress and boots are on loan from Fin."

"I'll have to seek Delphinium out and thank her."

"Did I hear my name?"

Beck swiveled and did a double take. Delphinium Bloom could easily have passed for Ami's twin. If her sister had been wearing mint green—instead of a dress the color of claret—he'd have been hard-pressed to tell them apart, especially from a distance.

The facial features were identical. As were the green eyes, hint of freckles across the bridge of her nose, and tan-colored hair. Fin's cut was different, more . . . jagged. And her dress probably cost twice as much as anything currently hanging in Ami's closet.

The differences were subtle but significant. Fin had the look of a big-city girl, with a polished smile and a wary—almost cynical— look in her eyes. She also exuded an energy totally at odds with her older sister's calm demeanor.

Ami had been right. There was something compelling—charismatic—about Fin that Beck knew many would find difficult to resist. He could. For one reason. She wasn't Ami.

"Welcome." She extended her hand in the manner of someone well versed in business etiquette, her gaze firmly focused on him. "I'm Fin Bloom. I don't believe we've met."

Before he could respond, someone called Ami's name and she turned.

"I'll let you two get acquainted," Ami said with an apologetic smile. "It appears I need to put out more cookies."

Beck watched Ami hurry off, then turned and gave Fin's hand a brisk shake. "Beckett Cross. I bought Muddy Boots last summer."

He offered her the bottle of wine. "A gift. For your father."

She studied the vintage and nodded approvingly. "Very nice. Thanks."

Though the event was supposed to be casual, most of the men roaming around wore dress pants and sweaters. Like him, they'd left their ties and sport coats at home.

"Well, Mr. Beckett Cross." Fin looped her arm through his as they strolled into the parlor. "I'm glad you were able to join us. I want to hear all about your relationship with my sister."

Her interrogation was cut short when Ami stepped from the kitchen with a huge platter of cookies and assorted bars teetering precariously in her arms.

"Excuse me," he said to Fin, then rushed across the room to Ami. "I'll take that."

She murmured a protest but he'd already removed the tray from her arms.

"This is much too heavy for you," he told her.

"I'm stronger than I look."

"I know, but you don't have to do it all. Not anymore. You can use me." His gaze met hers and he winked. "Any way you want."

She grinned. "Hold that thought . . . for later."

Fin had walked up. Beck wasn't sure how much she'd heard, but the smile hovering on the edges of her red lips told him it had been enough.

"Where would you like these?" Beck asked Ami.

"Follow me."

"It was a pleasure to meet you, Fin," Beck called out over his shoulder.

Like Moses parting the Red Sea, Ami forged a path through the crowd to two long tables positioned against one wall. There was a large, multitiered cake made to resemble stacked books of English classics. The top book looked like a Good Hope yearbook, and the dates on it matched the year her father started teaching and the current year.

At the very top, on a chalkboard made out of fondant, were the words "35 years of inspiring students." The nearby cupcakes, which Beck assumed Ami had baked, in the shapes of apples with red sugar crystals on top were almost gone.

The table where both the cupcakes and cake had been placed seemed designated for sweets, while the second table held an assortment of hot and cold finger foods, vegetables, and fruit.

Beck held the tray while Ami consolidated the items, making room for the platter he held.

While she fussed with the presentation, he glanced around the room. It amazed him to realize he knew most of the people in attendance by name. In little more than six months he'd become a part of this vibrant community on the shores of Green Bay.

He thought back to his old neighborhood in Bogart. Despite having lived in that house for over a year, he hadn't known any of their neighbors. Of course, he and Lisette had both worked long hours, and any free time was spent with family. That may have changed after the baby, but he couldn't be sure.

"Beck." Cory White, holding a towheaded toddler in his arms, strolled up. "It's good to see you."

The man was all smiles, as was the child in his arms, who was the spitting image of his father.

The familiar pang of loss stabbed at him, though it was now dull and manageable.

"Well," Cory said, when he caught his wife's beckoning hand. "If I don't see you before, merry Christmas."

"Merry Christmas."

"Ami, we're running low on punch." The unfamiliar voice had a husky, sensual quality. "Where did you put the bottles of ginger ale?"

Beck shifted his gaze to the pert-nosed sprite in a stretch black dress that emphasized a lean, well-endowed figure. Though her eyes were a brilliant blue and her hair a mass of blond curls, he pegged her as another Bloom. "You must be Marigold."

"My reputation obviously precedes me." She smiled brightly, her gaze sharp and assessing. "You must be Beckett Cross."

"It appears my reputation also precedes me."

Marigold glanced at her sister and a wordless message seemed to flow between them. When those dancing blue eyes returned to him, Beck couldn't help but smile.

"I'd love to stay and chat but I'm desperate to find the ginger ale." The harried look around her eyes told him this punch thing fell into the crisis category.

"In the garage, on the shelf to your right," Ami instructed. "There's a bunch of bottles. You can't miss them."

"On my way." Marigold gave Beck a jaunty wave, then hurried off, spiky red heels clicking on the hardwood.

"Tell me there aren't any more of them." Beck looped an arm over Ami's shoulders. "I'm staggered to see so many beautiful women in one family."

"It's wonderful having all my sisters back in Good Hope."

"Ami." Fin hurried up. "We're almost out of punch."

"I know." Ami's brows pulled together. "Marigold is getting more ginger ale from the garage."

"No, she's not. I just saw her. She's visiting with Etta Hawley." Fin gestured with her head toward a foursome.

"I recognize Etta and Clay." Beck narrowed his gaze. "Who's the tall older man with them?"

"Lars Svensen," Ami answered. "He used to be the principal at Good Hope High."

"We need to do something about the punch," Fin told her sister.

"Can I help?" Beck asked.

"I appreciate the offer." Ami flashed him a smile. "But Fin and I can deal with this."

"Then I'm going to mingle and let you two handle the punch." Beck couldn't stop himself from giving Ami's arm a gentle, supportive squeeze. God, how he'd missed her. "If you need anything—"

"I'll let you know," she said, taking her sister's arm and heading across the room in the direction of the garage.

After seeking out Ami's dad and offering his congratulations, Beck made the rounds. He was pleased to hear so many say that they loved that he'd started serving desserts from Ami's bakery. He made a mental note to discuss with Ami the possibility of continuing that practice after the holidays.

Several people commented on how nice his home had looked for the tour. He didn't have the heart to tell them the downstairs furniture had been borrowed and the movers had stopped by today to pick it up. The house seemed more cold and empty than ever before. Renovating and furnishing those rooms would go to the top of his to-do list for spring.

"Ho-ho-ho. Merry Christmas." Floyd Lawson strode up and clapped Beck on the back.

"Merry Christmas to you, Santa." Beck lowered his voice on the last word in deference to any children who might be nearby.

The movers had still been there when Floyd had stopped by to load up the gifts he and Ami had wrapped and stored. Somehow they'd managed to fit them all into Floyd's red sleigh, *er, his 1980s-era Dodge maxi van.* The jolly fat man and his "elves" planned to dress up and deliver the presents to Giving Tree recipients on Christmas Eve.

As Beck watched the man drive away, he felt proud of the part he and Ami had played in the event.

Speaking of Ami . . .

He caught her eye and smiled when she hurried over. "Crisis averted?"

"One of them, anyway. The punch bowls are now full."

The heavy sigh that punctuated the words had Beck furrowing his brows. "What's wrong?"

"Anita has embraced the hostess role and is running with it."

He searched her face, knowing how she felt about the woman. "Is that not okay?"

Another sigh. "Dad seems happy. That's what matters. And she did make him a fabulous cake."

"I'm partial to the cupcakes."

She chuckled. "I think you're a teeny bit prejudiced."

"Damn right I am." He snaked an arm around her waist and pulled her close.

When she rested her head against his shoulder and he felt her relax, Beck experienced a surge of satisfaction. One day she would accept that he'd always be there for her to lean on.

"It's a good crowd." He pulled his brows together when he saw who was standing next to Jeremy Rakes. "You invited Eliza?"

"She must have come with Jeremy." Ami shrugged. "It's fine. She—"

Before Ami could finish, Fin hurried over. She gripped her sister's arm and smiled apologetically at Beck.

"I-Need-a-Man is insisting on cutting the cake. Now." Fin's eyes flashed green fire. "We all decided to cut it at five, after Dad makes a brief speech and thanks everyone for coming. There are cupcakes out, so I'm not sure what her problem is, why she's wanting to rush the cake cutting."

Beck had a feeling that he knew exactly why the woman was so eager. "Too many people are talking about Ami's amazing cupcakes."

Ami rolled her eyes. "I'll speak with her." She turned back to Beck. "Catch me later?"

"Count on it."

Instead of leaving, Ami rose and pressed her mouth against his for a brief, sweet kiss. Then she hurried off to avert another crisis.

To Beck's surprise, Fin lingered behind and pinned him with her gaze.

"It's obvious my sister really likes you. Hurt her and you'll deal with me." The bright smile she flashed him was at odds with the warning glint in her eyes. "Chat later."

Beck grinned and, shaking his head at the sisters Bloom, he strolled across the room to get some punch.

Despite Anita's obvious desire to get her way and run the show, Ami had convinced the woman to back off on cutting the cake. The outcome of that discussion had been up in the air until her father had strolled up and mentioned how nice it was seeing two of his favorite women working together.

The piranha had smiled and agreed to wait. Though her father tended to prefer smaller, more intimate affairs, he appeared to be enjoying the afternoon's festivities. Part of his ease had to be because this was a party made up entirely of friends.

Except for Eliza.

Ami had kept tabs on the executive director of the Cherries since Beck had pointed her out. She'd watched Jeremy leave Eliza to saunter over to the table holding the punch and the wine, close enough for Fin to get a good look at him but not approaching her directly.

Fin, who'd been laughing with Clay Chapin, seemed oblivious to everyone else in the room, including Jeremy. That total concentration had always been part of Fin's charm; when she spoke to you, she focused solely on you, as if you were the most important person in her world.

Jeremy eventually returned to Eliza's side but appeared unable to keep his gaze off Fin. As if feeling the contact, Fin would shift and glance around before returning to whatever conversation she was having at the time.

Ami breathed a sigh of relief when she saw Lindsay approach Eliza. But Lindsay only paused briefly and shook her head when Eliza's hand closed around her arm. The floral designer pointed toward where Fin stood motioning to her.

Lindsay had barely left when the couple headed in Ami's direction, Jeremy with an easy smile and loping gait, Eliza with lips puckered and her back ramrod straight.

Seconds before the couple reached her, Fin rushed to Ami, her gaze fully riveted on her sister.

"Lindsay promised to keep her mother calm," her sister announced, her pretty face flushed, "but I swear to God, if I-Need-a-Man gives me one more order, I'm going to—"

Abruptly, Fin stopped midrant. She smiled brightly at Jeremy and Eliza. "Oh, hello."

Though Eliza was stunning in a wrap dress of off-white with boots the same shade of blue as the threads in the dress, Jeremy couldn't seem to take his eyes off Fin.

After a few tortured seconds of strained conversation about the "delicious" cupcakes and cookies, Fin placed a hand on Ami's arm. "I was just telling Marigold a moment ago that I'm glad I didn't stay in Good Hope. Ami is such a fabulous baker that I'd be eating sweets all the time. By now, I'd probably weigh a ton and you'd be rolling me out the door."

Jeremy's approving gaze lingered on her lithe figure. "You're even more beautiful than you were in high school."

"Have you had your eyes checked lately, Mr. Rakes?" Fin teased even as she preened, obviously pleased by the compliment.

His gaze locked with Fin's and that spark, that curious energy that surged whenever they were together, returned. "Just keeping it real, Finley."

Way back when, Finley had been his pet name for her. Only he had been allowed to use it.

Because she felt as if she were intruding on a private moment, Ami shifted her gaze. One look at Eliza told her she wasn't the only one aware of the connection.

Ami knew she needed to defuse the situation immediately. "Eliza, isn't it nice that Jeremy and Fin have remained friends?"

Eliza sneered. "I'm sick of the way everyone in this town thinks the Bloom sisters are perfect."

Confused by the vehemence and the comment, Ami blinked, then spoke lightly. "No one is perfect. Not my sisters." She added a little laugh. "Certainly not me."

"You're right about that."

The coldness that filled Eliza's almond-shaped eyes had Ami bracing for impact.

"I wonder what everyone here would say if they knew you were drunk when you wrecked that car and nearly killed Lindsay."

Chapter Twenty-Four

Eliza, former drama club president, had a voice that carried to the back row. It didn't fail her now. The accusation filled the room and conversation immediately halted.

Everyone turned to stare.

Eliza smirked, then once again projected her voice to the rafters. "I bet that wasn't the first time Ami drove after drinking, either. It was just the first time she hurt someone. Too bad it was her friend and not herself."

"Stop it." Lindsay quickly moved forward through the crowd. "I've never blamed Ami. That deer could have walked out in front of any car."

"You nearly died." Eliza's voice shook. "You were in a coma. I didn't know whether you were going to make it. Even when you regained consciousness, you had to fight to walk again. It broke my heart to see you struggle like that. And your face . . ."

A sudden sheen of tears appeared in Eliza's eyes, but the Cherries' executive director quickly blinked them back.

"The accident wasn't Ami's fault," Lindsay insisted.

"Why does she ride her bike and walk everywhere unless she knows she's guilty?" Eliza shifted her venomous gaze to Ami. "Lindsay may have forgiven you. I never will."

Ami's heart pounded so hard she felt lightheaded. She glanced around and caught Beck's eye from across the room. The expression on his face was everything she feared. The shock and the disbelief. Next would come the condemnation. She couldn't bear to see that in his eyes. She looked away.

"Eliza Shaw. I'm asking you to leave my home." Ami's father spoke in the firm, no-nonsense tone he'd successfully used to control unruly students for thirty-five years.

Anita stood beside him, a look of horror on her face. She leveled a glance at Ami. If looks could kill, Ami would be six feet under. "You were *drunk*?"

Her voice cracked with outrage.

Ami supposed she could deny it. But the secret had become a burden she no longer wished to carry. She gave a jerky nod. Then, because Anita's piercing gaze seemed to demand more, Ami took a shaky breath and found her voice.

"I had a wine cooler at the fish boil." Ami paused and swallowed hard. "There was also punch there—"

"Which everyone knew had been spiked with grain alcohol," Eliza interrupted. "Don't bother denying you drank that, too, because I saw you. I've only kept quiet all these years because

Lindsay made me promise. But no more. Everyone needs to know what you're really like."

"I had a few sips of the punch. I was told there was some champagne in it, but it was really strong, so I didn't have much. But what I did have may have been enough to slow my reflexes." Ami took a deep breath and met Anita's eyes. "I'm very sorry your daughter was hurt."

"Not simply hurt, *scarred* for life." Anita stepped forward, dark eyes flashing, index finger jabbing the air. "Because of you."

Her finger would have made contact if Steve hadn't taken Anita's arm and pulled her back.

Without missing a beat, the woman whirled to face her daughter. "Why didn't you tell me she was drunk? She should have been charged, made to pay. I—"

"I'd had a wine cooler, too, Mom. And some punch. All the kids were drinking that night." Lindsay turned to Eliza. "And Ami wasn't drunk. She didn't like the spiked punch any more than I did. It tasted foul. At the most she had two or three sips."

Eliza lifted her chin, opened her mouth, then shut it.

An awkward silence descended over the room.

Ami's heart pounded so hard it made her dizzy. She knew she should probably say something more, but her brain seemed incapable of forming the words.

"It's time to cut the cake." Prim stepped forward, a serene look on her face. Being the mother of twins had obviously taught her how to control her emotions in a crisis. "Anita, will you do the honors?"

Anita took the glass of wine from Steve's hands and downed the contents. After inhaling deeply and releasing her breath several times, she appeared calmer. She even managed to force a faux smile. "Of course."

Steve cast Anita a wary glance as she bustled off.

"We've got plenty of food and drink, and the cake is being cut," Steve Bloom announced in a loud voice filled with strain. He cleared his throat. "Knowing Anita, it will taste every bit as good as it looks. Which means it will go fast. You better get in line now if you want a piece."

Fin now flanked one of Ami's sides and Marigold flanked the other. The three sisters watched Primrose take Eliza's arm, obviously suggesting once again that it was time for her to leave.

Eliza stared unblinking at Ami for several seconds before jerking her arm from Prim's grasp and striding out the door.

Gathering her courage, Ami searched the room for Beck.

He was gone.

A murmur rippled through those who'd remained in the living room.

"Everyone." Prim clapped her hands. "Final warning. Grab yourself a piece of cake before I turn my boys loose on it."

Nervous laughter rippled through the crowd as the rest of the guests moved to join the line snaking around the cake table. On their way, many stopped to offer Ami a supportive word.

Even as her heart was breaking, she forced a smile. This was her father's celebration and she certainly didn't want to add to the drama by running off, weeping. She would stay strong and get through the evening.

Ami had to admit that when she saw Katie Ruth—gossip columnist to the Good Hope community—headed in her direction, she briefly considered bolting.

But as her high school classmate drew close, Ami saw only sympathy in the woman's gaze.

Katie Ruth placed a hand on Ami's arm and looked her straight in the eye. "I want you to know I won't be mentioning anything Eliza said in my column."

"Driving after drinking was stupid."

"Yes, it is," Katie Ruth agreed. "But you were young and didn't realize the spiked punch was that strong."

Ami lifted her chin. "That's no excuse."

The former high school cheerleader's gaze softened. "Ami, you ran into a bad batch of spiked punch and had a deer run in front of your car."

Ami thought of the woman who'd killed Beck's wife and baby. While not legally drunk, she'd been impaired. It was so easy to think an accident would never happen to you. Ami and Nina Holbrook knew differently.

"You often have people write guest columns." Ami spoke slowly as an idea began to form.

Clearly puzzled by the shift in the conversation, Katie Ruth pulled her brows together. "Now and then."

"I'd like to do a small piece. Is there room tomorrow?"

Katie Ruth grimaced. "Tomorrow is the day I list all the events happening in the area on Christmas Eve and Christmas Day, so the issue is pretty full."

"Please."

The pretty blond's gaze searched Ami's face. "If you keep it short and have it to me by eight a.m., I'll fit it in."

Ami took Katie Ruth's hand and gave it a heartfelt squeeze. "Thank you."

The *Open Door* editor shifted from one foot to the other. "Is everything okay between you and Beck? I saw him leave."

"We're good." Actually, Ami had no idea what Beck was thinking *or* feeling. While she was glad to have no more secrets between them, the fact that he'd walked out seemed an ominous sign.

But she couldn't think of Beck now. She had a party to get through first.

Her lips lifted in a humorless smile as she recalled Marigold's comment about not knowing what was around a curve until you made the turn.

Well, Ami had made the turn and found herself on an emotional roller coaster ride. There had been horror, then a surprising sense of relief when her long-held secret had been revealed. And when she'd confessed and taken full responsibility for her actions, the heavy weight of shame and guilt she'd carried for over a decade had lifted from her shoulders.

While Ami was wise enough to know she couldn't undo the past, she would fully embrace the gift of Lindsay's forgiveness and move on, knowing she was strong enough now to face anything.

Except a life without the man she loved.

Beck parked his vehicle in the carriage house but couldn't make himself go inside the house that held so many memories of Ami. Not when his thoughts of her were in such turmoil.

He locked the carriage house and started walking. Ten minutes later he stood outside the Flying Crane. Music spilled from the bar out onto the street and lights from the empty outdoor seating area illuminated the bay.

Squaring his shoulders, Beck shoved open the door and stepped inside. The music quickly became a pulsing beat in his head.

This was a mistake. How could he even think when surrounded by such noise? Even as he was tempted to leave, he made his way to the curved mahogany bar and ordered a beer.

Right now, *not* thinking sounded pretty darn good.

"Beck." Tucking an empty drink tray under her arm, a petite brunette with wavy hair and big brown eyes hurried up to him.

The woman, dressed in the familiar T-shirt and short skirt uniform of the Flying Crane, looked familiar. It took him only a second to place her.

"Izzie Deshler," he said, recognizing the talented painter who'd done such a great job on his walls. "I thought you'd be painting murals, not serving drinks."

"Have to pay the bills." She lifted a thin shoulder in a semblance of a shrug. Her gaze searched his face. "Is everything okay?"

For her to ask, Beck figured he must look as bad as he felt. He gestured to the seat beside him. "I've been better."

"I hear ya." She glanced at the bartender, signaled she was taking a ten-minute break, then confiscated the empty stool beside him. "Holidays can be difficult."

Before she could say more, the bartender, a burly young man with a shaved head and a sleeve of tattoos on one arm, placed a beer in front of Beck and a glass of water in front of Izzie.

"Are you staying in town for the holidays?" she asked when the silence lengthened.

"I am." He took a long drink of the beer he didn't really want. "How about you?"

"No time—or money—to go anywhere." She swiped the condensation off the side of her glass with a long, artistic finger. "My only day off this week is Christmas. That's only because the bar, as well as the rest of the businesses in town, is closed that day."

"If you're looking for companionship and food on Christmas, stop by the café." Beck swiveled on the stool to face her. "I'm keeping Muddy Boots open. We'll be serving a free Christmas meal for anyone without a place to go on the holiday."

A light flared in Izzie's gold-brown eyes. "That's nice of you."

"I'm a nice guy," Beck joked, then immediately sobered, thinking how he'd walked out on Ami at the party. He shoved the thought aside and refocused on Izzie. "If you come, you better be prepared. When people find out you're the artist who did the mural and the wall, you'll be fielding all sorts of questions."

She sipped her water. "Positive? Or negative?"

"All positive." Beck realized suddenly he should have been passing along the nice things customers had said about her work. And he should have made use of the stack of business cards she'd given him.

After all, neighbors helping neighbors was the Good Hope way.

"Max Brody—my accountant—has an office that definitely needs help from someone with your flair." Beck grimaced, thinking of Max's boring white walls. "He'll be calling you after Christmas."

Just because Beck hadn't made any referrals before didn't mean he couldn't now. After all, it was never too late to do the right thing.

"Thanks. I appreciate any business you can send my way." Izzie gestured to some strangers sitting at a four-top, enjoying a heaping plate of nachos. "I'm always telling out-of-towners to check out Muddy Boots."

Beck stayed until her break was over. He used the time to collect his thoughts, to make sense of what he'd discovered this evening.

About Ami.

About himself.

She'd kept the fact that she'd been drinking before her accident from him. Why had she been so reticent to share that part of her history?

It had to be because of what happened to Lisette. Ami must have feared he wouldn't forgive her, just as he hadn't forgiven Nina.

Physically, he and Ami had been as close as two people could be. Had he subconsciously placed invisible lines in the sand to keep them from taking that last step toward complete and total trust? Had he *wanted* to keep a little distance between them?

He couldn't discount the possibility.

If he let Ami fully in, would there be room for Lisette? He used to think of his wife multiple times a day. Now there were days when he didn't think of her at all. Times when he had difficulty visualizing her face.

If he forgave Nina, would that mean he was letting her off the hook for what she'd done to his wife? But he knew Lisette wouldn't want him to be bitter and angry.

Beck's head swam with questions. When he'd gone to the open house, he'd been ready to commit to Ami. The only thing he knew for certain now was that he had some hard thinking to do before he faced her again.

Chapter Twenty-Five

The next morning Beck hopped out of bed and hurriedly pulled on jeans and a sweater before he realized there was no need to rush. Tom was handling things at the café and Ami was spending the day with her sisters. Even if she hadn't been, he doubted she'd want to share a cup of coffee and a doughnut with him.

Not after last night.

Max had called and told him everything that had happened after he'd left the open house. Neither of them could understand why Eliza had done such a thing.

It was evident she believed Ami's actions had caused her friend's injuries, but apparently Lindsay didn't agree.

Where was Eliza's compassion?

Then again, where was *his* compassion?

After a restless night filled with dreams of Lisette, Nina, and Ami, all he wanted was a few minutes of solitude and a strong cup of his favorite chicory blend.

He reached the main floor and paused at the bottom of the steps. The house, which had pulsed with energy only days earlier, now looked hollow and forlorn.

The only sign of life, the only reminder of the vibrancy that had once filled this great room, was the Christmas tree. Beck crossed to it now, his footsteps striking on the hardwood like tiny slaps.

The tree filled the window with sweeping green boughs stretched proudly out, as if in welcome. His fingers curved around one of the ornaments he had purchased from the antique store. The form of the little doll gave him a cheeky grin. Ami had placed the ornament on the tree, her smile as bright as the doll's.

He remembered everything about that day: her laughing green eyes, the cinnamon-and-vanilla scent that was uniquely hers, and most of all, her joy. The way she embraced life with such optimism.

The sweet memory had him jerking back from the ornament as if the doll had gone red-hot beneath his fingers. He'd made many mistakes in his life, and leaving the party last night had been one of them. He'd let the woman he loved face a vicious wolf alone.

Not alone, he told himself; her family had been there. But he shook off the thought. *He* should have been the one to defend her, to support her. Instead, he'd let himself get so caught up in his own feelings that he'd failed her.

Shame flooded him. He began to turn from the tree but stopped abruptly, noticing for the first time there was a gift beneath the branches.

He squatted down and retrieved the neatly wrapped present, immediately recognizing his name written on the card in Ami's distinctive handwriting. Slowly, he traced the bold letters, imagining the delight she'd taken in slipping the gift unnoticed under the tree. The thought of his pleasure would have given her pleasure.

Beck expelled a breath and straightened, his fingers still curved around the brightly wrapped package. He flipped open the tag. *Wishing you the merriest, happiest Christmas ever! All my love, Ami.*

The message was so *her* that he had to smile.

Carrying the present with him to the kitchen, he placed it on the counter beside a stack of papers—most of them Victorian tour flyers the movers had picked up from the floor—then started the coffee.

His gaze returned to the gift. Today was only the twenty-third. Checking out the card was one thing, opening a present early quite another. Hopefully she'd be with him on Christmas and he'd open it while she sat beside him, a glass of wine or a cup of tea in her hand.

His laptop sat on the table and, because it was there, Beck powered it up and opened his e-mail account.

The first e-mail he saw was the one containing the latest *Open Door* newsletter. Beck's finger poised above the key to delete the tabloid rag when he remembered this was a special issue.

According to Katie Ruth, the December 23 release always included information on events occurring in Good Hope on the twenty-fourth and twenty-fifth. She'd heard about him keeping Muddy Boots open on Christmas and had inquired if he wanted that mentioned in the newsletter.

Beck clicked on the file, pleased to see she'd gotten the information correct. Actually, as he scrolled down, he found the newsletter jam-packed with useful information. He stopped scrolling when he saw Ami's name. The title of the article was "It Could Happen to You."

He thought back but couldn't recall Ami ever mentioning that she'd written an article. Of course, she knew he wasn't a fan of the newsletter. Not that he didn't think Katie Ruth was a nice person, and editorially, she did a fine job. But in his mind, the gossip portion of her newsletter tainted the rest.

It only took a few sentences to grab him and make him want to read more. The article was timely, focusing on the dangers of drinking and driving and the importance of having a designated driver.

He read the entire article. Ami pulled no punches regarding her role in the accident that had injured her friend. The bull's-eye was clearly that a single reckless action could have lifelong implications.

The well-written piece was short but powerful. While Lindsay's forgiveness was but a scant sentence in the article, Beck knew it was that forgiveness that had helped Ami heal and begin to move past that night. The fact that she couldn't get behind the wheel of a vehicle showed her journey was still a work in progress.

Beck surged to his feet, unable to sit any longer. Needing to rid his head, his house, of clutter, he scooped papers from the counter and opened the trash can with his foot. As the hydraulic lid slowly opened, he noticed a pale yellow envelope peeking out of the stack of flyers.

His stomach clenched, then released. He'd withheld forgiveness as a way to punish Nina and honor Lisette and their son.

But how did holding on to anger honor his wife, a woman who'd dedicated her life to healing? He thought of Nina. If her letters were to be believed, she'd turned her life around. Staying sober, speaking to groups about the dangers of drinking and driving. In a way, she was doing more to honor Lisette's memory than he was in holding on to rage.

It was time to make some changes.

With a hand that shook, Beck slipped the phone from his pocket and called a familiar name from his contact list. The man was a private investigator he'd often used in his law practice.

"James." The man's booming voice reminded Beck of Floyd Lawson. "It's good to hear from you. Last I heard you moved up north."

After a couple of minutes of polite conversation, Beck got to the point. "I need a cell number. Nina Holbrook. Spelled just as it sounds. She lives in Athens."

"Holbrook." The man paused. "Isn't she the woman who—"

"Yes," Beck confirmed. "Will finding the number take long?"

"Fifteen minutes, if that."

"Text it to me."

"Will do."

Beck pocketed the phone.

Needing a distraction, his gaze shifted once again to the present wrapped in paper covered in dancing reindeer with shiny red noses. Classic Ami. Whimsical and happy. God, how he missed her.

In seconds, the bow and paper littered the counter. He opened the box with an urgency one might use to open a suitcase full of money. But there were no stacks of hundred-dollar bills inside this box, just a crystal star the size of his hand, its sharp points jutting out in all directions.

According to the attached tag, it was a sun catcher. He held the star up to the window. The crystal prisms immediately caught the rays of the rising sun, scattering rainbows of light through the room.

While it was pretty, a sun catcher seemed an odd, almost impersonal gift. Then he recalled what Ami had said when she'd placed the golden star at the top of the tree.

A star signifies *home*.

With great care, Beck placed the star back in the padded box and shut the lid. He would hang the gift in the window once Ami was living under the rafters.

Because one thing he knew for certain, without her beside him, his house would never be a home.

Late that afternoon, after calling Joe Lyle with the good news that a resolution to his case was in sight, Beck made the short jaunt to Blooms Bake Shop. To his chagrin, Hadley informed him he'd just missed Ami.

Not dissuaded, he went back home for his car and headed to the bluff overlooking the bay. The trip to her father's neighborhood took less than ten minutes. Beck stopped short of the house when he spotted Steve and his grandsons at a ball field a half mile from the house.

Despite the chill in the air, they'd obviously been there awhile, if all the balls, bats, and gloves were any indication. The boys were red cheeked but dressed comfortably for a sunny day in the midforties.

Each of the twins had his arms full with baseball equipment. By the way they were dragging their feet, it appeared each ball, bat, and glove weighed a ton.

"Beckett. Didn't expect to see you." While his greeting may have been less than enthusiastic, Steve's expression gave nothing away.

"Do you have a minute?"

"The boys and I were getting ready to head home." He jerked his head toward the twins.

"Not home. You promised we could play on the equipment," the one in the red hat whined, apparently overhearing his grandfather's comment.

"Yeah, you promised," echoed the boy in the blue hat.

"They're like elephants . . ." Steve shook his head but he grinned. "Put the stuff nicely—don't throw it—in the back of the pickup. If you do that, you can have ten minutes at the park."

The boys cheered and hurried to the truck. Seconds later they raced side by side to the play area.

Beck waited.

Steve gestured with his head to a nearby bench with a good view of the play area. Once they were seated, the older man shot Beck a speculative look.

It appeared the proverbial ball was now in his court.

He met Steve's gaze head-on. "I plan to ask your daughter to marry me. I'd like your blessing."

"No."

For a second Beck thought he'd misheard. But the look in Steve's eyes told him there had been no misunderstanding.

He sat back, stunned. "No?"

"I watched you last night." A muscle in Steve's jaw jumped. "Just when Ami needed you most, you walked out the door and left her there to fend for herself."

"What Eliza said came as a complete shock to me. It brought back a lot of bad memories." Beck didn't want to make excuses, but he wanted her father to understand. "I didn't know what to think, much less what to say to Ami."

"You don't desert the woman you love . . . ever." Steve leaned forward and pinned Beck with a steely gaze that belied his mild manner. "Not for any reason."

Knowing her father didn't have all the information, Beck opened his mouth to explain further. But the older man didn't give him the chance.

"Do you think it was easy for me to sit beside my wife, the mother of my children, the woman I'd loved since she was sixteen, and listen to the doctor tell her she had only weeks to live?" Steve's hazel eyes flashed. "I didn't know what to say, what to feel, but I loved her. And I knew I wasn't the only one hurting. If you're a man, you suck it up and support the woman you love. You do whatever necessary to get through difficult times. What you don't ever do is walk away."

Beck closed his eyes briefly, swallowed his pride along with the desire to defend himself. "You're right."

"Ami's a gem." Abruptly Steve rose to his feet. Seconds later a shrill whistle pierced the air. When the boys spun around, he motioned to them, then turned back to Beck. "She deserves a husband who will be there for her, good times and bad. She deserves a man who won't let anything—or *anyone*—stop them from being together. Do I make myself clear?"

A warning and a challenge simmered in those hazel eyes.

Beck nodded, knowing he'd received the blessing he'd sought. The rest would be up to him.

The joy of the holiday season wrapped around Ami like a pretty ribbon. Only two days until Christmas and she was in a warm, fragrant kitchen surrounded by those she loved, doing what she enjoyed most—baking.

Yet her delight was tempered with melancholy. It was as if a critical ingredient in a recipe had been left out. Unlike the lavender cookies, Ami knew exactly what was missing . . . Beck.

Trying not to think of him had proved an impossible task. So she let the image of those dark brown eyes simmering with passion dance before her while she stirred sugar, butter, egg, and vanilla in a saucepan for tonight's bread pudding.

Nearby, Marigold rolled peanut butter in cornflakes for the balls that were her favorite. She heard Prim humming as she placed the M&M's in the "belly buttons" her boys loved.

Ami leaned over, snatched one of the buttons off the waxed paper. You didn't have to be a six-year-old boy to love a sweet treat made out of pretzels, Hershey's chocolate Kisses, and M&M's.

Fin had taken a call about some crisis in the office. Ami surmised the conversation hadn't gone well when her sister returned with a scowl on her face.

"Is everything okay?" Ami kept her tone light.

"At the moment, 'Take this job and shove it' seems an appropriate response to that question."

At Ami's concerned glance, Fin smiled. "I'm kidding. Just another minor crisis with a high-profile client. All is good."

"I wish I could say the same about my job." Prim popped the last M&M's into the chocolate Kiss and sighed. "Rumor is there's going to be another wave of layoffs where I work after the first of the year."

Marigold's blond brows pulled together. "Any chance you'll be out?"

"I don't think so." Prim's confident tone may have satisfied the other two, but Ami saw the worry in her eyes. "I hope not."

"I realize you love Milwaukee." Ami rested a hand on her sister's shoulder. "But remember you always have a place here."

"I sense a group hug coming on." Marigold's droll tone had Ami setting down her stirring spoon and moving close.

Fin rolled her eyes but obligingly closed the circle.

A "power of four" hug ended up being just what Ami needed on this brisk December afternoon.

"Is there room for one more in that hug?"

Ami stiffened. She stepped back from the sisterly embrace to regard Beck. "Who let you in?"

She wondered why she sounded cross when she was so wholly glad to see him.

"I let myself," he said sheepishly. "The door was unlocked."

Fin shot him a pointed look. "You could have knocked. Or, I don't know, rang the bell."

Prim chuckled before turning back to the belly buttons.

"I wasn't sure you'd let me in." Beck's dark gaze remained firmly focused on Ami. "Can we talk?"

Even as he saw her hesitation, he kept his gaze fixed on hers. "Please."

He didn't know what to think when she turned to her sisters.

"Your call." Prim spoke gently in a barely audible tone.

Marigold moved to Ami's side and touched her shoulder. "We'll support you, whatever you decide."

Fin also voiced her support before shooting Beck a withering glance.

Ami turned and studied his face for a long moment, her gaze searching his.

———————

Even as sweat trickled down his spine, he willed her to see the love that was in his heart.

Finally, she turned back to her sisters. "Can one of you finish up the bread pudding?"

Fin lifted the stirring spoon from Ami's hand and stepped to the stove. "I've got this covered."

"Thank you." Ami gave Fin's shoulder a squeeze, then motioned to Beck. "We can talk in the living room."

She sat on the sofa, taking a seat at the far end. She wore a simple green Henley, worn jeans, and UGGs. Her hair was pulled back from her face with two clips. He thought she'd never looked lovelier.

Beck removed his coat and laid it across a chair, then sat at the other end of the sofa. When he opened his mouth to speak, she held up a hand.

"There's a couple things I need to say first, that I want you to understand." She met his gaze unblinkingly. "I planned to tell you after Christmas that I'd been drinking when I was in that accident. Not knowing how you'd react, I wanted to wait so I didn't ruin your—or my—Christmas. I realize now that was a mistake."

She folded her hands in her lap, which he took as his cue.

"I read your piece in the *Open Door*." Beck rubbed his chin. "Writing that article took courage."

Her eyes widened. He could see he'd surprised her.

"It's not easy owning up to mistakes, much less making them public knowledge."

Ami's face remained solemn. "If just one person thinks before they drink and drive, perhaps something good can come out of my carelessness."

"Your article certainly made me take a hard look at myself." He cleared his throat, recalling his conversation earlier that day with Nina. "You were able to move on, while I've held on to my anger and pain as if it were a righteous shield. In the end, all that accomplished was keeping me stuck in the past."

Ami put a hand on his arm. "You had a good reason—"

"I called Nina Holbrook this morning. I told her I forgave her. She broke down and cried in gratitude." His eyes grew moist, remembering the woman's response. "It was the right thing to do. I feel like I've turned a corner and now I can finally move forward with my life."

"I'm happy for you, Beck." Her green eyes filled with tears. "That took real courage."

Ami began to rise, but he grabbed her hand and pulled her down beside him.

"I'm not finished." His tone was low and urgent. "I was wrong to walk out on you last night."

"You were shocked, disappointed."

Despite the soft-spoken, understanding words, Beck could see her father hadn't been the only one he'd disappointed.

"That's no excuse." His jaw jutted out. "A man doesn't walk out on the woman he loves."

Ami's gaze turned questioning.

"I love you, Ami." He smiled ruefully, wishing the pronouncement could have been uttered in a more romantic way. Taking her cold fingers, he warmed them between his hands. "I'm asking for your forgiveness for walking out yesterday. It won't happen again."

She pulled her hand away, her fingers fluttering to her neck. "I don't know what to say."

"Saying you love me would be a good start."

Whatever response she'd been about to make was silenced by the twins bursting through the front door, yelling that they'd seen a werewolf on the side of the road with fangs and glowing yellow eyes.

Ami rose to her feet and sighed. She shook her head at her dad. "Didn't I warn you not to tell the twins about the werewolf sightings in Jefferson County?"

"I think it was a big dog," was all he said. "Or a bear."

At the commotion, Ami's sisters spilled into the living room and everyone began talking at once. Beck heard the words *claws*, *dog face*, and *pointed ears* more times than he cared to remember over the next couple of hours. He accepted an invitation to dinner and pronounced the bread pudding excellent.

With everyone around, there was no opportunity for him and Ami to speak privately. On the way home, Beck consoled himself with the fact she'd given him an extra helping of dessert.

That, coupled with a kiss at the door, gave him hope there might be a merry Christmas in his future, after all.

Chapter Twenty-Six

"You didn't have to rush over here," Fin told Ami the next day as she pulled the car into Beck's driveway. "Just because he snaps his fingers doesn't mean you have to jump. Tonight's Christmas Eve. We've got dinner, church, and caroling in the town square. He needs to understand you've got a lot on your plate."

Ami had been at her father's house when she'd gotten Beck's call. "He didn't snap his fingers. He asked nicely. Besides, did you really think I wanted to hang around the house with Anita there?"

"Why do you think I offered to drive you?" Fin lifted a brow. "Five minutes around that woman and I-Need-a-Drink."

"Make mine a double." Ami laughed and reached for the door handle. "I'm sure Beck will drive me back to Dad's house. If not, I'll give you a call."

Fin leaned over, grabbed her arm. "He had that look in his eyes last night."

Ami cocked her head. "What look?"

"Just remember, if he wants you—and you decide you want him—make the guy do some groveling before you forgive him."

Ami only smiled. She stood for a moment in the drive, gazing up at the massive house that seemed so familiar. The sudden feeling of returning home gripped her as she navigated the last step.

The door swung open before she had a chance to knock.

Beck stood in the doorway, looking incredibly sexy in all black. His hair was slightly damp at the edges, as if he'd just stepped out of the shower. And he smelled terrific. Had he known the spicy scent he'd put on was her favorite?

Desire curled low in her belly, but she forced a serene, Madonna-like smile. It was safer if he didn't know how he affected her. She handed him her coat.

"Thanks for coming."

"Thanks for inviting me."

"You look lovely." The gleam in his eyes put a different spin on the simple comment.

Ami glanced down at the pencil skirt and cashmere sweater Fin had loaned her. She had to admit her sister had been right; the way the sweater hugged her curves added a certain allure to the outfit.

The footsteps of the heeled boots she'd also borrowed echoed in the empty foyer. She turned to Beck. "It looks so bare."

"We'll make it more beautiful than ever. I promise."

We'll? Ami's heart gave an involuntary leap when he put his palm against the small of her back and ushered her toward the stairs.

Ami glanced down the hall. "I thought we were having tea."

That's what he'd promised when he'd called.

"The pot of Earl Grey is waiting for us upstairs in the sitting room." He shot her an innocent smile. "I've got a fire going. We'll be more comfortable."

He was right, she thought, when she reached the upstairs. Through the lace curtains, Ami could see snow gently falling in large, white flakes. A cheery fire burned in the hearth, heating the room to a toasty warmth. It was cozy and intimate, the perfect place to relax on a cold winter afternoon.

She poured them each a cup of tea, then took a seat in front of the fire with her cup.

Beck seemed on edge, pacing in front of the fire while she sipped.

"Is something wrong?" she asked, growing concerned.

"You never gave me an answer."

Puzzled, she inclined her head. "I don't remember any question."

"I told you I loved you."

Just hearing him say the words had her heart breaking into a samba. But she covered the thrill by taking another sip of tea and lifting a brow. "That appears to be a statement, not a question."

"Don't be flippant." He raked a hand through his hair. "This is serious. I'm serious."

Make him grovel. Wasn't that what Fin said? But that wasn't Ami's style. Still, there was something she needed to make clear.

"Driving that night after drinking was a mistake. I learned from my mistake. I can't—I won't—be with someone who holds that against me."

He dropped down beside her.

Dear Lord, he smelled good.

"I made an even bigger mistake when I walked away from you the night of your father's open house. I learned from my mistake. I don't want you to hold that against me, to think I can't be trusted to stand by you."

"It hurt," she admitted. "But you'd just been smacked up the side of the head with a revelation you didn't expect."

"Sounds as if we're both human." A smile touched his lips. "I have a confession."

"You're not human?"

"Very funny. No, I opened your Christmas gift."

She shook her head and made a tsking sound. "You're as bad as the twins."

Beck rose and took the sun catcher from where he'd laid it on the mantel. It dangled from his fingers on a circle of fishing line. "A wise woman once told me that a star says 'home.'"

"That's exactly right." Ami glanced around. "Have you decided where to hang it?"

"I believe that's something we should decide together." Beck carefully placed the star back in the box.

"It's your home," she pointed out.

"My home is with you."

Ami was still processing the words when Beck moved to her side, dropped to one knee, and took her hand in his. He caressed her palm with his thumb, then cocked his head as if listening.

"Do you hear something?"

"Thankfully, no." He chuckled. "I really don't want anyone spoiling this moment by rushing in with talk of werewolves on the side of the road."

Their gazes held and Ami found herself smiling at him.

"I think we're safe." She was amazed she could respond so coherently with the blood rushing in her ears. "You may continue."

Her control nearly shattered when he brought her hand to his mouth for a kiss, his dark eyes burning with emotion.

When he spoke, his voice was low, raspy, and not quite steady. "From the first moment you walked through the door of Muddy Boots, I knew there was something special about you. I wasn't looking to fall in love, but there you were."

His gaze, so full of love and tenderness, had tears springing to her eyes.

"I can't imagine going through life without you by my side. You bring out the best in me and make me want to be a better man. My life is richer and fuller, beyond measure, and the only thing that could make it more complete is if you'd be my wife."

He paused, and searched her face as if trying to decipher her expression.

"I would give you the world if I could."

"I don't need the world," she began.

His fingers closed over her lips before she could say more.

"I know you wanted to turn the house into a bed-and-breakfast, but I would like it if this could be our home, where we trim the Christmas tree together and have friends over for barbecues on the back patio, where our children can run up and down the stairs in their pajamas." He spoke quickly, as if determined to get it all out. "If you're set on running a B and B, I've heard the Dunlevey house might be coming up for sale. We could—"

"I don't want to turn our home into a B and B. I don't want to run one, either. I love the bakery."

He arched a brow as if that surprised him. "You said you'd always dreamed about turning this house into a bed-and—"

"Because that's the only way I thought I'd be able to afford this house." Still, seeing uncertainty on his face, she continued. "Don't you see that this will be *our* bed-and-breakfast?"

As comprehension began to dawn on his face, she cupped his cheek briefly in her hand. "We'll go to bed together every night and have breakfast together every morning. I can't think of a sweeter, or more wonderful, life."

"There's only one thing missing from that picture."

"What is it?"

"A ring and a promise." He reached into his pocket and flipped open a black velvet case. Nestled inside was an emerald-cut diamond in brilliant platinum.

Tears slipped down her cheeks. Happy tears from a heart overflowing with joy.

"I love you so much. I can't imagine anything better than spending my life with you here in Good Hope, building a home, a family, and a life together. If you love me even half as much as I love you, I'll be a happy man. Will you marry me?"

"I love you, James Beckett Cross. More than I ever thought possible to love anyone. And yes, I'll be happy and proud to become your wife."

He slipped the ring on her finger. "Forever."

Then, before Ami even had a second to breathe, Beck's lips were on hers, exquisitely gentle and achingly tender, with the promise of a long and happy life together.

$\mathcal{E}$pilogue

Snowflakes, large and fluffy, were falling when Ami stepped into Muddy Boots on Christmas morning, her fiancé at her side. To her surprise, her entire family had already arrived and was hard at work.

Ami stood for a moment in the doorway, inhaling the scent of pine from the small, decorated tree someone had placed in the corner of the café. With Beck's arm draped around her shoulders, she soaked in the melodious croon of Bing Crosby and the excited chatter of familiar voices. A wave of contentment washed over her.

The past twenty-four hours felt like a dream. A very nice dream. Last night, over a meal of smoked whitefish chowder and crusty French bread, her father and sisters had toasted her and Beck's engagement. After enjoying coffee and their choice of dessert, they'd all headed off to church.

There had been one hard moment, when Anita had appeared and taken a seat in the pew beside their father. As their dad had made it clear earlier in the day that, while he would always love their mother, he was ready to move on, Ami and her sisters had done their best to make the woman feel welcome.

Like a dollop of fresh whipped cream on a perfectly made cherry pie, the night had been topped off with caroling in the town square.

Being together had been such a joyful experience that the Bloom family had decided to spend Christmas Day giving back, which meant Beck had a whole troop of volunteers for his first annual Muddy Boots Family Christmas Dinner.

When Fin had asked last night why he'd called it a family dinner, Beck's answer had only made Ami love him more. In addition to blood ties, family, he told his future sister-in-law, could be those brought together by community.

Since family wasn't expected to pay when they came to your home for a holiday dinner, the meal was free. Although a Giving Tree donation jar sat on the counter, there was no pressure to donate.

Red and white carnations in bud vases, donated by the Enchanted Florist, decorated the tables and added to the festive atmosphere. Tom manned the kitchen with Hadley's and Izzie's assistance.

Ami and her sisters had brought the pies while Anita had furnished the cakes. She'd also brought Lindsay and Dakota along to help serve.

"Have you thought any more about when you'll tie the knot?" Prim asked as she and Ami cleared a table to make room for another family.

"We discussed it last night." Ami glanced in Beck's direction. When he gave her a wink, she grinned like an idiot before turning back to Prim. "It'll take some quick planning, but we decided on a June wedding."

"I'd marry her tomorrow if it were up to me." Beck stepped close and wrapped his arms around his fiancée, lifting her hair to plant a kiss on the back of her neck.

Laughing, Ami pulled away, and the large diamond on her left hand caught the light. "Mind your manners. There are children present."

Beck glanced at the twins, who were busy swatting each other with cloths originally meant to clean the tables. "I don't think we need to worry about them."

"I'll be back." Heaving a weary sigh, Prim hurried across the dining room. "Boys, stop that this instant."

Ami chuckled. "God willing, that will be our life in a couple of years."

As Beck watched the twins dodge their mother, a thankfulness for all his blessings swamped him.

He tugged Ami close and kissed her softly on the mouth. "I can hardly wait."

About the Author

Photo © 2013 Marti Corn Photography

Cindy Kirk started writing after taking a class at a local community college, but her interest in the written word started years earlier, when she was in her teens. At sixteen she wrote in her diary, "I don't know what I would do if I couldn't be a writer."

It took Cindy years to return to her first love—writing. Unlike some authors, Cindy wasn't interested in shorter works; she jumped feetfirst into book-length fiction. She loves reading and writing romance because she believes in happily ever after.

An incurable romantic, Cindy loves seeing her characters grow and learn from their mistakes and, in the process, achieve happy endings.

Cindy hopes that once you read her books you'll be able to tell she is an eternal optimist, one who truly believes in the power of love. She invites you to kick off your shoes, pick up one of her books, and get to know her.

She and her high school sweetheart husband live on an acreage in Nebraska with their two dogs.

Made in the USA
Las Vegas, NV
13 January 2022

41269245R00176